WYNDSPELLE'S CHILD

The Wyndspelle Trilogy
Book Three

Aola Vandergriff

SAPERE
BOOKS

WYNDSPELLE'S CHILD

Published by Sapere Books.

24 Trafalgar Road, Ilkley, LS29 8HH

saperebooks.com

ISBN: 978-0-85495-587-9

For
SMOKEY AND JUDY
with love

PROLOGUE

Reverend Ian Mackenzie's desk was littered with paper. The stub of a candle, stuck in a saucer beside him, burned low. He looked at it ruefully. Both candle and writing materials were church property, and, therefore, should not be wasted. He must either accomplish what he set out to do, or forget it. There must be no more false starts.

Pulling a fresh sheet to him, he dipped his quill in ink and set down the date again. *January 21, 1815.* Then he wrote, for what must have been the tenth time, *My Dear Niece Megan…*

The first few paragraphs were devoted to the usual pleasantries he exchanged with the young girl he had not seen since she was five years old. At last, reluctantly, he divulged his reason for writing on this day:

I am a lonely old man, with neither kith nor kin on this side of the waters. While you, in your present position as neither guest nor servant in your English cousin's home, may be in similar case. It has come to me that we may be of comfort to each other.

He paused, the flickering candle scoring the laugh wrinkles in his lined face, as he wondered how to proceed.

This, then, is what I have to offer: A Scottish gentleman, whose wife and infant son perished, innocent victims of our recent war, has taken a great house nearby on the coast. He was left with an afflicted child, a girl. It is this child who needs someone to care for her, a companion, of Scottish descent preferably. Though exacting, it would be a fine and noble work, and I immediately thought of you.

Here, Reverend Mackenzie stopped, swallowed hard, and went on, stating that a letter of credit upon a London bank accompanied his message, and giving directions, should the girl find the position suited her at this time.

You will sail for Boston, thence to Gloucester. There you will be met by my conveyance to bring you inland to me.

I, myself, will take you to Wyndspelle.

There! It was done. Making up the packet, wrapping it in oiled silk, he took it to an outer room, where he gave it to the man who waited.

And it was gone. Too late to call back, even if he wished. His mouth felt dry, and it was hard to swallow. Had he done the right thing, as a man of God? Surely, the Megan he knew from her letters might be salvation for this poor mind-wounded child!

Or had he contrived the whole situation to suit his own selfish ends? With the knowledge of approaching death upon him, he longed for one of his own kin.

He picked up the letter the messenger had brought to him and read it again.

I am coming to you for aid, Preacher, though I do not want your prayers. Our physician has brought my daughter's need for a companion to my attention. As you know, the local females avoid Wyndspelle like the plague. Nor are they wanted here.

I should like you to find a good Scottish woman for this purpose. One who will care for the child, mind her own business, and leave me secure in the knowledge that I have discharged my fatherly duty. I shall be grateful for your assistance, but not to the point that you need feel called to save my soul. A letter of credit is enclosed. Signed, Craigh Stewart.

The pain that Ian Mackenzie had lived with lately intensified, racking his short stubby frame. Dropping the letter he held, he wandered to the window, looking out into the night. He could not see Wyndspelle. It was much too far away, but he knew that it was there, crouching on its promontory like some great evil beast.

There was death in that house. He had felt it on his one and only visit there, a visit of welcome and condolence. And he had not even managed to get past its doors. He had been turned away.

Yet this was where he'd thought to send a young, defenseless girl. He had been wrong! Wrong! Perhaps the messenger had stopped at the Publick House to fortify himself with ale. Perhaps he was not yet gone on his way —

Frantically, the Reverend Mackenzie scrubbed at the misted window with his sleeve. But the night was black as pitch. There was nothing to see.

Only lightning in the direction of the great house called Wyndspelle, the haunted house of Wyndspelle with its spilled blood and its many secrets. A zigzag of light flashed across the sky, with a crack like the opening of hell.

And in the Reverend Ian Mackenzie's room, the candle guttered and went out.

CHAPTER 1

The air was hot and still. Too still. A vacuum waiting for a storm to fill it. Megan Alisdair, Scottish by birth, but come to this country by way of England, allowed herself a moment of affectionate frustration at the slowness of the rider ahead of her. How she would love to dump this miserable side saddle in a ditch, straddle the horse, and ride like the wind — as she had ridden the shaggy Highland ponies in her childhood. That would stir up a breeze!

But it might also shock the cassock off her uncle, the Reverend Ian Mackenzie. Better to bide her time, brush the clouds of hovering midges away, and try to bring a smile to his lips when next they paused to rest. For surely, the black mood was on him today!

A wayward branch, catching her bonnet, sent her carefully pinned-up hair spilling around her shoulders, and she forgot her ladylike decision.

"Drat!" she exploded.

"Eh?" The small man ahead turned his horse on the narrow path. "Something wrong, lass? Ye called?"

"I said — my *hat*." Her voice was meek, but the gray eyes that studied the ruined bonnet sparked with anger that turned them almost black for an instant. The bonnet was the only one she owned and had to suffice with both her gowns. And she had planned to look most respectable upon her arrival!

Her ire didn't last long. It never did: her sense of humor always seemed to come to the fore. The gentleman who was to employ her through her uncle's good offices might just send her back as damaged goods! A spring of laughter bubbled forth. "Look at me," she chortled. "I'm a mess, for true!"

The answering smile she invited was not forthcoming. The old man climbed creakily from his horse, his face still shadowed with whatever was eating away at him. "Aweel," he sighed, "'tis time to rest a bit. Give ye time to set yourself to rights."

Megan climbed down obediently. Setting the covered basket she carried upon the ground, she opened it to release a small bristly dog. It ran in circles about her, rejoicing madly in its temporary freedom.

"Don't go far, young Angus," she cautioned the puppy. "'Tis a wilderness you're in, now, filled wi' bogles and ghaisties that would welcome a tasty morsel like yersel'!"

She busied herself at pinning her hair back into some semblance of neatness, thinking as she did so how apt her description of this place had been. The trees meshed overhead, allowing only a sickly green light to filter through. The very silence seemed unnatural and depressing. From the corner of her eye, she looked at her uncle, leaning against a tree trunk like a small, dejected gnome.

How different he was today. Yesterday, upon her arrival at his cottage next to the church, he had greeted her with warmth and exuberance. His eyes had sparkled as he hugged her; his cheeks had been rosy and his smile beaming. And last night — they had sat up nearly the whole of it, exchanging memories of Scotland, of home, re-telling old family tales until he wiped his eyes and chuckled, "Lass — lass, I cannot recall having laughed so much in a long time."

But this morning, he had been somber, puttering about, stalling the beginning of their journey, though clouds in the distance portended a coming storm. Now he looked even more miserable. As if he were reluctant to continue the rest of the way.

Perhaps I am not what he expected, she thought. *Maybe he expected to have a fine lady to introduce as his relative. And instead, here's a great gawk of a girl, dressed like a servant!* She looked with distaste at the gray woolen gown, a cast-off of her English cousin's. She should have used the additional money sent along for her passage to acquire something more suitable to wear.

Instead, she'd thought to be thrifty, to return what was left to her new employer. Surely a man who'd had so many troubles would have need of it! She'd taken only enough to purchase Angus, the little dog, for the poor sick child who would be her charge.

Her loyalty to her new-found uncle rallied. He was not the kind of man to be ashamed of the way she dressed. Was he not poor himself? True, she had dined well at his cottage, but she'd noted his larder was empty. And last night, when they'd finally retired, she was given his cot while he made himself a pallet before the fire.

No, it was something else that put the black mood on his shoulders. She moved toward him, seeing that his face was drawn and gray.

"Uncle Ian — are you unwell?"

Her voice stopped uncertainly as he turned toward her, his eyes dark with something that looked like pain — and fear.

"Nay, lass. It's just that I've been thinking. I want you to return home with me." His words were tumbling forth now, his accent growing thicker with emotion. "I'll find a way to repay the mon for yer passage. I dinna know how, but I will! 'Tis a wrong I've done ye, but naught I canna set aright."

His face had turned a fiery red now, with an unhealthy choleric flush. Megan was afraid for him. She put a calming hand to his shoulder, feeling the fragility of the bones beneath his cassock. "I don't know what you're talking about, Uncle Ian. If you would just explain —?"

He sagged at her touch. "I'm sorry, lass. Gi' me a wee bit to collect myself." He turned away for a moment, then, facing her, a greenish pallor about his mouth, he said, "Sit ye down, lass. I hae a tale to tell ye."

He told of his own boyhood, as they sat together on a mossy rock. Youngest of seven brothers, he had a younger sister whom he adored — Megan's mother, who had left their home on the northern coast to wed the Alisdair.

"I visited Alisdair Castle once, when you were a wee one. Remember? We talked about it last night."

She smiled, recalling the way he had joined her in mischief. An adult partner in crime. How *could* she forget?

"You were your mother all over again," he said. "'Twas the last time I saw her. My father died, leaving me little. And I came here to serve the Church." He was silent for a moment. "When I heard that your family had drowned and the castle had passed into your uncle's hands, I wanted to send for you. I heard you were sent to live with your English cousin, but it was the dream of my life to have you with me. But the living I make here — you saw — is a poor one. Then this offer came. Forgive me, lass!"

"I don't understand, Uncle Ian. It seems providential."

"Aye, so it did to me. But there were things I put in the back of my mind!"

He paused. The dog, Angus, returned and whimpered at Megan's feet. She picked him up, holding him close as she waited for her uncle to continue.

"There are things I have not told you. The master of Wyndspelle is a godless man, his mind crazed by his grief —

or," he lowered his voice to a whisper, "or something *worse*. And the hoose itself! 'Tis a dreadful place, Megan. Wicked things have happened there, lass. 'Tis said that it is accursed!"

So that was all! Megan's laughter pealed forth again. "Uncle Ian! You have forgotten — I grew up at Alisdair, remember? It is only a small castle, I'll admit, after seeing the great houses in London, but it has a bluidy history for a' that. Roderick slew his brother Jock in the north tower, remember? And Bruce was slain at table in the great hall, by his own son! Cameron died in the buttery, where he had slipped down for a liaison with a dairymaid. They all are supposed to walk the castle at night! And there is our headless lady, the Lady Anne —"

Ian's face lit up, and he began to grin. "I had forgotten! There is a rhyme, isn't there? *Lady Anne to Duncan wed —*"

He stopped, and Megan finished the rhyme. *"He found her in the coachman's bed. And then the lady lost her head —"*

Now it was her turn to pause. She swallowed, blushing. It was not exactly a verse suited to a clergyman's ears. But to her surprise, the old man chuckled, his eyes twinkling naughtily. Her laughter joined his, and their friendly rapport was established once more.

"I had forgotten your background," he admitted finally. "There was something about the hoose that frightened me. And there are the tales the gossips tell. I began to think of myself as a selfish old mon, bringing you here, and it began to weigh heavy on my conscience. But if ye are not afraid?"

"I am not afraid," she said. "In fact, at my cousin Elizabeth's house in England, nothing *ever* happened. I found it most dull."

He laughed again, drily. "I recall your cousin, and I can believe you. Then, I take it, you wish to go on?"

"I do," she said.

There was a flurry of activity, gathering up the reluctant Angus and pressing him back into his basket, mounting the horses, and they were off. She had lied a little, Megan thought ruefully, but only a little. The doleful tales of age-old happenings at Alisdair had not frightened her as a child, but she'd had a peculiar sensitivity to certain areas of the castle. The north tower had a chill about it. Once, at dinner in the great hall, she looked at her father at the head of the table — and saw death in his face. She avoided the buttery, and she'd imagined she saw the Lady Anne…

Now, in spite of the heat, she felt cold inside, chill bumps on her arms. No doubt about it: her uncle's words, coupled with the atmosphere of this dismal, brooding spot, had troubled her.

She stiffened, clutching the basket that contained Angus a little tighter. There could be no truth in what he had to say. And if there were, if Wyndspelle should, indeed, prove to be a frightening, haunted place, she still had no choice. She was indebted to the man who had sent her fare. Despite Uncle Ian's promises, he would never be able to save up enough to repay him. And she was morally indebted to care for a sick child.

And if they turned back, there was no place to go. Uncle Ian had barely enough to survive upon himself. And while Cousin Elizabeth might be able to send her the fare home, it was out of the question. She had run away from there — and only just in time!

With a sick feeling, she thought of her cousin's husband; how he had pawed at her so disgustingly that night — in the very room where his sleeping children lay! And how Elizabeth had appeared at the door —

"George! What is it? What are you doing?"

The man was frozen, guilty, beyond answering. Megan had answered for him, clutching tightly to the letter in her pocket. The letter she had had no intention of considering. The letter from Uncle Ian.

"He — he was kissing me goodbye, Elizabeth. I just told him I am leaving. I am going to America."

She had certainly done nothing to encourage the man's advances, but now her cheeks flushed with at the recollection. It was a scene she'd like to erase from her mind, but she knew it would haunt her forever. Elizabeth had not believed her, but she had pretended to. She'd had no other recourse. And though Megan hadn't been particularly fond of her cousin, there were the children. They had become part of her life.

She was so absorbed in her own thoughts that she didn't notice the wind come up, the branches above her swaying in a sigh. The gust was followed by a spate of dust, then a chill wind carrying a few scattered drops of rain that struck her face like sleet.

Ahead, her uncle reined in, calling back over his shoulder. "Megan, girl? We're going to have to make a run for it, lass. The storm's coming."

Whipping up his ancient nag, he finally managed to settle her into a sedate trot. Megan followed close behind, thinking how otherworldly he looked in the gloom cast by the approaching weather. Like a little troll, bouncing along on his steed, leading an enchanted princess into fairyland.

She giggled a little at the thought of herself as a princess, then took a firmer grip on Angus's basket. Most likely Wyndspelle held no resemblance to the castle of her dreams. Still, it was ahead of her, it promised a new life, and she had no place to go. If it were not the home she looked for, then she must make it so!

She lowered her head against the wind and the rain, lifting it only when the Reverend Mackenzie stopped, barring her way.

"We must be careful now," he shouted above the shrilling wind. "Be certain your hold on the rein is sure." She looked first at his face, which had taken on a new grimness, then in the direction of his pointing finger.

Her heart stopped still at the sight before her.

They were on the edge of a precipice. A narrow trail led downward to a bowl-like depression surrounded by the horseshoe-shaped cliff on which they stood. The depression stretched for a space, carpeted with sparse, scant grass and twisted, stunted trees. Then it climbed steeply to a promontory overlooking the sea.

On this promontory stood a house, looking as if it grew from the rock on which it was situated: fully three stories high, the bell tower topping it pierced black, boiling clouds that moved in from the waters. A mystic, eerie scene.

"'Twould be the Castle of Cailleach," Megan gasped, "or surely, the home of the De' Danann!"

Her uncle frowned, his face black with disapproval. "What are you saying, lass? Has the devilish place already got to you? *Cailleach,* the earth mother … her people, the *De' Danann,* to whom she gave the gift of magic? Surely you do not hold with pagan beliefs?"

"No," she said in a troubled voice, "those are only tales. 'Tis just that the place is so beautiful. Beyond description. And yet—"

She did not finish her sentence, but sat awed until her uncle guided his horse down the narrow path and she was forced to give all her attention to the rain-slick path her own horse must follow.

As they reached the foot of the curving pathway, they rounded a stone and came out into the hollow behind and below the towering mansion, facing the sea. Here, the storm struck with its full force, deluging the travelers with sheets of water driven by swirling winds. Megan licked her lips, tasting both wind and the sea, barely conscious of a low building on her right where a whickering sound proclaimed it a stable.

"The back door," Ian Mackenzie gasped. "We'll never make it to the front."

At last they fetched up against what seemed to be a solid wall. The old man assisted Megan from her horse, and she clung to him, thoroughly chilled, her hair wet and streaming, plastered against her pale face, the dog's basket clutched to her.

"Ye will not reconsider?" her uncle shouted in her ear. "No? Then I will leave ye here."

"No," she gasped, "please — wait!"

His arm about her waist, Ian Mackenzie led Megan to a windowless door, set in walls of stone. Still holding her, he battered the wood with his fists, raising his voice in a mighty ministerial shout. After what seemed an eternity, the door opened with a creaking sound.

Before them stood a tall, raw-boned woman clad in somber black. The light of the lamp she carried delineated her strong dark features: a tight mouth with a faint down on the upper lip, black hair pulled back tautly, black expressionless eyes. *So she would look if she were in her coffin,* Megan thought, with a shudder that was not entirely from the cold. Dimly, she heard her uncle introducing her, explaining their presence here.

His words seemed to have no effect on the woman. She just stood there, solid, unmoving, as if to block their way. Suddenly, there was a fluting voice from the darkness behind her.

"What is it, Constance? Is someone there?"

The woman, Constance, stepped aside, allowing Megan a glimpse inside. The door led to a kitchen, a huge cavern of a room with walls of the native stone upon which the house was built. There was a smell of dampness, and the light from a fireplace at one end of the room made the stone walls glisten. The same light illuminated a figure that stood halfway down a set of stone steps leading from above. Megan gasped.

The woman on the steps was the most beautiful lady she'd ever seen.

"He's done it, Miss Fiona," Constance said in a harsh, mannish voice. "This is the preacher from down in the settlement, and he brought this girl. Says she's here to take care of Miss Lea."

"Oh, my!" The woman above placed her hands to her cheeks and stood thinking for a moment. Then she came gracefully down the stairs. "Step in and let me look at you."

Megan obliged, feeling awkward and clumsy before the woman's scrutiny. Her clothes were sodden, and a puddle was forming about her feet.

"So young," the woman said in a little bird-like rush. "Too young to have such responsibility. This is not a happy house, Miss —?"

"Megan. Megan Alisdair."

"This is not a happy house, Megan. And I'm sure the position is beyond your capabilities. Between Constance and myself," she shot the other woman an affectionate look, "we have managed quite well without — help. You're perfectly free to go. I shall explain —"

Megan lifted her chin. She did not know this woman's place in the household, but she knew that passage money had been sent her by a man. It was to him she owed her allegiance. To him and to her Uncle Ian, who stood shivering behind her, not quite out of the reach of the rain.

"It is Master Stewart I must speak to," she said, positively. "It was he who employed me."

The pretty woman exchanged another glance with Constance and sighed. "Very well, then, if you insist." Touching Megan's sleeve, she drew away. "My dear, you're soaked to the skin! Come with me."

Megan twisted her head to look back. "Uncle Ian —"

"He will be all right. Constance will see to him. Come along."

Megan was led up the stone steps into a lavishly furnished small room that served for dining, and thence into a great hall that put the one at Alisdair to shame. A fireplace at the right of their entry dominated the room. Before her at the far end was a huge door that must front on the sea. To either side of the door twin staircases curved gracefully upward to a balcony that surrounded three walls of the hall. Alisdair, with its twisty corners and cubbyholes for children and ghosts to hide in, was never like this!

Conscious that she was gawking like a country girl, Megan flushed and looked at her companion, noticing a faint smile of amusement on the woman's lips.

"I am Fiona Dunstan," she said. "Master Stewart is my brother-in-law. My brother, Aherne, and I make our home with. him. In addition, there is my personal servant, Constance Bagley, whom you met downstairs; the cook; and a deaf-mute who serves as maid-of-all-work. So you see, this can be a lonely place for a young girl." Seeing Megan's jaw set stubbornly, she sighed again and said, "If you insist on seeing Craigh, stay here by the fire. I will see if I can find him."

Then she was gone. Megan moved to the blazing hearth and stood close to the fire. Strangely, the shuddering cold that still possessed her seemed to intensify. For a moment, she was a small child again, hiding from her brothers in the north tower at Alisdair, the ill-fated tower where brother slew brother.

In the covered basket she still carried, Angus made an eerie whining sound. *He feels it, too,* she thought. And she remembered Uncle Ian's words. *Wicked things have happened there … 'Tis said that it is accursed!* That was what had brought about her wild imaginings! That and the chill she'd taken. Was she to be kept standing here forever in these sodden clothes? And her uncle in the kitchen was fully as drenched as she. How was he faring? It would only take a moment to see.

With an upward glance at the balcony above, seeing no one in its shadows, she retraced the way she'd come, running lightly down the stairs that led to the kitchen. It was empty except for Constance and a stout woman stirring something at the fire. Megan studied the room in bewilderment. There seemed to be no other entry to the rooms above.

"My uncle," she asked, "where has he gone?"

The servant didn't deign to reply, merely indicating the door with a wave of her hand.

"Gone? Gone without a chance to dry himself? A cup of tea to warm him?" Megan's voice was incredulous. "What were you thinking of to let him leave like that? He's an old man! Unwell!"

"No man of God is welcome in this house," the woman said, tight-lipped. "I only obey orders."

"Whose orders?" Megan was no longer cold with the fury that raged within her.

"A house has only one master," was the insolent answer.

Megan stared at her for a moment, then rushed to the door, opening it on a world of blinding windblown rain. "Uncle Ian," she called into the darkness. "Uncle Ian! Can you hear me? Come back!"

Her voice was drowned in that of the tempest, the roar of the surf on the rocks below the promontory, the keening of the wind that screamed about the house like a lost soul seeking sanctuary. *The ban sith,* Megan thought, trembling. *The banshee!* And, turning to look at Constance whose fire-lit features seemed to wear a smug satisfaction — *Black Annis! Morrigan! Destroyer of men!*

Pagan beliefs! She shook her head, recalling her uncle's concern. *"Has the devilish place already got to you?"* he'd said. In a way, she felt she had betrayed him — and perhaps she had misjudged the power of the servant before her. Uncle Ian had not wished to enter with her. He might have decided to leave of his own accord. He was a stubborn, strong-willed little man, secure in himself. As she must be! Secure in herself, and strong in her faith, if she were to aid the ailing child who would be her charge.

A child in the house! Megan's heart lifted suddenly. She had been making much of nothing. A strange house in a new country, a surly servant, a storm. Tomorrow, everything would be brighter.

Fiona appeared on the stairs to say that Craigh Stewart would not be available for consultation this night, but that Megan should follow, since her room was now prepared. The girl could not resist turning at the top step to look back.

Constance Bagley looked up at her, something frightening in her eyes. *Black Annis! Morrigan!*

Knuckles white on the handle of her basket, Megan followed Fiona through the shadowed house.

CHAPTER 2

Megan woke to a rain-washed morning. She had lain sleepless for a while the night before, worrying about her uncle out in the storm-filled darkness. And she had been concerned about the fate of Angus, too, for the woman Fiona was shocked to learn what the basket contained.

"I have cats, you know."

"But I will keep him by me," Megan said, obdurately.

Fiona sighed. "Oh, my, you are a stubborn young lady. Suppose we compromise? My brother, Aherne, loves animals. He will feed the dog and find it a place in the stables for the night. Craigh, of course, will have the final say as to its disposition. I'm certain he didn't propose you bring your pet with you."

"Angus is not mine," Megan said, perilously close to tears after this frightening night. "I brought him for the child."

"For Lea?" Fiona looked startled. "Oh, my dear, did Craigh not inform you? Lea is not — is not like other children," she finished lamely. "She is an invalid — in body and in mind."

"I didna know," Megan said, lapsing into her native brogue, so intense was her feeling. "But perhaps," her face brightened, "perhaps Angus can work a miracle. 'Tis like that, sometimes, with something to love."

Fiona turned away, picking up the dog's basket. "I shall attend to this immediately," she said, briskly. "And on this one occasion, I will have hot water brought to you, and a tray. After that," she shrugged prettily, "since we are so understaffed, you must attend to your own needs."

The water had been welcome, the food was delicious, and Fiona had been kind. Still Megan had been unable to relax as she lay listening to the strange breathing sound the house made. Fiona had explained it, earlier, as a phenomenon — a combination of the storm, wind, wave, and the peculiar situation of the house, built as it was to bridge a chasm that led to the sea at the foot of the promontory.

A rational explanation, it was true, but there was something in the sound that resembled the last harsh efforts of the dying.

She had a vision of her uncle, his slow horse plodding through the lashing rain. She said a prayer for him and, at last, fell asleep.

In the morning, Megan's usual good spirits returned. Droplets sparkled on the window of her room. From below came a whickering sound. Leaping from her bed, she ran to the window. She had been given a third-floor room at the rear of the house, overlooking the stable and the small paddock beside it.

Beneath her, a pale-haired young man — about her own age, she would assume — had just finished saddling a spirited mare. Megan gasped in admiration. Such a beautiful animal, its silken coat shining copper in the sun. And the boy who tended her so lovingly, laying his cheek against the soft muzzle, must be Aherne, Fiona's brother who loved animals so.

And she had been concerned about Angus! She was concerned about a lot of things last night, and now this beautiful day! She laughed softly at her own foolishness and leaned farther from the window. She would like to see Aherne's face. But he had turned away from the animal and was looking down at his boots, shoulders slumped in a sullen attitude.

Another man, clad in black, had come from the house. He approached the horse and, putting his foot in the stirrup, swung up into the saddle. Megan gasped, for the man's hair was the same copper color as that of the mare. Mounting as he did, they seemed to become one, a creature half-man, half-beast.

Did the small sound she made carry? Or had he intuitively sensed her eyes upon him?

He raised his head, and for a space she received a quick impression of slanting electric-blue eyes set in a dark face. Then he seemed to flinch at the sight of her. With a twitch of the rein, the mare spun and was off in soaring flight; the horse and rider seemed more than animal, less than human, as they flew up the precipitous horseshoe cliff.

It would be Craigh Stewart, the master of this house, her employer. Of that she was certain. But why had he looked up at her so strangely?

Megan backed away from the window, conscious of how she must have appeared, leaning out as she did: hair down, streaming across her shoulders, and in her nightdress! He must think her a depraved creature! Cheeks flaming, she hastened to don her clothing. It was going to be difficult to face him.

At last, dressed in her second-best dress — a dark thing she disliked — Megan went downstairs, taking note of her surroundings on the way. The upper floor, where she had slept, consisted of closets and small empty rooms opening off a T-shaped hall. Servant's rooms, no doubt. At the base of the T, a ship's ladder led upward to a trap door, and thence, Megan supposed, to the bell tower above.

The steps led downward into a small room with a door opening onto the balcony. Here, she paused to look at the scene that had so impressed her the night before. The windows of the great hall below were velvet-draped, the place shadowy even in the day. The furnishings seemed somehow incongruous — delicate gilt chairs, couches with intricately carved backs, all cushioned with silken material shot with sunbursts of metallic thread.

It was truly a feminine room. She could see Fiona's hand here, but not a man's. No, never a man's preferences. The furniture looked fragile, temporary — as if one might blink an eye and all would disappear. A heavy, long table might be more suited to the spot before the fireplace, for example, with huge baronial chairs.

Megan laughed at her thoughts. Surely, the decoration of this house was none of her business! Tearing her eyes from the scene below, she moved along the balcony toward the stairs. Here, the last room on the right, was the child's room. Fiona had pointed it out the night before. How Megan longed to meet her!

Could she not just open the door and peep inside? No, she decided. It might frighten the little girl. She would have to wait until she was properly introduced.

Going down the gracious stairway, Megan touched the smooth curving balustrade. It was just such a stair that the hall at Alisdair boasted. She recalled sliding down it, at play with her brothers, and landing in a giggling heap on the stone parquet below. Even now, it was tempting — and there was no one to see! She looked about surreptitiously, caught herself, and began to smile. She was an adult, now. More than twenty years of age. Such things as sliding down handrails were behind her. Was she not to be given full care of a sick child?

She went decorously down the steps, pausing at the foot to orient herself. Two doors opened at either side of the fireplace. One led to Craigh Stewart's study, where he would no doubt interview her today. The other opened on the small dining room, with its stairs to the lower regions of the house. From the second door came the sound of voices. Feeling awkward and shy, Megan opened it and stood framed in the doorway.

Breakfast was in progress. Fiona and Constance were at table, together with the pale-haired boy Megan had judged to be Aherne. A blank-faced woman, neat in pinstriped cotton and a white apron, was serving them. Fiona looked up, smiling.

"Good morning, Megan."

"Good morning," Megan clumsily searched for a method of address and settled on "ma'am. I didn't mean to intrude. I was on my way to the kitchens —"

The woman rose gracefully. *"Fiona,"* she corrected Megan. "And do come in. Craigh insists you take your meals with the family, though I decided to let you sleep in this morning, after yesterday's arduous journey." She waved Megan to a place at the foot of the table. "You've met our Constance, of course. And this is my brother, Aherne."

Megan ducked her head in greeting, but the boy did not look up. His face was bent close to his plate. He was eating swiftly, voraciously, like an animal forced into human company through hunger, intending to satisfy it and escape.

Her judgment was correct. The boy stood up, shoving back his chair, nearly toppling it in his haste. "Outside," he muttered, and was gone.

Megan was startled. The boy was either angry about something or definitely rude. She looked at the others. Fiona seemed unruffled; apparently, Aherne's behavior was an accepted thing.

She took the seat Fiona had indicated, still feeling gauche and poorly dressed in the poised, doll-like woman's presence. The moment Megan's plate was set before her, Constance rose.

"I am quite finished, Miss Fiona. If you will excuse me, I will see to Miss Lea."

Without a glance in Megan's direction, Constance left the table. Her attitude had been deliberately insulting, and Megan bristled with resentment. Fiona leaned to place a slim white hand over Megan's strong fingers.

"Don't let Constance upset you, my dear. Perhaps we've spoiled her a little. She's been with us for years, even before Morna married Craigh. My sister and I were her whole life. Now, with Morna dead, she's transferred much of her affection to Lea. I suppose she feels threatened by your presence."

"There's no need for that. I am only here to care for the child. I do not intend to alienate her affections. I — I would like our relationship to be a friendly one." Megan's voice was a little stiff.

"I am certain there will be no problems. I've explained to her that you are only here in a somewhat token capacity — to ease Craigh's conscience. Once she knows you do not plan to interfere —" Fiona stopped at the expression on Megan's face. "Oh, my! I've put that badly, haven't I?"

"I don't understand," Megan said, bewildered.

Fiona sighed. "As much as I dislike discussing family affairs, I shall have to be honest with you, Megan. Lea's type of illness involves the mind, and Doctor Potts, our physician, holds no hope for her recovery. Craigh cannot bear the sight of her, and Constance and I have devoted all our time to her care. I think that Doctor Potts, in recommending a companion, was but considering the state of my own health. Truly, though, I fear the presence of a stranger will only upset her."

Megan had stopped listening at the beginning of Fiona's explanation. *Craigh cannot bear the sight of her,* the woman had said. Craigh Stewart, the child's own father! All Megan's instincts were revolted at the thought. Was he, himself, so perfect that he could not stand imperfection in others? Megan knew, already, that she would not like the master of this house!

"So, you see, it would be far better if you left us. We are so isolated here. It is lonely, there is nothing for a young girl to do."

"I will stay," Megan said.

"In that event, we shall do our best to entertain you," Fiona said, carefully replacing her napkin at her plate. "You and Aherne will have much in common, I am sure, and you may use a horse from the stables, should you care to ride."

"I will not have too much free time," Megan said, quietly, "since I am here to care for the child. Now, if you please, I would like to know more about her condition. Has she always been afflicted as you say she is now?"

Fiona smiled wryly. "You are a stubborn young lady," she said. "I suppose I will have to repeat the story, though I try to avoid thinking of the past with its painful memories." A fleeting expression of anguish touched her features as she continued.

"When Craigh and Morna came to this country, Aherne and I came with them. Lea was but a babe, then. Though Craigh is a man of independent means, he chose to settle in Michigan Territory, near Detroit, with the thought in mind to build small vessels for use on the lakes. Five years ago, his son was born. His — his worship for the boy was close to idolatry. And then the war came."

Fiona's voice dwindled, and she reached for the teapot. Filling her cup, she sipped at it delicately as if to gain courage to go on.

"There was danger from both British and Indian attack. Craigh decided to remove the family to the coast, where he believed it to be safe for us. We were all to travel together, but Lea fell ill. Craigh came on ahead to find a dwelling for us. The night before he returned, our home was burned to the ground. Morna and the little boy died in the fire."

So that was the reason for Craigh Stewart's indifference to his daughter's well-being, Megan thought, her eyes brimming with tears. Because of Lea's illness, the family had stayed behind, and he'd lost his wife and adored son. And he'd held a little girl, a sick little girl, to account for it. No wonder the child was troubled.

Fiona was still talking, telling how she was away at the time, gone to a ball at the Detroit fort. Aherne was visiting at a nearby farm. They returned to find the house in flames, Constance wandering in shock, with Lea in her arms. Craigh Stewart had returned the next morning.

"And Lea has been the way she is ever since," she finished. "Speechless, unable to walk, given to occasional frenzies. We came here, to the home Craigh purchased for his family, and since then she has been a constant care."

Megan shoved her plate away. "I am quite finished with my breakfast. I would like to see the child."

"Have it your own way." Fiona shrugged. "Perhaps after you have met her, you will change your mind. Her — infirmity does not tend to make her a lovable child. And I must warn you, Constance will not take kindly to interference."

Leaving the table, Megan followed Fiona up the curving stair. Constance stood on guard at Lea's door, bristling at the thought of intrusion. "I fed her," she said, "and bathed her. Now she's asleep."

Fiona interposed, offering to give Megan a guided tour of the house, and she accepted. But this day, Megan told herself determinedly, she would assume her rightful duties. First, she intended, if possible, to have a brief conversation with the man who withheld love from his own child.

As they walked along the balcony, Fiona pointed out the various sleeping chambers. Constance slept next to Lea, in a room with an adjoining door. Here was Fiona's bedroom. She flung open a door, revealing an opulence of silks and satins all in blending shades of blue. Aherne's room was next, then Craigh's. The two rooms at the far end of the balcony were locked, never to be opened except for cleaning. One was fitted as a nursery, the other as Morna's sitting room. The sight of those closed doors seemed to point up the sadness in this house as mere words could never do.

Megan was glad to follow Fiona down to the kitchens. There, in the cavernous room with its steam-slimed walls, she was introduced to Mollie Sharp, the cook; a brutish-looking woman, who, Fiona whispered, was a former convict but adequate at her job. The deaf young woman who had served at table was known as Della. Seeming to understand the introduction, she lost her blank expression momentarily as she bobbed and smiled.

"Now you've seen the lot," Fiona said, "except for down there." She pointed to the floor at her feet. "That's *his* private realm." Megan looked startled, and Fiona laughed. "Oh, my! It sounded as if I were speaking of Satan himself. No, dear — I meant *Craigh*. Those steps along the wall lead down to the wine cellar, thence to the chasm this house bridges. There is a cavern midway where Craigh indulges in his hobby — and his desire to be alone."

"Is he down there now?"

"If he has returned from riding, I should imagine so."

"Then do you suppose I might speak with him?"

Fiona's face sobered. "A word of caution, Megan. Craigh is not — himself. No one is allowed below. Should he be disturbed — I would hate to think what the consequences might be."

Megan paled, recalling Ian Mackenzie's words: *The master of Wyndspelle is a godless man, his mind crazed by his grief — or something worse.* Though she wished to confer with him, she had no desire for a confrontation in some eerie subterranean room. It was possible the man was mad. His treatment of his daughter would indicate that he was.

"I shall go outdoors, then," she finally smiled at Fiona. "I am certain that you have things you must attend to. I will go to the stables and check on the wee dog."

"You do that," Fiona agreed. "In the meantime, I will try to speak with Constance."

Megan pushed open the door by which she had entered the previous night, daunted a little by the scene before her. Though the sun was shining, the area was still a sea of mud and scattered stone, the scant growth that graced it offering no dry footing. At a distance were the ruins of what might have been a pergola or summerhouse. A stone bench lay broken, tipped upon its side. This morning Megan had been too interested in her first sight of Aherne and the horseman below her window. Now, she had to admit, dismally, the house she thought so impressive was situated in a setting of utter desolation.

The sound of barking claimed her attention. Lifting her skirts clear of the muck that coated her shoes, Megan went in search of Angus.

She found the pup and the boy, Aherne, together. An unused stall had been partially boarded up, and the floor covered with fresh straw. An almost-empty dish indicated the small animal had been recently fed. Aherne knelt on the floor, playing with Angus, his odd, triangular face alight with enjoyment until he heard Megan's voice.

"What a nice place you fixed for him," she said cheerily. "I appreciate your kindness."

Aherne froze, his shoulders slumping, his head ducking between them as if for protection.

Megan entered the small space and knelt beside him to pet the little dog. She still had the impression that there was a wildness in Aherne; that if not approached quietly, he would flee.

"He's a bonny wee dog, isn't he?" she asked.

His answer was a sullen mumble, but he reached out to Angus shyly. The little dog, overcome with joy at so much attention, whirled and wagged and tumbled like a clown. Megan was pleased to see that Aherne's face wore the beginnings of a smile.

"I took note of the horses as I came through the stable," she said softly. "They are so beautiful and well kept. I understand you're responsible for their fine condition."

This time the smile reached his eyes. *He* is *nice,* she thought as he looked at her directly for the first time. Though behind his smile she sensed a suffering, sensitive spirit.

"Fiona said I might ride one of the horses sometime." He nodded his head. "Princess is gentle."

Megan was delighted. She had found a way through his shyness. "I ride well," she said, "so any horse will do. I would give my life to ride the mare I saw you saddle this morning. Though I could never ride like Master Stewart. I have never seen such a handsome sight —"

With a growling sound, the boy leaped to his feet. He frowned at Megan for a moment, then slammed out of the stall. She heard his running feet outside the stable and sat, numb, small Angus whining at her side, wondering what had happened between his two best friends.

Angus was not the only one to wonder.

Whatever the problem was, it had to do with the last thing she had said. For a brief space, naked hatred had flashed from Aherne's eyes. And it was at the mention of Craigh Stewart's name.

Fiona was right: this was not a happy house. There were undercurrents here that brought clouds across this sunny day. Constance, jealous of anyone who might supplant her with Lea and Fiona; Craigh Stewart, who could not bear the sight of his own daughter; Aherne, who loved small creatures, but hated his brother-in-law with a depth that frightened her.

For a moment, she thought wistfully of the life she'd left behind her in England. True, it was a rather dull existence: Elizabeth querulous, the children spoiled, yet somehow endearing. But her cousin's husband had made remaining there an impossibility. Far better if she could have remained with Uncle Ian. Though his house was sparsely furnished, there was something home-like about it — comforting.

Angus whined as she closed the door to the stall. "Dinna fret," she whispered. "I'll be back soon. And as soon as I talk with Master Stewart and get a few things settled, you'll be sleeping in my room!"

It was a promise, she thought drearily, that she had no right to make. From what Fiona had said, Megan would have no authority in this household at all. Craigh Stewart might not even allow Angus on the premises. If such were the case, she would go.

CHAPTER 3

Megan's attempts to meet her charge were blocked, gently, by Fiona. The girl was sleeping or having one of her nervous spells. Wait. And, finally, she was told that it would be best to talk to Craigh first, in order to learn the extent of her responsibilities. Megan spent her morning refurbishing her two sadly inadequate gowns, waiting for the noon meal when the master of the house would surely appear.

He was not present, however, and his absence seemed to go unquestioned. Having braced herself to meet the man, Megan was sick with disappointment as she tried to ignore Constance's brooding face and Aherne's sullenness. Fiona dominated the table with gracious serenity, talking to make Megan feel at ease.

"Are you not too warm in that woolen gown, Megan? Surely you brought lighter garments with you for the summer! You did not?" She turned to Constance. "Perhaps we could make something up for her. Is anything remaining of the bolt we bought for Della? The blue stripe?"

Constance shook her head, a smug smile playing about her lips. Megan burned with embarrassment. The woman was enjoying the fact that Megan was placed in the same category as Della, the servant, though Fiona had only been thinking of her comfort. Megan felt a wave of gratitude as Fiona added, sadly, "If I only had something that would do for you —"

The idea was so ludicrous that Megan almost giggled. Fiona was diminutive, graceful; Megan, with her long arms and legs, her coltish awkwardness, would never fit into the woman's delicate frilled gowns. She could almost hear the sound of ripping seams!

"I sew quite well," she offered. "Perhaps I can find dress materials in Wychboro."

Fiona's face set. "We do not deal with the merchants there. They seem to hold some grudge against Wyndspelle. A grudge so old they've most likely forgotten what it is. They are a hidebound people. No, I shall ask Craigh to buy something suitable for you when he next goes to Boston. Something dark and serviceable, I think —"

"I will be most grateful," Megan said in a small voice.

Fiona waved her thanks away. "It should not be long. He should go in the next week or two, and you will be able to finish something before the summer heat *really* sets in. It will give you something to occupy your time."

"I intend to spend much of my time with the little girl," Megan said quietly. "I had thought to speak with Master Stewart at the noon meal —"

"Oh, Craigh takes most of his meals apart, especially when he's working at his hobby, as he is now."

"Will he dine with us this evening?"

"I have no idea." Fiona's face was suddenly shadowed. "It depends upon his mood. Sometimes he must be alone for maybe a week or two. I cannot answer for his actions."

There was something in the woman's voice, a tone that penetrated Megan's senses. *She loves him,* Megan thought with astonishment. *Fiona loves him! And his attitude is hurting her, as well as Lea!* Craigh Stewart had to be the most selfish, unfeeling man in the world.

"Do you read?" Fiona asked, suddenly.

"I am quite fond of books," Megan admitted.

"Then you will be interested in seeing the study," Fiona said, pushing back her empty plate. "Come. You may choose something to keep you occupied the rest of the afternoon."

Shortly thereafter Megan found herself ensconced in her room, several ancient leather-bound volumes at hand. Normally she would have been ecstatic, but instead, she felt like a prisoner. It was quite clear she had been pushed off up here to keep her from interfering with Lea in any way.

Unable to read, she wandered to the window. Below, she could see Aherne. The boy was playing at hide-and-seek with Angus, hiding behind a corner of the stable, leaping out to confront the scrappy little bundle of fur. Aherne was unaware of her presence, his odd face almost handsome as he knelt to ruffle the dog's coat.

For some reason, Megan felt suddenly better.

She went down to dinner, secure in the knowledge of what she intended to do. If Craigh Stewart did not appear, she would insist upon seeing Lea. After all, she had crossed an ocean in answer to Master Stewart's plea for help. He had had all day to spare her a moment of his precious time!

Dinner was much the same as the other meals had been. The master of the house was absent, Constance silent, Aherne staring into the burning candles as if hypnotized. Called to attention by Fiona, he left the table. He was soon followed by Constance, ostensibly to take the sick girl a tray. It was then that Megan delivered her ultimatum.

"Oh, my," Fiona said. "Constance will be —" She stopped, then made a placating gesture. "Very well, I suppose we can go up now."

Following Fiona through the shadowed hall and up the balcony stairs, Megan felt a pity for the woman. Outwardly poised and serene, she was like a petal dropped into a dark pool, drifting along the surface, at the mercy of the turbulent emotions that stirred it. Did she ever feel like standing up to the other members of the household? Screaming at them to stop their sulking and hating? Telling them that a home needed laughter, warmth, and love? Or was this her method of survival, this gentle drifting?

Perhaps, Megan thought glumly, it was because Fiona was a *lady*. Something she could never be.

Reaching Lea's door, they stepped inside. Megan was immediately aware of the stuffiness of the room. The heavy curtains at the windows were drawn, and a fire blazed in the fireplace. Constance sat hunched beside a high bed, blocking the figure on it, making small coaxing sounds. In her hand she held a spoon.

"Constance," Fiona said.

The woman turned and glared at them. Once her attention to the patient was diverted, a flailing hand rose, striking out with deadly accuracy. The spoon flew into the air, scattering its contents. Constance was livid with fury. "Look," she said, glowering. "Look what you made her do!"

But Megan was already at the bedside, looking down. The figure beneath the bulky comforters was that of a child, but the face was more like a wizened old woman: sharp-chinned, eyes blue-circled, bones visible beneath the taut skin. An arm lay outside the covers, burn scars visible where the sleeve had fallen back. But the eyes of the child held Megan's, slanting eyes of an electric blue that brought the horseman of the morning to mind. And those eyes were alive, filled with intelligence — and hatred.

"Lea?" Megan's voice was not quite so certain, now, as she bent above the small, emaciated body. "Lea, I'm Megan —"

In answer, the girl spat upon her, full in the face.

Megan staggered back, sick with instant revulsion. The deed had been done with aforethought. She had seen the flash of cunning that preceded it, the look of calculation.

Megan drew herself up to her full height. Carefully removing the spittle from her cheek, she smeared it, deliberately across the face of the child, oblivious to the gasps of horror behind her.

"Now," she said, calmly, "we are even. So now we can be friends. Think on that tonight. I will see you in the morning."

Turning, she bade a polite goodnight to Fiona and Constance who still stood frozen, brushed past them, and climbed the stairs to her room. There, she scrubbed furiously at her face, using the cold water left in the bowl. How could she have reacted in such an ugly way? It was something Fiona would never have done. And the elusive Master Stewart was probably hearing of her deplorable actions at this very moment.

Well, let him! If she were to help his daughter, they must first establish a bond of mutual respect.

Her hair unpinned, she carried a candle to the small dresser to search for her brush and caught a glimpse of herself in the mirror. She halted with a sharp indrawn breath. For the face that looked out at her so briefly was her own — but not her own. It was a woman's face, framed by glorious red-gold hair, lips curved in an irresistible, dimpling smile — but the eyes held a mute appeal —

The candle tipped in Megan's shaking hand, spilling hot wax, and she flinched with the pain. In that short space the face was gone.

Megan frowned into the glass, seeing only her own familiar self; tip-tilted nose, with freckles dusted across it, too-large mouth, soft brown hair that showed red only when struck by the sun. The apparition had only been a trick of light and shadow, caused by the candle in her hand. It might be a good idea, she thought ruefully, to have a candle with her always if it made her look like that.

Readying herself for bed, she slid beneath the blankets to discover she could not sleep. Her mind was filled with the events of the day. The way Craigh Stewart looked up at her this morning, something like shock in his strange eyes. The story Fiona had told her; the knowledge that Craigh could not bear the sight of his own child. Aherne, so tender in his love for animals, but with something in his nature that was warped and frightening.

And the child, Lea. The terrible, pitiful child!

At last, Megan fell into a restless sleep, to waken long before dawn. The silence of the dark house seemed sinister, and sleep would not return. Finally she rose and moved toward the window, opening it to let in the breezes of the night.

And she heard the screams from below.

Megan stood transfixed for a moment at the terror that shattered the darkness. The cries were bloodcurdling, the ultimate in fear and horror.

And those shrieks were made by a child!

Megan snatched up her cloak, still crumpled and damp from her journey, threw it over her nightdress and ran barefoot down the stairs, the flickering candle she lit hastily casting monstrous shadows around her. She paused momentarily, sensing that she was not alone, then hurried on. Reaching the balcony, she could see a faint ray of light from a door that was slightly ajar.

Lea's room.

She raced toward it and flung it open, uttering a choked cry at the scene before her.

The room was filled with smoke, dense and smothering. The girl's small body was obscured by a black figure bending over it. Constance! She appeared to be strangling the child —

Megan threw herself forward, grappling with the woman, flinging her back and away, interposing herself between Constance and the child on the bed.

"Are ye daft?" she screamed. "God in heaven! What were you doing?"

Constance stood mute, her face sallow, her eyes dark with fear as Megan raged on. "You were trying to kill that child," she accused. "I saw you!"

With apparent effort, the woman pulled herself together. "It's not what you think," she said, sullenly. "She had one of her spells. I was only trying to help her."

Megan whirled toward the girl on the bed. Lea lay unmoving, her eyes wide with horror, face marble-white. She appeared to be dead. Megan drew an unsteady breath, then placed her hand on Lea's breast. She was still breathing, thanks be to God.

"Lea?" Megan said, her voice trembling. "Lea?"

There was no answer. Lea stared at the ceiling, oblivious to all but her own private terror.

"Leave her alone," Constance said harshly. "Won't do you any good. She's always like this, after. Sometimes for days."

"After *what*? After you've frightened her out of her wits?"

"After she's had one of her upsets," the woman said. Then, insolently, "Seems to me *you* were the one who upset her."

Megan stared at her until she lowered her eyes. "You're lying," she said. "I don't know what you were doing, or what is taking place here, but I intend to find out —tonight! I'm not leaving you here to do further damage. Open those windows!"

The woman complied, and when the air had cleared, Megan took one more look at Lea, who lay as still as though she were in her coffin. "Now," she told Constance, "walk ahead of me, out into the hall. I'm going to wake Fiona."

"You do that." Constance smiled ominously. "You just do that. But I can tell you she isn't going to thank you for it!"

Megan followed at the woman's heels until they reached Fiona's door. There, she hammered at it furiously. If it wakened the other sleepers, let it! Surely they would have heard Lea's screams if they carried to her floor? Why had no one else rushed to help the girl?

Fiona's door opened almost immediately. She stood before them in a sweeping blue peignoir, a sleek black cat cradled in her arms.

"Oh," she said to Megan, "did she wake you?" Then, across Megan to Constance, "I was going to see if I could help you. Was it — bad, this time?"

"Bad enough. Might have Doctor Potts take a look at her tomorrow. I was going to call you, but — *this* one — she indicated Megan contemptuously, "came in and attacked me. Got the idea I was trying to murder the child!"

"Oh, Megan!" Fiona's voice held a mingled note of concern and amusement. "The very idea! But I suppose it's understandable. We should have explained earlier that Lea is subject to these … spells. She screams and thrashes about, and Constance is the only one who can handle her."

"And she needs me now," Constance snorted. "So I'll go back to sit with her."

Megan put out a hand, impulsively, to stop her, then felt a tide of embarrassment sweep over her. What a fool she must look to both Fiona and Constance. She was suddenly conscious of her sleep-tousled hair, the wrinkled cloak, her bare feet. How stupid she must have looked, galloping to the rescue of someone who was in no danger at all! Constance had cared for Lea for years. And she, Megan, had been in this household only a night and a day. Yet she had dared to make snap judgments of another's actions.

"I … I'm sorry," she began. But before she could finish, the door to the next room opened. Aherne stepped out, hastily buttoning the shirt that covered his thin boyish frame, his pale hair standing on end, eyes fogged with sleep and something else: terror.

"I heard Lea," he said. "I smelled the smoke. It was *her,* wasn't it? She's come again!"

"You're dreaming," Fiona told him. "Now go back —" Her words ended in a little wail as a bristly bundle of fur appeared between Aherne's feet. Angus, whom he'd evidently slipped in for the night.

Mad with delight at seeing Megan, the small dog charged toward her, barking furiously. The black cat in Fiona's arms clawed its way free and shot down the stairs with a piercing shriek. Angus streaked after it.

Megan stood stricken for a moment, then followed suit.

The animals circled the great hall below, Angus ignoring Megan's coaxing calls. He seemed to have decided it was a new kind of game, and he liked it. The cat found the open door to the dining area and was through it in a flash, Angus close behind. When Megan reached the door, the two combatants had already disappeared into the kitchens below.

Megan ran down the steps, her heart pumping furiously. She didn't think the puppy would injure the cat, but whatever happened, Angus was only at Wyndspelle on sufferance. Why had that wretched boy brought him in tonight? She quelled her irritation at the memory of the boy's evident loneliness. She could not blame him.

But the animals were no longer in sight. Where could they have gone? The door that led to the warren of rooms off the kitchen was closed. But the one at the foot of the stair leading to the wine cellars yawned open.

Gingerly, Megan descended the dank steps that led toward the forbidden regions, Craigh Stewart's domain. She found herself in a cavernous, echoing chamber that seemed to be hewn from the rock itself. The sound of the ocean boomed in her ears as she turned about, holding her candle high. Its light was lost in the shadowed, irregular walls. Permeating the air was the odor of a century of damp and mold. The atmosphere was the same as that of the buttery at home, where Cameron was slain — an aura of old wrongs, and evil unavenged.

Shivering a little, Megan walked forward to where a lighter shade of gray marked an opening, a square in the center of the floor, where a trap door had been turned back on its hinges.

Peering down, she saw a flight of rough-hewn steps falling steeply to the sea, water surging and frothing at the base. Torchlight flickered on the craggy walls, creating an illusion of moving shadows.

Surely the animals had not gone down there! It was difficult to imagine living creatures descending, easier to believe the steps were created for something to come *up*: some slime-coated monster, escaping from the sea —

But human hands had set fire to those torches, though why they burned so wastefully at night, she could not guess. And she heard Angus's bark from below, the sound of it magnified, echoing up to her.

Resolutely, Megan set foot upon the stair.

Holding carefully to the walls, though they were wet and repelling to the touch, she made her way down. *It's like descending into hell,* she thought. *The devil himself might dwell here, or one of the old forgotten gods of the Netherworld —*

As the notion touched her mind, she heard a cry of rage — and on the right-hand wall before her, opposite the flaring light that must mark the cavern she'd been told of, appeared a monstrous shadow. A shadow of a man, magnified to gigantic size, one arm swung high above his head. And in that hand, he held a weapon — a club of some kind —

Angus! Dear God, wee Angus!

With an incoherent cry, Megan threw herself forward, forgetting all caution as she rushed frantically down the slime-slick, treacherous stair.

CHAPTER 4

As Megan reached the natural cavern that opened off the steps midway, she lost her footing and found herself falling toward the waters that lapped hungrily at the foot of the stair. With a violent effort, she managed to throw herself to one side, landing on the floor of the rock-walled room in a small, ignominious heap. She drew a long, sobbing breath, then looked up at the sound of an oath.

The shadow-maker stood above her, his weapon still upraised. As her dazed eyes focused, Megan recognized the man as Craigh Stewart, his face blazing with anger at her intrusion. He hardly looked human. More like some pagan god. He was shirtless, his bronze body gleaming in the torchlight that turned his hair to copper. In one hand he held a mallet, in the other a chisel.

She was on her feet in an instant, pummeling at his chest with her fists. "Dinna hit him!" she screamed, lapsing into a thick brogue. "Ye damn girt hulkin' brute!"

He gave way before her onslaught. "I assure you, young lady, I had no intention of striking the beast. Though I would suggest you take him and go." His voice was tinged with ice. "I allow no one down here. Were you not told?"

She was still trembling with fury. "I didna wish to come here! 'Tis only my wee dog I've come to fetch!" She glared, indicating the mallet. "An' ye were goin' to hit him, ye damn … ye damn…!"

He sighed, wearily. "If you will take note, I am an amateur sculptor. These are the tools of my trade. I was quite peacefully at work when I suddenly found myself involved in a dog-and-cat fight, then set upon by a rather untidy-looking female, whose language is unladylike to say the least. What do you expect of me?"

Megan wilted, seeing the great stone behind the man from which two shapes were emerging. The black cat was perched atop the taller one, while Angus waited, whimpering a little below. Master Stewart must have had quite a surprise! She felt a smile twitching at the corners of her mouth as she imagined the scene. Then the identity of the stone figures struck her. One was that of a woman. Beside her, a small child. A little boy.

Craigh Stewart was down here creating his lost ones in stone, while upstairs a little girl, his daughter, was dying for lack of love!

She had wanted to talk with him, and now she had the opportunity.

"If you are quite finished," he said coldly, "take your dog and go. I will be sure the trap door is closed hereafter." He turned away indifferently, and she seized frantically upon the opportunity to speak.

"I am sorry you were disturbed," she said to his bare back. "I am Megan Alisdair, your daughter's new companion. I have been wanting to confer with you, to discuss my duties." He did not turn, and her anger flared until she could contain it no longer. "Master Stewart, I said I wish to speak with you!"

"There is nothing to discuss. Fiona will explain your responsibilities. Now, if you will excuse me —"

Megan set her chin and stood tall. "I will not excuse you! Master Stewart, you are an unnatural father, and in my opinion, a very rude and obnoxious man. I insist upon doing the job I came to do. I want full charge o' the wee lass, a cot in her room, and a hand in her discipline, else I canna abide in this house! If this be your attitude, to the devil wi' ye!"

The minute the words were out of her mouth, she wished them back. This was the master of Wyndspelle she'd had the temerity to address in such fashion! A tremor ran through her body as he turned. His eyes were expressionless, but she had a feeling he was laughing at her. When he spoke, however, his voice was as cold as before.

"We will discuss the matter on the morrow, Miss Alisdair. This is neither the place nor the time."

He scooped up the little dog, handing him to her. Somehow she managed to make her exit, though her knees were weak as water. On the steps, she could not resist the temptation to look back. He was staring after her, his eyes blind and unseeing, wrapped in his own tortured thoughts. He had the look of a man who was weary unto death.

Holding Angus close, Megan climbed the stairs. Reaching the balcony, she opened the door to Lea's room and peeped in. The girl was as she had left her, with Constance sitting beside the bed. There was only a faint smell of smoke. Apparently all was well. Megan closed the door, gently, without disturbing the occupants.

Passing Aherne's room, she heard Fiona's voice in conversation with him. Probably comforting the boy, with his wild imaginings. Megan frowned, remembering. *I smelled the smoke,"* he'd said. *"She's come again!"* Who in the world had he been talking about?

The smoke, however, had filled the room in a choking cloud. That had not been explained. Perhaps the fireplace was not drawing properly. She thought of the sweep Cousin Elizabeth employed from time to time, with the grimy little lad who cleaned the flues. Perhaps they did not have such services available here.

Back in her own room, Megan made Angus a bed upon the floor. She would return him to the stables in the morning, which, from the appearance of the sky, should not be overlong in coming.

Abed at last, she lay restless for a time, reviewing the events of the night. At least she had achieved an objective — a conference with the man who employed her — but she had no notion of how it would develop.

Would he be angered at her forwardness this night? Tell her she must go? Or would he actually consider giving the sick child into her charge?

That would be unlikely, she thought. For the story of the spitting incident would be carried, not only to Craigh Stewart, but to the physician who was due to call on the morrow. What would *his* reaction be?

She twisted her head on the pillow, sick with worry and embarrassment. What she had done to the child had come naturally, but was it wrong? Had it been a childish way of meeting the problem?

Closing her eyes, Megan felt the night breeze caress her forehead with cool fingers, like the touch of a soothing hand. And on it came a drift of faintly familiar perfume.

With a thumping heart, she recalled Lea's room tonight. When she entered it, there was a strong smell of smoke, but there had also been this same underlying scent. At the time, it had been frightening, but now it was vaguely comforting.

Megan drifted into a deep and dreamless sleep.

CHAPTER 5

When daylight flooded her window, Megan awoke instantly. It seemed important to return Angus to his quarters in the stable where he would be out of sight — and, she hoped, out of mind — after the fiasco of the previous night. She dressed hastily and stole through the still-sleeping house, the animal clutched in her arms. Passing through the great hall, near the fireplace with its smell of dead ashes, she felt a momentary qualm. There was evil here. She felt it. And she also felt very small and alone. She hastened her steps, almost running through the dining room, down the stairs into the kitchens, and out into the day.

Settling Angus, she dawdled before returning to the house, pausing at each of the stalls to speak to the horses, introducing herself, rubbing their velvet muzzles. Though Craigh Stewart's mount was graceful and spirited, there was one she would choose for herself, a small stocky brown that reminded her of the sturdy Highland ponies of home. She stood feeding it wisps of hay, which it took delicately from her hand, until she could force herself to return to the waiting house.

Mollie Sharp was in the kitchen, and with her presence Megan's courage returned. Though all she received from the cook was a scowl, the oppressiveness she'd sensed when she was alone had gone. In the dining room she found only Aherne at breakfast, Della hovering over him, attending to his needs. With a smile, the young woman returned to the kitchens to bring Megan's food. Aherne did not look up, and Megan took her place at table, a little nervous.

"I took Angus out to the stable," she said finally.

A twitch of the boy's shoulders indicated that he'd heard, but he did not answer.

"I'm sorry about the commotion last night," she continued. "I do hope Fiona isn't angry."

Aherne swallowed the last bite on his plate and pushed back his chair. Suddenly it seemed important that he not leave her. Megan stretched forth a hand in a pleading gesture.

"Please, Aherne, I want to be friends! We both like the same things, horses and dogs…"

He lifted his eyes to meet hers, and she saw something in them, a wistfulness, as though he wanted to believe her.

"I'm a stranger here," she rushed on, "and I'm so confused. I don't understand what happened last night. Lea screaming, the smoke —"

Aherne flinched, a shutter seeming to close over his eyes, but Megan plunged ahead, recklessly. "What did you mean, *She's come again*? There's so much that I don't know, and if I'm to help Lea —"

His eyes went beyond her, and Megan turned to see Fiona in the doorway. "Gotta feed the horses," Aherne mumbled, and was gone.

Fiona entered, taking her customary place at the table, a smile of apology on her face. "I'm sorry I'm so late," she said, "but Craigh insisted on having a private conversation this morning. I understand you found your little dog?"

Megan nodded, her throat tightening. What had Craigh Stewart told Fiona? Did he mention the way she'd struck out at him? Or the language she'd used, so unbecoming to a lady? Her face reddened at the memory of the things she'd said and done as she waited for Fiona to reveal the gist of the

51

conversation. Probably she would be told, most politely, that she must go.

But the words that followed Fiona's thoughtful pause were not what Megan expected. "I wish to apologize for my young brother's actions last night," she said in a sad, soft voice. "He, too, felt the impact of our tragedy to a great degree, blaming himself, me, Craigh for being away. He has dreadful nightmares, in which he insists Morna is still alive. And sometimes he has periods of irrationality. He adores Lea, yet we cannot allow him to visit her — for both their sakes." A single crystal tear appeared at the corner of one eye, and she dabbed at it, ineffectually, with a lace-bordered handkerchief. "I'm sorry," she whispered, "but it is difficult to say such things of one's own brother."

Megan sat silent, wishing there were something she could say or do to comfort the woman. But after a moment Fiona lifted her head, smiling bravely through her tears. "We must talk of pleasanter things," she said. "Are you enjoying your breakfast? Constance will be with us presently. She has been delayed. Craigh wished to confer with her, too, before he rides into Wychboro to ask Doctor Potts to come to Lea."

Fiona could hardly have chosen a *less* pleasant subject, Megan thought morosely. At this moment, Constance was probably dwelling on Megan's inadequacies and misdeeds, blaming her for Lea's condition. And after his one and only meeting with Megan, Craigh Stewart would be inclined to agree with her. No, she was *not* enjoying her breakfast! How could one enjoy something one could not swallow? The meal stretched interminably as she endeavored to make polite responses to Fiona's gracious conversation.

When Constance came, she wore an expression of triumph. "He just asked some questions," she told Fiona, "and I told him what I thought. Now he wants to see her." She pointed an accusing finger at Megan. As Megan left the room, she heard Constance say, "He's going to get rid of *that* one."

And Fiona's placating answer: "Now, Constance, remember that whatever Craigh does, it is his decision and you must accept it. And you must not be so certain where he is concerned. He never fails to surprise me."

Crossing the great hall, Megan knocked at the study door, her heart hammering with apprehension. Hearing Craigh's command to enter, she turned the knob, suddenly blind with terror, and tripped on the edge of the carpet that covered the study floor, going down to her knees. It seemed she knelt there for an eternity before a large hand gripped her arm, lifting her to her feet.

"Do you always enter a room this way?" the man demanded. "Or it this strictly for my benefit? Though I find it entertaining, it is quite disconcerting."

Megan pulled away from his supporting grasp, her face scarlet. "I tripped," she said with some confusion.

"Obviously. And now that the preliminaries are over, we shall have the talk I promised last night. Will you be seated?" He gestured toward a chair.

"I prefer to stand," she said, stubbornly.

"Very well, then, since a gentleman should not seat himself while a *lady* remains standing, I shall stand, too."

Megan wished she could take her words back. Though her legs were over-long and she felt awkward in Fiona's presence, Craigh Stewart towered over her, making her feel at a disadvantage. She stood as tall as she could, though the man turned away from her, hands clasped behind his back, looking out of the window.

He paused just long enough for her nerves to tighten to a fine edge, then said, "I have considered your requests and am inclined to grant them. You are to have full charge of the child. I shall inform Fiona that you will occupy the quarters adjoining Lea's, with Constance to be removed to the upper floor. The exchange of rooms will take place today."

Megan gasped with astonishment, and he raised a silencing hand.

"Obviously, you will be unable to handle twenty-four-hour care alone. Therefore, Constance will be required to sit with the girl two hours in the morning, and two in the afternoon, thus leaving you time for diversion. On Thursdays, you are to have the whole day free, from eight in the morning until eight at night. Do you consider the arrangement fair?"

"M-more than fair," Megan stammered.

"There is only one other stipulation. In assuming charge of Lea, you also assume all responsibility. If any question as to the child's state of health arises, you are free to summon Doctor Potts. I do not wish to be troubled with small details or prolonged discussion. Is that clear?"

The enormity of the man's proposition struck Megan with horrifying clarity. He was ridding himself of his sick daughter, shuffling her off as he would an outworn cloak, giving her into the hands of a virtual stranger. Anger blazed inside her, and it sounded in her voice. "Master Stewart!"

He turned, sighing wearily. "If you intend to launch into any further dissertations on my character, Miss Alisdair, you may spare yourself the trouble. I believe you did that quite thoroughly last night. And frankly, I do not give a damn for your opinions. I have stated my terms. You have only to refuse or comply."

Megan faced him, glaring, her hands clenched at her sides while her mind raced wildly. Craigh Stewart had made his demands quite clear. Now she had only to choose whether to go or to stay. She could return to Uncle Ian. Every fiber in her body urged her to do so. But if she did, Lea would be left at the mercy of the possessive Constance — and delicate, weak-willed Fiona. She thought of the scene the night before, of Constance bending over Lea's bed. Perhaps the woman *had* been trying to harm the girl. Rather than lose her to Megan's care, Constance would prefer to see her dead —

Megan shivered. She would stay. She would have to! She would do as much for an animal. But she did not intend to let Craigh Stewart have the last word.

"If I remain," she said, her jaw set stubbornly, "the dog stays, too. He will share my room."

The man's lips twitched with what may have been amusement. "Granted," he said.

"Then 'tis settled." Megan turned and walked, stiff-backed, from the room, careful to avoid the treacherous carpet as she went. She closed the door behind her.

By noon, the change of rooms had been effected. Constance was silent, casting baleful glances at Megan as they passed, each carrying her own possessions. She had earned the woman's undying hatred, Megan knew. And left alone at last with her small charge, she began to wonder if she had been right in her decision to accept Craigh Stewart's terms.

Lea's catatonic state of the previous night had lessened, the expression of horror leaving the eyes that were so like her father's. Now she seemed a little feverish, dazed and uncomprehending as Megan attempted to feed her soft foods from her tray.

"Eat up, hinny," Megan whispered, slipping into the soft tones of her own childhood nurse. "When ye're yerself again, I hae a giftie for ye!" The child showed no reaction to her voice, but Megan kept talking in a low murmur, warm with a tenderness for the unloved girl.

When she'd managed to spoon down enough food to sustain the child, Megan wiped Lea's lips, fluffed her pillows, and was gratified to see her eyes close in a restful sleep.

Wandering to the window, Megan looked out. This room, at the front of the house, had a view of the sea. Leaning outward, Megan could see a strip of beach at the foot of the promontory, studded with boulders. For an instant, she seemed to see a tall shape slant across the sands. She blinked, and it was gone. Her nerves, she thought, seemed to have affected her vision.

Turning from the view of sand and sea, she jumped to see Constance in the doorway. She had been so intent upon the scene below that she had not heard the sound of the opening door.

"You have your two hours," the woman said, harshly, "and I am to tell you there's something left for you in the dining room. Miss Fiona's in her room. A sick headache." Somehow her tone managed to accuse Megan, as if she'd caused problems by not coming down to dinner, and Fiona's discomfort was in some way to be traced to Megan, too. In spite of herself, Megan felt an instant's guilt.

She thanked Constance and left the room hastily, pausing outside the door for a moment of amusement at her own feelings. She was not answerable to Constance in any way! She, Megan, had full charge of the child. And if tender, loving care would bring Lea back to health, Megan certainly intended to supply it. She had a vision of Lea restored to the glowing sturdiness that was the birthright of every young girl, and of herself leading her to Craigh Stewart, showing him how wrong he'd been in his rejection. She stopped with her hand on the stair rail, imagining a new Lea, a tomboy Lea, a girl such as she had been as a child, partaking in all sorts of lively activities.

Like sliding down a curving rail, she thought, running her hand along the polished wood, her eyes bright with memory. What a marvelous sensation it had been! Like flying!

Temptation nibbled at her. Well, why not? Constance was sitting with Lea, Fiona confined with her illness. Aherne would be out and about. Craigh Stewart was to have gone to fetch Doctor Potts. Who was there to see?

Cheeks pink, she swung one leg across the railing, adjusting her clothing to suit, facing upward as she did as a small girl, and let go, glorying in her speedy descent.

She did not hear the front door open, but she did hear a loud masculine exclamation.

"Good God!"

It came just at the time she should have clamped her knees together, slowing herself at the curve of the rail before shooting off into space. Panic-stricken, she released her grip and felt herself propelled into the air and into what seemed to be a tangle of bodies.

When she dared to open her eyes at last, she was seated on the floor of the great hall, her limbs exposed in most unseemly fashion. Apparently she had taken two men down with her in her landing: Craigh Stewart, who rose, dusting himself off, his face impassive, and another gentleman whose brown eyes stared at her in shock.

Still seated, Megan scrambled for her skirts, arranging them decently around her. Before she could rise, the master of Wyndspelle performed the amenities.

"Miss Alisdair, this is our good doctor. Doctor Potts, this is the girl of whom we've been speaking. Lea's new companion."

The shaken doctor rose, and Megan looked up at him, helplessly. Youngish, his dark face saved from being handsome by strong lines that formed parentheses from nose to mouth, the physician was obviously upset.

"This will not do," he said. "I had in mind someone older, more mature —"

"Miss Alisdair is quite mature," Craigh Stewart said. "'Tis only that she has a habit of entering a room — precipitously." He held a hand to Megan, assisting her to her feet, and the doctor frowned.

"You shouldn't move her, man! She may have sustained an injury. If you will call one of the women to attend, I shall examine her —"

"No," Megan exploded. "I mean, thank you, sir, but I am quite all right." It was a lie, she knew. There were bound to be bruises — but at least they were where they would not show! "I am very pleased to make your acquaintance, Doctor," she continued, her face crimson.

But the physician was not looking at her. "I repeat," he said to Craigh, "this girl will not do. She is little more than a child herself, as she has proven by this performance."

"Perhaps Lea needs a young companion," Craigh said, lifelessly. "You said yourself, that Constance is a gloomy, smothering influence on the girl."

"I'm not thinking of *Lea*," the doctor said, his voice low and even. "I am thinking of Miss Alisdair. You know the dangers here! We need to find some sturdy country woman, strong —"

"I can vouch for Miss Alisdair's strength," Craigh interposed. "Also, that she has some considerable talent in the art of fisticuffs. In addition, her vocabulary has a pungency that would put the driver of a team of mules to shame. I beg you, good friend, not to be misled by appearances."

Megan flushed hotly, wanting to retaliate, but held her tongue. Doctor Potts eyed her with new interest.

"She is older than she appeared at first impression," he said grudgingly, "but I must insist she be prepared for what she must face in the handling of my patient, else I refuse all responsibility."

Craigh's face darkened. "Very well, Doctor." He gestured toward the study. "Discuss all that you will. However, do not disturb me. I am going below."

When he had gone, the physician led Megan into the study, indicating a chair. She sat gingerly, beginning to really feel the effect of her fall. He started to seat himself at Craigh's desk but instead went to the window.

"Craigh has given me his version of Lea's hysteria last night. I would like to hear your impressions."

Megan told of hearing the girl's screams, of rushing down to find Constance struggling with her, of the smoke-filled room.

"Ah," he said, "smoke. Craigh didn't mention it. Tell me, was there anything strange about it? An odor of brimstone, perhaps — like gunpowder?" His face had a strange, avid expression.

Megan shook her head. "I smelled a kind of fragrance," she said, "more like a perfume, a scent."

The man looked oddly disappointed. He came back to the desk, seating himself in Craigh's chair, crossing one long-boned leg over the other. "Now," he said, "tell me, how much do you know of the tragedy?"

"Only that Master Stewart's former home was burned, killing his wife and son. It was supposedly set fire by natives, the night Detroit fell to the British." She paused, looking at him questioningly.

"That is the story as it was told," the man said, heavily. "And I must ask that you regard anything I tell you further as confidential."

"Of course."

"Fiona and Aherne were both away at the time," he continued. "They returned to find Constance wandering outside, in shock. Apparently, the two had escaped through an open window in Lea's room."

Megan nodded. "Fiona told me."

"But did she tell you that the door was bolted from the outside, both front door and back? Did she tell you Lea had been punished severely for playing with fire the day before? That she was intensely jealous of her baby brother, and of her beautiful mother? That she knew when her father was due home?"

Megan's eyes were dark with horror. "You can't mean that! Are you trying to say that a seven-year-old child —?"

"Murdered her mother and brother? Yes. And what I'm going to say may even sound more shocking. It was I who suggested Craigh approach Reverend Mackenzie, hoping to bring a touch of sanctity into this godless house! I have a strong religious heritage, Miss Alisdair, and I hope you will persuade Craigh Stewart to take the only course by which he can save that little girl."

"I do not understand."

"Exorcism, Miss Alisdair. Exorcism." His brown, near-handsome face was anguished. "I have tried everything known to medical science — leeches, purgatives, tonics, but to no avail. The child is possessed of a demon. There have been other instances to prove it. *The child is possessed.*"

CHAPTER 6

"Balderdash!" Megan said flatly, when she could get her breath after his startling pronouncement. "I have never heard such — such idiocy in my life!"

Doctor Potts stiffened, his deep brown eyes showing hurt, and she hastened to amend her words.

"I'm sorry, I didn't mean to sound so adamant. I suppose it is possible that the child set the fire that ended in tragedy, but I cannot believe it was with any idea of vengeance. An accident, perhaps, a very sad one. Don't you see? She is punishing herself! She needs love, affection, understanding —" She stopped, swallowing. "*Possessed?* The very idea! And you call yourself a man of science, sir?"

The physician's face reddened with angry confusion. "And you, young lady, are a newcomer to these parts. I would suggest you do not leap to conclusions on things that you know nothing about! My education tells me that demons do not exist, yet my background, growing up in this area, tells me that they do. This house, itself, is a haunted place. Accursed! Yet my medical training brings me here to treat a child, though my personal belief leads me to feel myself in mortal danger. Would you have me suggest you remain here without giving you at least a warning to take care?"

"I'm sorry," Megan said again, "and I appreciate your thoughtfulness on my behalf. But," and she set her jaw, stubbornly, "you are very wrong in thinking such dreadful things of a poor sick child."

Rising wearily, Doctor Potts mumbled something about having done his duty, then informed Megan that he was traveling down to Boston to replenish his medical supplies and would be gone for a few days. Lea would have to be her full responsibility in his absence. It left her with a shivery feeling, a sense of inadequacy that frightened her.

Afterward, Megan sat beside her charge, holding the small hand that was cold, limp, unresponsive. Angus pawed at her lap. She picked him up, taking comfort in his warmth, his eager, bewhiskered face. "Can we help her, lad?" she asked him.

He whined.

Possessed! Megan still would not believe it. Yet *something* haunted the child, and the darkness must be cleared away.

Morning, when it came, was like a new beginning. Megan rose, dressed, and entered Lea's room, throwing open the windows to catch the fresh smell of the sea.

"'Tis a lovely day," she sang to the girl on the bed. "We must be letting some of it in!" To her delight, Lea's eyes blinked against the brightness she was unaccustomed to. The first involuntary movement since the night of her strange spell.

She needs the sun, Megan thought. *Poor thing, cooped up in an airless prison. She needs the sun, the smell of the sea and of growing things.*

Megan scanned the room thoughtfully. It was a pleasant enough place, with its muted shades of rose, but there was nothing in it to indicate that it belonged to a girl of Lea's age. No poppets or mementos of the past. No ribbons or gewgaws suitable to a twelve-year-old.

She went to the wardrobe. It was empty, but a large chest held a selection of plain white utilitarian gowns such as the child was now wearing. What if she had a day gown, Megan wondered? Something bright and pretty! And supposing she were lifted and seated in a chair by the window, where she might look out and see the changing colors of the sea and sky? And she needed something that would make this room her own. Megan resolved to ask Fiona if anything had been salvaged from the fire.

Della brought hot water, and Megan sponged the sick child's body, aching at the sight of her emaciation. Lea's copper hair was like Craigh Stewart's, except that it lacked its snapping vitality. Megan brushed it into a fan against the pillows. It had been kept braided tightly, and she guessed it might be soothing to have it free.

When the trays were brought, she fed the sick girl, fretting at the tiny amounts she was able to get her to swallow. Her diet did look unappetizing. Curious, she tasted a bit of the custard from Lea's tray, gagging on it. No salt, no sugar! It had the consistency of a paste of flour. Sipping the brew that had been brought to the girl, she puckered her lips in distaste. Some sort of herbal concoction, as bitter as gall.

Taking the tea from her own tray, Megan laced it liberally with honey and held it to Lea's lips. Though it was a slow process, she managed to get her to drink half a cup. She wondered if it were only her imagination, or if there was truly a bit more color in Lea's pallid cheeks.

"I will speak with the cook," Megan whispered. "There will be good food for you. You will eat it, and grow strong and rosy! Then we will go down to the beach, below. My father was a Highland laird, but my mother came from near the sea — and she taught me the games the fisher children play! We will play them together."

Was there a spark of interest in Lea's eyes? Megan could not tell. She wandered to the window, looking out at the waters below.

"I see a stone in the sea," she said, "much like the one at Portessie, called Scatt's Craighs. When the tide is out, the children stand upon it and shout:

'I warn ye once,
I warn ye twice,
I warn ye three times over.
Tak oop yer wings
An' flee awa',
For fear o' Johnny Rover.'

"Then they jump from the rock and run and run as fast as ever they can, until they are tired. We will do that, Lea, I promise you."

"A promise you cannot keep!" said a voice from the doorway. Megan turned to see Constance, her face set with anger. "The child will never walk again. Doctor Potts says so. 'Tis a cruel thing to speak to her in this way. And you have the windows open! The air from the sea is not good for her. The bright light will harm her vision."

The woman strode past Megan, slamming the windows closed, drawing the drapes, her body rigid with fury. Megan promptly opened them again, staring Constance down. "I am in full charge of Lea," she said, tight-lipped. "If you do not wish to accept my orders, you may go to Master Stewart. I intend to do as I think best for her."

Constance looked at her, her face a battleground of mixed emotions. There was hatred there, fear, perhaps, and something that resembled hope. *She does love the child,* Megan thought, *but in such a strange way! Wanting to keep her here, abed, a prisoner in a darkened room.* Maybe she believed that, if Lea should recover, there would be further incidents such as Doctor Potts had mentioned.

"Constance," Megan asked softly, "the fire that killed Lea's mother and brother — do you think Lea had any hand in it?"

Fear blazed in Constance's eyes, effacing her other emotions. "It was a raid," she said, finally. "The war —"

"I have heard differently. And you should know. You were there."

The words came from Constance's throat in an agonized cry. "I don't know," she said. "I can't remember. I can't remember!"

She sounded so upset that Megan had to believe in her sincerity. "You're here to sit with Lea, while I take several free hours?" she asked. "Then I will carry these trays down to the kitchen."

Leaving Constance hovering over the girl, she took down the trays, bearding Mollie Sharp, the cook, in her own domain. "Miss Lea's breakfast was sadly lacking this morning," she told the woman, who stood with arms akimbo, frowning at her.

"Fix what I'm told to fix," the cook grumbled.

Had Doctor Potts ordered the child's diet, Megan wondered? To her way of thinking, strengthening foods were in order. Porridge, sweetened tea, a coddled egg at breakfast. And for the other meals, beef or mutton broth, sieved vegetables, honey custards, milk with beaten egg —

"Fix what I'm told to fix," the woman said again, her forehead creased in an ugly scowl.

Megan lost patience. "Then the meals will be as I have suggested," she said, firmly. "For I am *telling* you."

"Well, hoity-toity! Two days here, and you're the mistress of the house. Maybe Master Stewart will have something to say about that!" The cook advanced toward Megan, her hand clenched on the poker with which she'd been stirring at the fire. And Megan remembered what Fiona had told her — that Mollie Sharp had a prison record behind her. A wave of fear threatened to weaken her knees, but she stood her ground.

"Speak to Master Stewart if you will," she said with a feigned indifference. "You will find that all pertaining to the child is in my care. That includes the food she will eat. I suggest you either take my word or risk his displeasure at being disturbed on such a small detail." Mollie Sharp stopped, gave a gesture of acquiescence, and turned away, mumbling to herself.

Megan had won her point, she knew. But she also knew she had made an implacable enemy.

Crossing the kitchen, she opened the door that led to the grounds at the rear. As she stepped out into the morning light, she looked down to see small Angus at her heels. She had forgotten him, yet he had been with her all the time. Somehow it was a comforting thought.

Now, however, he deserted her, rushing toward the stables in search of his other friend. Megan followed, smiling at the little stab of jealousy she felt. Angus had enough love to go around, and it was possible that Aherne needed some of that affection as much as she did.

The boy was not in sight when she reached the stables, but Angus was scratching and whimpering at a rough door at the end of the long room. Megan opened it, let the little dog inside, and followed him into a dark enclosure hung with bridles and harness. A small window at one end shed a dusty light down upon the pale hair of Fiona's young brother. He stood at a bench-like table, working at something he turned quickly to conceal.

"What are you doing?" Megan asked as she approached. "Why, Aherne, that is *beautiful!*"

The object he'd been so intent upon was a hand-carved box, a small chest, perhaps thirteen inches by eighteen. The interior was painstakingly lined with velvet, and he'd been at work upon the lid, which had not as yet been affixed.

Megan studied the fine scrollwork, seeing the initial that graced the center of the wood. A letter, L. "I've never seen anything so lovely," she said, honestly. "Is it for a gift?"

He mumbled something about a birthday.

"Is this for Lea?" Aherne shot her a look of fear and turned away. "I think she will be pleased," Megan said.

The expression of fear was exchanged for one of hope. "Will you give it to her for me?"

"I think," Megan said, "that you should give it to her yourself."

"But they won't let me —"

"Lea is in my charge," she said, crisply. "And it is up to me to make such decisions."

Tears formed in the boy's eyes, and Megan walked back to the door by which she had entered, giving him time to get himself under control. "I would like to ride this morning. Do you suppose I could take the small brown horse? And perhaps you'd like to ride with me?"

He said nothing, but after he'd saddled the pony she'd chosen, he readied a horse for himself.

It was a pleasant ride. They crossed the barren lands of Wyndspelle, rode past the big stone at the foot of the horseshoe cliff, and climbed up into the cover of the trees that lined its rim, following the trail Megan and her uncle had traversed coming to Wyndspelle on that night that seemed so long ago.

The forest had seemed oppressive then, heavy with the feel of a coming storm. Today, small bright birds flashed through the trees like embroidery, and the day smelled fresh, green, sweet.

"How I wish Lea could be with us," she burst out.

The boy's eyes touched her face with a new trust. "Do you think she ever will?" he asked.

"I pray so."

He was silent for a long while, the only sound that of the horses' hooves, the creaking of saddle leather. Then he said, "You don't think *she* would hurt Lea, do you? The way Lea is — it's not *her* fault!"

Megan jerked up her head. "You mean Constance?" His expression told her she'd hit the wrong key, and she went on, "Mollie Sharp? Della? Not Fiona!"

"No," he shouted, his voice raw with frustration. "Her! I'm talking about *her*!"

They stared at each other for a moment, then Aherne dug his heels into his mount's side, turning it, and was off like the wind in the direction of Wyndspelle.

Megan remained still for a moment, bewildered and confused. This was Aherne's second reference to some mysterious woman. For a space there, he had seemed to be on the verge of madness. Perhaps, as Fiona had explained, he was having one of his irrational moments. It would have to happen just as she thought she'd made a friend of him. Perhaps they were right in keeping him away from Lea!

She thought about it as she rode slowly back to Wyndspelle, the light suddenly gone from the day. But when she reached the stables, Aherne was waiting for her as though nothing untoward had happened. He helped her to dismount, and she thanked him, gathering Angus up to return him to the house.

Feeling a touch on her arm, she turned to see Aherne gazing at her with anxious, troubled eyes. "I — I wanted to tell you," he said with an unprecedented rush of words, "if you — if you want a box like that, I'll make you one."

"Thank you, Aherne," she said, her eyes brimming with unaccountable tears. "I would like that. I would like it very much."

CHAPTER 7

Megan returned to relieve Constance at her post beside Lea's bed. When the child's lunch arrived, it was more nutritious and better tasting than the other meals she'd been served. Megan was delighted at the amount the sick girl was able to swallow. The wizened face seemed to be taking on color. It had all contributed, Megan thought: the good food, the light, the bracing sea air that had cleared the stuffy room.

Though Lea still lay in a kind of coma, unseeing, unhearing, Megan kept up a running one-way conversation, telling of her own childhood, the mischief she had got into, relating the old Celtic tales that had been told to her by her mother.

When Constance appeared again for her two-hour stint, Megan spent a few minutes with Fiona, now recovering from her ailment but still pale and wan. Then Megan went for a walk on the grounds, noting how very depressing it all seemed. It was strange, she thought, how the sadness of the people in a house affected its whole environment. It was as if the land, itself, were blighted. The grass grew sparsely. Here and there, an occasional tree had gained a foothold in the bitter soil, reaching up a few skeletal branches, only to die.

She thought of the forest one entered upon climbing the horseshoe cliff. There had been flowers there. Birds. A smell of fresh sweetness. It was as though some evil aura hung over Wyndspelle lands, keeping beauty at bay.

Reaching the stone at the turn in the path, Megan leaned against it. It felt warm to her back, and she felt strangely at peace. She noticed she stood on a narrow strip of fresh green grass, starred with tiny blue-eyed flowers. So her idea of evil rampant had been a silly one. Perhaps one day the greenery would spread to Wyndspelle's door, flowers would bloom, and there would be the sounds of young laughter.

She shut her eyes, imagining how it would be, and stood lost for a time in a dream of beauty.

Guiltily, she realized her free time had ended. She must return to Lea's side. And since the child could not come here, she would take a bit of this place to her. She knelt to pluck a few blades of grass, one of the fragile blooms —

And she realized she had been standing on a grave.

She backed away, looking at the oblong carpet of tender shoots of green. The stone she had been leaning against, had something carved on it. A name... Time and winds had eroded it until it could not be read. The grave was old. Perhaps a century had passed since the name had been inscribed there.

Just beyond was what seemed to be another grave site. Above a sunken spot, where a leafless briar grew, was a second obliterated name. Megan looked at it, shivering a little at the thought of the difference in the two plots. There was no reason for one to be so verdant, and the other —

Ridiculous! It surely had something to do with the slant of the sun.

At any rate, she had lingered too long. She hastened back to the house and to Lea.

That night, she tucked the sick child up for sleeping, still marveling at the color returning to Lea's cheeks. Having made her as comfortable as possible, Megan stood for a moment looking down at her. On impulse, she bent and brushed a kiss against the now-warm cheek. *"Ghaist nor bogle shalt thou fear,"* she murmured. *"Thou'rt to love and heaven sae dear, Nocht of ill may come thee near, My bonnie dearie."*

Was it her imagination, or did she detect a flicker of a smile?

Returning to her own room, Megan got ready for bed. It had been a most peculiar day, what with Aherne's outburst and the eerie discovery of the two graves. Yet she felt she had accomplished much. Lea was being given proper food, and she would benefit from having light and air in her sickroom. Tomorrow, she would see if any of the girl's possessions had been salvaged from the tragic fire. Tomorrow —

Tomorrow, she had planned to ride into Wychboro to see Uncle Ian, to discuss Doctor Potts's theory that Lea was a child possessed.

But was there any need for that? Lea was only a haunted, unloved little girl. If she had set the blaze through jealousy, as was believed, she must be made to forget through affection and forgiveness. After all, the evidence against the child was only circumstantial. Lea, herself, was the only one who really knew. And until Megan had proof, she refused to believe the little girl was guilty of such a dreadful deed.

The visit to Uncle Ian could wait until another Thursday.

Megan realized that she had not caught a glimpse of Craigh Stewart all day. Not that she *cared*. Yet there was something unhealthy in the way he shut himself off from everyone.

She closed her eyes, but still his face persisted in her mind. It irritated her. She forced herself instead to think of Doctor Potts with his serious dark features, his deep brown eyes and quiet comforting presence. He seemed to be a fine, dedicated man. She flushed, recalling what a fool she'd made of herself at their first meeting. And afterward, she had practically called him an idiot in his theories about Lea. When he returned —

Megan drifted into sleep.

She dreamed of Uncle Ian. He was standing before her in his dusty cassock, gesticulating, trying to tell her something. She couldn't understand. His stubby pipe was clenched in his teeth, the smoke from it rising above his silvery hair, growing more profuse until his figure was almost obscured.

"Uncle Ian," she said, coughing a little, "your pipe!"

She coughed again and woke to blackness. The candle she'd left burning at Lea's bedside had gone out, yet the smoke of her dreaming was a reality. The air was heavy with it. And there was a rustling beside her. Megan froze, still halfway between sleep and waking.

"Uncle Ian?"

In answer, there was a rush of movement. Hands clasped about her throat, tightening with an unbearable pressure. Megan tore at them, sobbing for breath, her body thrashing beneath the restraining comforters as she fought for her life. At last, she felt her limbs weaken, her body quivering at the verge of death, and her mind began to slip away.

"Mama!"

The child's sobbing cry was part of her dream. Uncle Ian was there, reaching out a hand to her, but Megan was falling, falling into darkness —

She came back to consciousness slowly and painfully. Dawn was gray at the windows. It had been a nightmare, a terrible, painful dream, so real that she could not swallow. Sitting up, Megan put a hand to her throat. It was bruised, aching, feverish. And the room still held a taint of smoke.

Dear God, Lea!

Dragging herself from her bed, Megan stood, tottering as she reached for a supporting chair. It seemed an eternity before she could make her way to the adjoining room.

Lea's bed was empty.

Stifling the scream that tore at her wounded throat, Megan rounded the bed. And there the child lay, crumpled on the floor against the far wall. Megan dropped to her knees beside the limp body. Lea was breathing, thank God! But she was hurt. There was blood on the white gown.

Megan found the source. The child's thin, weak wrists were scratched and torn. As if by someone fighting for her life against a pair of strangling hands.

"No," Megan whispered. "Oh, no!"

Lea could not have tried to kill her! Lea was sickly, weak. And the fingers that had closed over Megan's throat had had a demonic strength…

The words of Doctor Potts returned to Megan's mind. She shook her head to clear it and said, painfully, "No, hinny! Ye didna do it! And naught will make me believe it of ye! Naught!"

Lifting the emaciated child in her arms, she carried her to the bed, then returned to her own room. She dressed in the gray, which would prove too hot and bulky by noon but would serve to hide her bruised throat. Her logic began to assert itself. Lea, as well as Megan herself, was the victim of a mysterious attacker. Someone wanted them both dead. And Megan would ride to discuss it with Uncle Ian, this day.

It was later than she expected when Megan finally managed to leave the house. She had cleansed the child's scratches, and was surprised to find Fiona and Constance accepted them so easily as self-inflicted during one of her spells. As for her own pale appearance and husky forced speech, Megan used the excuse that she was unaccustomed to the climate and suffered from a cold.

When she announced her intention of taking a prolonged ride, Fiona refused to hear of it. It was only after much fussing about and a dosing of hot strong tea that Megan was allowed to go at all. "It is going to be very warm today," Fiona said at last, capitulating.

And she had been right, Megan thought as she turned her horse on the path that led upward toward the tree-fringed cliff. There was no air stirring, and the sun boiled down until she felt like a sodden mass in the gray woolen gown. She was glad to reach the green shelter of the trees. She must do something about her clothing, she thought dejectedly. For since summer was only beginning, it was clear that what she owned would never do.

Out of sight of Wyndspelle, the forest closing in about her, her spirits lifted. Megan felt free to throw her leg across the saddle, with no one about, and bending low to escape the branches, she urged the little horse to speed.

Red-cheeked and disheveled, she stopped at the outskirts of Wychboro to tidy her hair and arrange herself in more seemly fashion before entering the town, if town it might be called. As she rode slowly in the direction of the church, she looked about, recalling what Uncle Ian had said of this place. Once it had been a Puritan community, then a more or less hidebound little town of merchants and farmers. Now it was a city of old people, all the young ones having left for greener pastures. It was the Reverend Mackenzie's conviction that one day the town would fade away.

It was true, she thought. The hundred-year-old buildings were tumbling down, the newer ones falling into disrepair. There was something sad about it.

Reaching the little house that was Uncle Ian's, close by the church, Megan reined in, dropped to the ground, and tethered the pony to a post provided for that purpose. Then she forgot sedate demeanor, and, yearning for the sight of her uncle's friendly, loving face, ran to the porch.

Hammering at the door, she called his name but was disappointed to receive no answer. Then it came to her. He would be at the church, of course!

She tied her pony and walked the few feet along the dusty lane, stopping before the church. How *homey* it looked, she thought, with its graying boards, steps bordered by hollyhocks, and the small cemetery with ancient, lichened stones spread out behind it. A friendly place.

Stepping inside, the scent of old wood and tattered hymnals assailed her nostrils. It was dim, shadowy, dust motes dancing in rays of light that crisscrossed from the windows. There was an air of hushed waiting about the place. And her uncle was not there. *Probably calling on a parishioner,* she thought, regretfully. She would go to his house and wait for his return.

But as she turned to leave, she ran headlong into a gentleman who had entered behind her.

"I — I'm so sorry," she stammered as the man caught her elbows to steady her. "I ... was looking for someone."

"I am Reverend Saunders," the newcomer said. "Perhaps I can help you?"

"My uncle," she explained. "I am Megan Alisdair, Reverend Mackenzie's niece. Perhaps you would know —"

"Of course! I will take you to him. Won't you follow me?" Megan obeyed as he went down the aisle between the narrow, hard-backed pews toward the altar. Turning, he led her to a small door set at the side. It opened on the out-of-doors. A few feet farther along, Reverend Saunders worked at the latch of a rusty gate. It swung open, creakily, and he ushered her through. She found herself standing in the small cemetery she'd glimpsed from the lane.

There was no sight of Uncle Ian anywhere.

"This way," the minister said. She followed on his heels, through the old part of the graveyard with its leaning stones, to a section which was still open meadow. And at last, her guide stopped short, gesturing ahead of him.

"There," he said, with satisfaction. "And, it may please you to know, we have ordered a stone."

As Megan stood looking at the heaped-up mound of earth, scattered with the remnants of dead and dying flowers, the horror that she'd been suppressing since they had entered the gate was at last made fact.

Uncle Ian was dead. This was his grave. She felt numb with shock, too numb for tears.

"I say, miss, are you ill?" The anxious voice of the man beside her returned her to her senses. She turned toward him, her face still blank and bewildered, feeling her knees crumple beneath her.

"If I might sit down?"

He led her to a stone bench beneath a tree and hovered over her as she fought to regain her senses. Her eyes closed tightly, she could see her uncle's face before her, hear his voice telling her how he'd longed for someone of his own.

And she thought of her last sight of him, a small figure making a puddle in the doorway of the Wyndspelle kitchen, dripping with rain, his white hair plastered to his skull, a dead pipe clenched in his pugnacious jaw.

And they had sent him away. Out into the storm. On Craigh Stewart's orders, they had sent him away! She looked up at the minister who stood over her.

"Murdered," she said, flatly. "My uncle was murdered!"

The man flinched, staring at her as if she were mad. "Oh, no," he said, in a shocked voice. "I was not here, of course, but they say it was his heart. Reverend Mackenzie asked for an assistant or replacement some months ago, when he became aware of his condition. I was shocked to learn of his death upon my arrival. But after all, he was getting on in years —"

Not inside, Megan thought. Inside, he was like a young man. It was only his body that was old. Too old to be turned out into the darkness and the storm.

"Who would know?" she asked, dully. "Who cared for him at the end?"

She was directed to the home of Unity Deaton, Ian Mackenzie's neighbor at the other side of the parsonage. Thanking Reverend Saunders, she let herself out at the creaking gate. Sometime she would return to Uncle Ian's grave. She would bring fresh flowers, and she would say a prayer. But not today. Today, there was no room in her heart for anything but anger at the waste of a good man. And for that waste, Craigh Stewart was surely to blame.

Going up the path to the vine-covered cabin where she had been directed, Megan could see that the flowers that made the church so lovely had come from here. The place was a tangle of flowering vines, hollyhocks rising from the deep grass, a wall painted with sweet peas and trumpet vine. Butterflies fluttered everywhere, drunk with honey, bees droned, and there were ruby-throated hummingbirds.

A woman, sitting in an ancient hand-woven rocker, a coverlet over her lap, dozed on the rickety porch. She was the oldest person Megan had ever seen. Sparse white hair was braided in a coronet above a time-lined face. Wrinkled hands were clasped on the coverlet as if in prayer. Her eyes were closed, and Megan stood still, not wishing to intrude upon her solitude.

Could this be Unity Deaton? How could she have cared for Uncle Ian? She looked too old and frail to even care for herself! And after·all, what could the woman tell her? Nothing that she did not already know. Megan shifted, hesitant in her decision to leave this place, and the old lady's eyes flew open, surprising alertness in their faded blue depths.

"I am looking for Unity Deaton," Megan said, reluctantly.

"Yes."

"My name is Megan Alisdair. My Uncle Ian —"

"I know," The woman on the porch smiled back at her. Rising, her aged body erect and exuding vitality, she extended a hand to Megan. "He told me you'd come, and I've been waiting for you. Come in, my dear. We'll have a nice cup of tea."

CHAPTER 8

When Megan left the little house, it was late afternoon. The four-o'clocks beside the overgrown path were in their full glory. With a twinge of surprise, Megan eyed the skies. Unless she hurried, she would not reach Wyndspelle before darkness fell. With a hasty goodbye to Unity Deaton, she sped down the path to where the stocky little horse still waited.

The woman's words were heavy in her mind as she rode through the town. Only a few people were in sight. Those she saw in the yards or on the single rutted road turned their faces from her. She'd thought nothing of it earlier, realizing she was a stranger here. But now, after her conversation with the older woman, she understood their reasoning.

Megan Alisdair was not a stranger. They knew who she was and from whence she had come. She shivered a little, thinking about what she'd been told.

Unity had ushered her into her home and they took tea in a bright and spotless kitchen. "How did you know I was coming?" Megan asked.

"I did not think you would go too long without inquiring about your uncle's health. Not if you are the girl he thought you to be. And when you did, where else would they send you? Where but to a wicked old woman like me?"

Megan couldn't help smiling at the old lady's twinkling naughtiness. "I cannot believe you are wicked," she said, "not if you were Uncle Ian's friend."

"'Tis many a rare argument we had," Mistress Deaton admitted. "Though he was more tolerant than the Puritan family into which I was born." She pulled down her mouth in an imitation of her dour, disapproving parents. "I fear my people could not have been too holy, else they would not have been rewarded with such an offspring. I'm sure I was a trial to them! At any rate, I feel most religious when I am among my birds and flowers. And if I get my heavenly reward, 'twill be because God, Himself, has a sense of humor."

"I do not think you and my uncle differed too much," Megan laughed. "I'm glad he had someone like you for a friend."

"He was a friend. A friend to many. A pity that memories are short."

"Tell me." Megan leaned forward. "How did he die?"

Unity did not reply for a moment. Going to the hearth, she took the kettle off the hob and poured it over the tea leaves in the little pot. Then she set herself to slicing and buttering fresh-baked bread. At last she said, "He has had an indisposition of the heart for a long time. Did he not tell you? It was bound to happen."

"I was afraid it had something to do with me," Megan confessed. Her eyes had brimmed with tears, and she told how Ian Mackenzie had escorted her to Wyndspelle and had been turned away into the stormy night. She feared his death was a result of that journey.

When the woman spoke again, she seemed to choose her words carefully. "I believe I can say that he suffered no ill from being wet or chilled. As for dying because of his journey, perhaps he did, perhaps not. It is the general opinion here that his death was due to his exposure to that house and the people within it. Wyndspelle is an evil place, my dear. It and its inhabitants have been avoided by the people of Wychboro for more than a century." Unity stopped short, looking from the window. "Look at my hummingbirds," she said, smiling. "Now, *there* you see God's handiwork!"

Returning to the subject, she spun a tale that, to Megan, was beyond belief.

Unity Deaton had been born in 1718 of staunch adherents to the Puritan faith. For years young Unity believed, along with them, that Wyndspelle was the abode of the devil himself. The minister, Reverend Potts, ancestor of young Doctor Edward Potts, was a terrible raging old man with a shock of white hair. Each Sabbath day he made at least one allusion to the witch of Wyndspelle — a girl, properly tried and accused, who had been tied to a stake at the foot of the precipice where the great house now stood.

The girl had called out to the demons who were her gods, and they came for her. It was that witch who cursed Wyndspelle's blighted lands.

"I can recall his very words after all these years," Unity said. Her eyes glazed with memory as she recalled his sermon in a hypnotic half-chant.

"And then she cried out, the smoke rising around her. She called to the spirits of the wind and the sea. A wind came, and a great wave. And when it was gone, it had taken her and those who stood on the sand. Jemmie Wheeler. Jenkin Haymes. And John Cooper, her accuser. Those who watched from the promontory above saw a gull rise against the black sky as the fires of hell crackled around them, and they smelled the fumes of the netherworld, of fire and brimstone, of evil…"

The old woman swayed as if in a trance as she uttered the chilling words. Megan sought for an answer and at last said, "But that was long ago! Surely a happening so ancient could have no effect today!"

"Could it not? Consider what has happened since! Some years later, a blind pirate came to those shores to build the house that stands now, high above the sea. It bridges a chasm in which, 'twas said, he consorted with the demons of the deep.

"In that time, which is within my memory, two young girls — one the adopted daughter of Reverend Potts — were drawn to that house after being accused of witchcraft. Neither returned. There were rumors of bloody deeds. Another great wave came, inundating the land. Had you not noted that no flowers bloom there?"

Mistress Deaton poured another cup of tea for Megan, her wrinkled hand shaking visibly, the good humor gone from her face.

"The house stood empty for a while. Shunned. Then, before the great revolution, a fisherman purchased it for his bride. His sympathies were with the colonies. Hers for the King. She betrayed him and his men, who were smuggling goods for our country's defense. His fishing fleet was sunk in view of the house, the lives of many good men lost. "And," her voice grew lower, "'tis said the house itself ran red with blood, and that on stormy nights, the bodies of the dead attempt to climb the steps in the chasm below, seeking vengeance."

Megan's mind whirled as the old woman's voice quavered on. "The lintel above the fireplace in the great hall — 'tis the very stake to which the witch was tied. It was left standing in its cairn of stones when the great wave had gone away. It suited the builder of the house to use it in this fashion. 'Tis said that all who dwell at Wyndspelle are possessed. They have the evil eye and can bring illness and death to those with whom they come in contact. And now Ian Mackenzie is dead!"

A tear ran down her lined face and she made a harsh, sobbing sound. It broke the spell that had held Megan.

"You cannot believe that, Mistress Deaton. I, myself, dwell in that house! Doctor Potts comes and goes!"

The old woman flushed. "You are right, of course. I am only telling you what my neighbors believe to be true. So truly that, without me, your uncle would have died alone. And you will find you are not welcome in any house but mine. If having you as my guest is a danger — well, I have lived long enough! Now, let us speak of happier things. Have you ever seen such roses? Once the Reverend Mackenzie put his nose to one, and there was a bee —"

The conversation went on in such vein until it grew late, then turned back to Wyndspelle once more. "I beg you," Megan's hostess said, "for Ian's sake and for mine, take care!"

"I shall," Megan told her. "Now I must go. I do not wish to be caught in the forest after dark."

"Wait a moment," Unity said. "I have something for you. Reverend Mackenzie asked me to give it to you when he knew the end was near. He said it was all he had of your mother's. He kept it as a remembrance and a good-luck charm." She rummaged in a sewing basket filled with yams and came up with something in a twist of paper. Shaking it out, she held up a necklace of amber beads.

"A lamer," Megan said, her eyes filling with tears. "They're worn by the children of Scotland in some areas to ward off ill luck." The necklace blurred before her eyes as she reached for it. The beads felt warm in her hand.

Had Uncle Ian's last thought been to leave her something that her mother had worn? Or had he feared for her safety, believing she would have need of them?

She clasped the strand around her throat. It fit tightly, too tightly, since the flesh beneath her high collar was still swollen and bruised. Megan dropped it into her pocket.

Thanking the woman once more, she had taken her leave. Now, with only Wyndspelle and a darkening sky before her, the things Mistress Deaton had told her burned in her brain. Riding alone through the whispering forest, she thought of the cold places she'd felt in the house, how she'd not been able to warm herself before the fire in the great hall. And the people at Wyndspelle, each with his own warped, tormented emotions!

Now she was returning to that house and, for the first time, she admitted to herself that she'd hoped never to return again, that Uncle Ian would say, in the light of the attempt upon her life, her obligations to the sick girl had been ended. Her only avenue of escape had been removed with her uncle's death. She had nowhere to go.

Could she go to Craigh Stewart with the tale of what had happened the previous night? Tell him of the strangling hands that had closed about her throat, of Lea's scratched wrists? It would only serve to throw further suspicion upon the girl, and Megan could not believe she had the strength. Then who?

Only time and watchfulness would tell. In the meantime, Megan would have to be on guard.

The horse beneath her balked a little, and she scolded him, tightening her grip on the rein. It was just a shadow, but the shades of night were falling fast. A quavering sound from the darkness set Megan a-tremble until she realized it was only an owl's cry.

But other things than owls came forth at night, did they not? Scottish-born and English-reared, she did not know these woods. It had been a mistake to stay with Mistress Deaton for so long a time. If only she dared straddle the pony and ride as she had at the beginning of the journey! But there was danger after dark, with the overgrown path and low-hanging trees that might sweep her from the saddle.

Head down, lost in thought, she forced herself to endure the plodding pace. At last, the pony stopped. She could feel a tremor that ran through its body; heart in her throat, she flicked the reins, urging him ahead. And rounding the turn in the path, she discovered the way was blocked by a huge figure, black against the night.

A startled cry was forced from her before she could recognize the apparition for what it was. Only a man on horseback! But her relief at the recognition was short-lived.

For a giant cloaked figure flung himself from the saddle and approached her, placing hands like iron bands about her waist, dragging her from the pony. Her outcry was hushed as those hands moved up to her shoulders, shaking her until her hair fell down about her face.

"You fool," a voice roared. "You damn little fool! What do you think you're doing out here at night? Don't you realize you could lose your way? Die out here?"

Megan's knees gave way beneath her, and she began to cry. At the moment, she found herself, sobbing, in Craigh Stewart's arms.

CHAPTER 9

Megan's first sensation when she recognized Craigh Stewart was one of relief. Now, seated on the pony which he led, as though she were a child, she thought of his interrogation, and her anger began to mount.

"Where have you been?" he asked.

"To Wychboro."

"And why, may I ask?"

She was mutinously silent. After all, it was none of his business. Besides, she couldn't bring herself to mention Uncle Ian's death — not yet.

He sighed. "You don't have to answer. It is enough to say that we, at Wyndspelle, have no dealings with the people there. And you are forbidden to return."

"I shall do as I please on my free days," she said.

"Then you will walk, since I do have control over my own stable. I'm certain there is nothing in Wychboro that is so vital to your needs. Unless, of course, you are dallying with one of the young yokels there?" Megan gasped, clenching her fists, and he went on. "I have stated my opinions, and you may regard them as demands. You will not leave the premises of Wyndspelle alone. If you ride, it will be in Aherne's company — or failing that, mine. You are my responsibility while you are under my roof, and I will not have you losing yourself here among the trees. I have wasted enough time looking for you as it is."

Megan was infuriated and humiliated at being led home, like a rebellious child. Led *home*? Nay, led to prison! For with

Master Stewart's terms, that was exactly what Wyndspelle had become. A prison where she dared not sleep, for fear of being murdered! Was that so preferable to losing one's way? And if it were so easy to wander off the path, to lose oneself in the darkness, why was not that a consideration the night Uncle Ian was sent, cold and wet, into the night?

Mistress Deaton might choose to put the blame on a heart condition, or on a house that was cursed long ago, but the decision to turn her uncle away had been Craigh Stewart's. That she knew!

At last they emerged from the wood, to rest their horses before beginning the precipitous descent down the horseshoe-shaped cliff. Ahead of them, Wyndspelle loomed black. There would be candles lighting the rooms, Megan knew, but the shades were drawn. And the effect from here was to make the house seem the cursed, doomed structure Unity Deaton had claimed it to be.

Megan's hands tightened, her breathing harsh and constricted at the idea of returning here. She knew she had the mystic senses that she'd inherited from her Celtic forebears, but she'd always been able to make light of it before. Now, she admitted that she'd always felt a wrongness about the place. Witches and curses, murders, a house that ran with blood...

As Craigh Stewart turned his horse down the steep path, leading hers behind, Megan plunged her hand into the pocket of the woolen gown she wore, closing her fingers fast about the lamer, her mother's string of amber beads. She prayed it would protect her.

Reaching the stable, Craigh halted. Megan slid from her horse before he could offer his assistance again. Craigh, too, swung down, moving in front of her, blocking her path. "I apologize for my harshness," he said tightly, "but we have been concerned. And the people of Wychboro are an unsavory lot — unfriendly, bigoted gossips —"

"And you were afraid I'd learn something about you, were you not? Well, perhaps I did."

His hand closed over her arm, grasping it roughly, his blue eyes gleaming slits in the darkness. "What are you talking about? What kind of tales are being spread?"

"Tales? Or truths?" Megan shivered, recalling Uncle Ian's raw new grave, thatched with dying blossoms. "What I learned, I know to be a fact. And I have certain proof."

"Proof of what?" His voice was harsh, a hint of danger in it.

"That you're a bloody murderer," Megan cried.

Pulling away from his grip, she ducked around him and ran into the house, slamming the huge door to the kitchens shut behind her. Up the steps that led to the dining room she hurried, only to stop, aghast, as she reached the doorway. For in her first quick glimpse of the room where only a single candle burned, she saw a scene of horror and decay. Tattered curtains hung at the windows, and cobwebs festooned the corners where shadows moved —

Only for an instant, then the room seemed to turn, righting itself. The terrifying sense of ruin and desolation was gone. Megan looked at the delicate furnishings that bespoke Fiona's taste, at the muted colors of walls and silken draperies, and passed a chilled hand across her eyes. The day had been too much for her. Now she was seeing things that did not exist.

Megan hastened through the hall and up the stairs to Lea's room, her feet winged with fear. She was almost glad to see Constance sitting by the child's bed, waiting to be relieved for the night. Closing the door against the woman's departure, Megan leaned against it for a moment. She was tired. So tired. If only she dared creep into her own bed, to sleep.

But she could not. She feared for herself, and for Lea. Miserably, she took the chair Constance had vacated, still stricken with grief over her uncle's death and sick with horror at the things she'd learned this day. Unity Deaton's tales had affected her more than she cared to admit.

The wind came up outside, and the house, in its peculiar situation, began to breathe. The candle at Lea's bedside guttered, casting elusive shadows across the girl's face, contorting her features in an eerie way.

"She didna do it," Megan said stoutly to herself. "She's but a child! I dinna care who says different. The look of innocence is upon her."

Still, as she sat wide-eyed through the night, watching over the sick and haunted child, Megan kept her hand in her pocket, fingers clasped tightly about a string of amber beads.

CHAPTER 10

Megan was sound asleep when the knock sounded at Lea's door. When gray dawn crept into the room, she had finally relaxed her vigilance. Now a ray of sunshine lay across Lea's bed. She was awake, and Megan, rising, saw an odd look in the girl's eyes, a look of curiosity, speculation.

Answering the knock, Megan discovered Constance waiting in the hall, carrying Lea's tray. With a look of satisfaction, the woman informed Megan that *she* was to feed Lea this morning, on Master Stewart's orders. Megan was to breakfast with the family.

Megan's heart sank. Perhaps she was to be let go, after her comments of the night before. And Craigh Stewart had chosen this time to deliver his ultimatum. With Uncle Ian gone, cut off from everyone she knew, and in a strange country, where could she turn? Why had she never learned to control her rebellious tongue?

No matter. Whatever came, she must face up to it. But now, and in this condition? She looked down at the disheveled gray gown she still wore. It surely smelled of horses and of dust. And her hair! She put her hands to it, trying to arrange it. Mumbling an excuse, she fled to her own room and closed the door, performing a hasty toilet. It would have to do.

Descending the stairs, she forced herself to walk proud and tall. She entered the small dining room to feel a wave of relief. Craigh Stewart was not present at the table. Just Fiona and Aherne.

"Oh, my," Fiona said in a shocked gasp, "you *do* look terrible! Craigh was quite correct in thinking you should have some relief from today's duties. And he said you'd ridden all the way into Wychboro, without telling a soul where you were going. Megan, that was very naughty of you!"

"I'm sorry I gave you cause for concern," Megan told her, sincerely. "I … I but wished to visit my uncle."

Fiona nodded. "The little man who brought you to us. We have cause to be grateful to him, do we not? But I must ask you, Megan, to not ride out unaccompanied. Aherne will be most happy to go with you. Now, if you will excuse me, I will tell Cook you are here."

Rising, she left the table. Megan felt Aherne's eyes upon her face and, looking up, caught a glimpse of something that was almost worshipful before his expression became guarded again.

Megan said, breaking the silence, "You cared for Angus in my absence? I hope it was not an imposition."

"No," the boy mumbled. "I like him." Then, his face lighted from within, he added, "I … I like you, too. And I want to be your friend." He colored, rose from the table, and was gone.

She would never understand this young man, Megan thought. One moment he was wild with hatred, then crazed by fear. Now, he confronted her with calf-like adoration. What had brought such a change about?

Suddenly she knew.

He had been in the stables last night when she returned in Craigh Stewart's company. He had heard her denounce the man. In their mutual dislike of Master Stewart, they had become allies. Perhaps Aherne might even bring himself to confide in her, so she could better understand the situation here. His enforced company as escort when she rode would give her the opportunity to gain his full trust. She could use it to her advantage.

Except not today. Her throat still hurt from bruises inflicted by hurting hands. She was stiff from her ride of yesterday. Today she would rest.

Fiona returned to the table, followed by Della, bearing Megan's tray.

"Drink your tea while it is hot," Fiona chirped. "Craigh was so concerned about you. But I promised him we'd take good care of you while he's away."

"Away?" The word issued from Megan's tortured throat in a croaking sound.

"Oh, did I not tell you? He's gone to Boston on business. And I did ask him," Fiona's brow creased in a little frown, "to find some suitable materials to make up for you. Though I suppose he will forget." She shrugged her delicate shoulders and managed an apologetic smile. "Men! You know how they are."

No, Megan thought, she did not. She had memories of her father, a gigantic, laughing man; of her uncle who took his place as Laird of Alisdair upon his death, sending Megan into a sort of polite servitude. And there had been Cousin Elizabeth's husband, with his roving hands, then kindly Uncle Ian.

No, she could not pronounce herself an authority where the masculine gender was concerned. But she answered Fiona's look of mock hopelessness with a smile of her own. "It really does not matter," she said, lying a little. "I have sufficient clothing. But if he does remember, it will be most kind."

And to herself she said that she'd rather wear her ancient hand-me-downs to the grave than be beholden to that man! Though she would decide how to deal with it when the time came. There was no point in upsetting the kind Fiona. Megan felt a surge of pride. She *was* learning to control her tongue.

She ate her breakfast, a little ashamed of her appetite in view of Fiona's delicate nibbling. After yesterday's exertions, she was hungry. That thought gave rise to concern over what Lea's breakfast tray had held. Was the child well fed in her absence? She would make certain, from now on, tasting a bit of each dish to ascertain if it were edible. And there were other things she planned to do.

"Fiona, forgive me for returning to a tender subject, but the house that was burned — was anything salvaged? Any of Lea's personal possessions, perhaps a plaything?"

Fiona stiffened, her face taking on a look of tragedy. "Why do you ask?"

Megan told of her notion that the girl's room lacked identity. "It is a sickroom, that is all. I thought perhaps if there was something familiar around her, it might prove to be a restorative."

"How nice," Fiona whispered. "What a kind thought! And how ashamed I am for not noting it myself. But Lea has been so ill, and all our efforts have been directed toward helping her to survive."

She looked so troubled that Megan put out a hand of pity, but Fiona rallied and went on. "There are some things in the stair room, I think. In a little room that opens beneath the steps. Lea's playhouse was untouched by the flames; also a small storage shed behind the house. You might find something there. It may be locked. Constance will have the key. And it will be dark there. You will need a candle."

After breakfast, Megan climbed the stairs, a lighted taper in her hand. If the door were not locked against her, she wouldn't disturb the surly Constance. To her delight, it opened at her touch. Stepping inside, bending to avoid the intruding stairs, she was pleased to find a veritable treasure trove. Chests and trunks sat about, dust-covered, cobwebbed. It was clear that they had been set in here and left alone for years. The lid to one chest had been sprung. Opening it, she found a litter of tarnished objects that made a pretense of being jewels. Paste, and base metals, she thought. Could these belong to Lea? Jewelry for play?

She decided not. Green with age, some of them melded with time, they must have been here almost as long as the house.

Behind the chest was a large, framed canvas. Megan drew it forth, brushing away the dust that furred it with the hem of her skirt. It had been damaged, slashed with some sharp object, but gradually a face emerged, a face with strange, haunted-looking eyes, a scar marring the forehead and one cheek.

The clothing gave her a clue to its identity. The man in the portrait wore a white silken shirt with full sleeves, the shirt open nearly to the waist, exposing a brown, muscled torso. There was a sash about the middle, a jeweled dagger thrust through it.

The blind pirate who built this house, using a stake from a witch's burning pyre for the lintel above his hearth. The first master of Wyndspelle!

Megan breathed a little unevenly. There was no resemblance between this man and Craigh Stewart. Even their coloring was different. Yet there was something … a similar look — as though both were demon-driven!

Megan carefully replaced the picture, turning the tragic face to the wall. Yet, as she continued her search, she had the feeling that she was being watched by the portrait's blind eyes.

She moved to another chest, opening it, and reeled a little, feeling suddenly faint. It was filled with a woman's clothing, fine things, of a fairly modish style. The slightest stirring of the garments elicited a faint perfume, a familiar scent: the odor Megan had detected underlying the smoke in Lea's room.

Retreating to the open door, Megan held her candle high, studying the shadows in the closet-like room. In her mind, she could hear Aherne's words: *"She's come again!"*

The chest held Craigh's dead wife's apparel; of that Megan was certain. The colors were bright, gay, unlike the pastels Fiona affected. And the scent the chest held was more vivid than the one Fiona wore.

Yet that odor had lain beneath the smoke, and had once permeated Megan's own room. *How?* The woman was dead! And she had never lived in this house.

Imagination again. She would get what she'd come for, Megan thought stubbornly, and go. Yet, as she tiptoed forward to slam the lid on the box that contained Morna Stewart's clothing, she felt suddenly cold. It was as if, in the dusty portrait turned to the wall, in the chest with its richly frivolous apparel, these people still lived. A storehouse of souls.

Setting her jaw, Megan turned her attention to other boxes. First she found a box of baby things, and knew they had belonged to the little dead boy. At last, she found what she was looking for: a chest that held little dishes, a gigantic hand-sewn poppet with shoe-button eyes, a child's diary.

Slipping the diary into her pocket, she carried the rag doll to Lea's room, propping it up on the girl's dresser before Constance was aware of her presence. The woman looked up, resentfully, then her eyes flickered as she saw the resurrected doll. For a space, her impassive face broke up, her eyes blurred. Her face became that of a heartbroken, ageing woman.

"Where did you get that?" she croaked. "Where?"

"From a storage closet." Megan picked up the doll, handing it to Constance, who took it, touching it with almost reverent fingers.

"I made it for the child," Constance said in a voice that quavered with emotion. "Sewed every stitch! From bits of material left from Miss Morna's gowns, and Miss Fiona's." Then, her expression changing to one of fierce anger, "Why did you have to bring this here? Why?"

"I thought it would help the girl to have familiar things around her, things from her childhood," Megan said, stoutly. "Perhaps it will help her regain her senses."

Constance stood up, her eyes bleak, her voice heavy with a sick despair. "You're a fool," she said, flatly. "A fool! Leave her the way she is. Don't you understand? She doesn't want to remember her past. And she must not! Not if I'm to keep her safe."

"Safe?" Megan stared at the woman. "What do you mean? That something she might recall would place her in danger?"

Constance's face closed like a fist. "Morna's dead," she said harshly. "The little boy, too. Leave them that way. And don't torture Lea with something that cannot be remedied. Take my advice, Miss Megan, and *leave this house!* You brought trouble with you when you walked in the door. I sensed it. Trouble — trouble!"

The woman put her hands to her head, uttering the words in a kind of chant, swaying. Alarmed, Megan stretched out a hand to her, but Constance struck it away. With a rustling of dark skirts, she was gone.

Dismayed at the reaction the doll had produced, Megan turned to place it again upon the dresser. Turning back she beheld a sight that made her stop dead still.

For Lea's eyes were fastened upon the poppet, with its silly, embroidered smile and floppy limbs, and in those eyes, Megan saw a look of sensibility and recognition. It lasted only for an instant, then the fragile lids closed. But along one cheek, leaving a tiny trail of dampness as it went, rolled one single silver tear.

CHAPTER 11

For the next few days the weather was soft, balmy. The sea from Lea's window was blue silk with a froth of white lace. Megan ached for the girl, bound to her sickbed, and kept up a running commentary on the scene.

"There are white clouds," she said softly. "They look like fluffy lambs, just lying up there in a blue-sky meadow. And did you know there is a huge rock out there in the midst of the water? Birds must nest there, for I can see so many. There is one now, he is turning in the sky above it, like this."

Megan lifted one arm, lowering the other, to show how it pivoted on one wing.

"Just think," she said, "before long, you and I — and Angus — will go down to the beach below, where we can watch them. And we will run and play and throw stones in the sea."

Did Lea take in what she was saying? Megan did not know. But there was an expression now in the formerly blank eyes. A questioning look. And when Angus was lifted, Megan placing Lea's hand on the little dog's bristly fur, she was certain the girl felt an affection toward the small animal. Once, she thought she caught a fleeting smile.

These moments were balanced by periods when Lea seemed consumed with unreasoning anger. Her mouth would work as if she wished to speak, to shout her fury to the world, and she would strike out with her hands, spilling food from the spoon Megan raised to her lips. Once she upset a bowl from her tray.

At these times, Megan thought of the doctor's dark statement that the child was possessed. Then she tried to imagine herself in Lea's position. What if *she* were forced to lie in that white bed, unable to walk, to communicate? She, too, would lash out in pure frustration. She was sure of that.

Then came the morning of the miracle.

Megan was brushing Lea's hair, preparatory to braiding it, the child's hair ribbon lying on the coverlet. Like a rubber ball, wee Angus bounded from the floor, catching one end of the ribbon in his teeth as the alarmed Megan snatched at the other end. The little dog growled and tugged mightily, rolling end over end as Megan let the ribbon go.

And from Lea's lips came a tiny, silvery sound. A giggle, such as any child might make.

Megan enfolded her in her arms, her cheeks damp against the girl's hair. "Oh, Lea!" she said, joyfully. "Oh, Lea!"

Megan's first impulse was to find Fiona and tell her what had taken place. When Constance relieved her at her post, she saw that the door to one of the forbidden rooms at the end of the hall stood agape. Recalling that Fiona had mentioned tidying the rooms, she hastened along the balcony, bursting into the room, still filled with excitement over Lea's improvement.

"Fiona?" she called.

There was no answer. Fiona had been here, for there was a small basket of cleaning supplies. Apparently she had just stepped out. Megan started to follow suit, but turned to look at the room once more. It was tastefully furnished. A tall harp stood in one corner; its strings seemed to quiver as if touched with the dead player's hand. But it was the portrait directly before her that caught Megan's eye, a likeness of a beautiful young woman with a crown of glorious red-gold hair. There was something familiar about the face, lips curved in a dimpling smile, eyes laughing; flirtatious, yet appealing —

Megan stepped closer, recalling the fleeting mirror image she had seen. It was not possible. And yet, this must be Morna…

A scent of perfume drifted past her, and the harp hummed as a breeze from somewhere touched its strings. Megan stood paralyzed until Fiona's voice stirred her to action.

"Megan! You mustn't be in here! Craigh will be livid!"

Megan stepped out on the balcony. "I'm sorry, Fiona. I was searching for you. I have something exciting to tell you.Lea—"

"Will it keep, dear?" Fiona was surveying the work that remained to be done. "I must finish here. I should have left the door locked, but I was called so suddenly. Doctor Potts is below. He wishes to speak with you and then see Lea."

So the physician had returned. For some reason, the thought gave a lift to Megan's spirits. She hastened down the stairs, blushing as she recalled their first meeting, to find the doctor waiting at the foot of the steps. He made an apologizing gesture for the condition of his dusty clothing.

"I was returning to Wychboro," he said, "but turned aside on the way to see how the child is progressing. Has there been any change in her condition?"

"Indeed there has," Megan said, happily, "and I would like to discuss it with you. But first, I'd like for you to see her."

Leading him up to Lea's room, Megan dismissed Constance and stood by while the girl was examined. She saw Doctor Potts's look of surprise as he noted Lea's color. And though Lea lay quiet, it was impossible to mistake the signs of returning life to the small face.

Folding his stethoscope, Doctor Potts gestured to Megan and stepped outside.

"I cannot believe it," he whispered. "What have you done?" Then, to Fiona, who had joined them, "I believe this girl is a miracle-worker. She —"

He was interrupted by a sound of joyous barking. From where she stood, Megan watched as the little dog bounded to Lea's bed, to tug at one of the pale braids in mock battle. And before Megan could move, the child's laugh rang out, followed by a cooing word.

"Awn — goose," Lea said, lovingly. "Awn — goose." Megan recognized an imitation of her own speech. *Angus*. Lea was saying the dog's name.

"Blessed God," Doctor Potts whispered. "Did you hear that? Did you *hear* her, Fiona?"

But Fiona had turned away, running down the hall toward Constance. "Lea just spoke, Constance. She's regaining her speech."

The woman only stood staring at Megan with accusing eyes, and Megan thought of her frightening words. *"She doesn't want to remember her past. And she must not! Not if I'm to keep her safe!"*

At last Doctor Potts drew in a shaky breath. "Come away," he said to Megan. "I would like to discuss this with you further. As for Lea's speaking, perhaps we should not let her see that we know. Let it develop naturally."

"I think that might be best," Megan admitted.

Constance returned to sit with Lea in Megan's stead, and Megan followed the physician downstairs, looking upward to see Fiona going back to the locked, forbidden rooms.

At the doctor's suggestion, he and Megan went outside, to walk and talk upon the barren Wyndspelle grounds. "I do not like it much better out here," he admitted, "but I must admit I prefer it to the house. 'Tis said that none of my blood should come here, due to an ancestor of mine and an ancient curse."

"I have heard the tale," Megan admitted, "though I do not believe it. The past cannot rule the present. That is as we make it."

"Can it not?" He looked at her sternly. "This has always been an unhappy place, a place of damned souls. Can you not feel it? The house smells of evil! It drove my ancestor, the founder of Wychboro, mad. And sent my great-uncle — a teetotaler, mind you — to drink!"

There was something so ludicrous in this gaunt raven of a man, croaking out his doomsday words, that Megan giggled. He looked so bewildered that instantly she was penitent.

"I'm sorry," she said. "You sound so grim! And look, the sun is shining. How could anything be evil on such a day? Come, sir. Smile!"

He flushed, and then complied. It was amazing what a rare smile did for his doleful countenance. Again she thought, *He is a handsome man.* Not with Craigh Stewart's overpowering masculinity, but nice. Kind.

"May I call you Megan?" he asked, suddenly.

"Of course, Doctor."

"Edward. Now, come. Tell me how you've been treating our patient."

Megan told him of insisting on an improved diet, of the constant running conversation she'd carried on with Lea, telling her of the things they'd do together when she was well. She told him of Angus, and his affection for the child; of the doll she'd retrieved from the storage room in an effort to bring past and present together.

And at last, she told him of Constance; how the woman believed Megan was doing Lea an injustice, that if the girl remembered the past, she, Constance, would not be able to keep her safe. "Safe from what? From whom?" Megan asked.

Edward Potts shook his head. "I have no idea! Even if he believes that Lea is responsible for the death of Morna and the little boy, Craigh would not harm the girl. Constance is a strange woman, doting on Morna and Fiona, transferring some of that affection to Lea. Perhaps Morna's death drove her a little mad — and she thinks by keeping Lea dependent, she can watch over her, making her totally her own."

There was some truth in his theory. Megan had to concede that. But she felt there was more to it.

"What if," she said, carefully, "Lea was *not* guilty of starting the fire that killed her mother and brother? What if she has knowledge that might expose the person who did? That would be a reason for not wanting her to remember."

The doctor looked startled. "Unlikely," he said. "It would have to be one of the members of the household. Constance is ruled out. She worshipped Morna, according to Fiona. And Fiona ... well ... that is beyond imagining! True, Aherne is a strange lad —"

Megan shivered a little, recalling the boy's hatred of Craigh, his preoccupation with fire that she had noted several times. But she had seen his love for Lea in his eyes.

"No," she said, "I do not think so."

"Then we are left with one suspect," Edward Potts said shortly. "The child's own father. And though he's the most haunted, bedeviled man I've ever met, I cannot see him as a murderer."

"He killed my uncle," Megan said softly.

The doctor jumped and stared at her in bewilderment. "What in the name of God are you saying?"

With tears running down her cheeks, Megan recited her story, telling of coming to Wyndspelle and Uncle Ian being turned away, out into the night and the storm, and now he was dead, and lying behind the church in Wychboro.

Edward Potts was silent for a moment. "I'm sorry to hear that," he said finally, "though 'twas not unexpected. Ian

Mackenzie was living on borrowed time, Megan. I attended him shortly before I left on my journey. It was his heart, Megan. Of that I am sure."

"His heart," Megan said obstinately, "and chill and fatigue. Craigh Stewart killed him, though not by his own hand."

They had reached the door that led to the kitchens at Wyndspelle. Megan noted that the physician paled, visibly, as they entered. Retrieving his medical case, he said a rather formal farewell, then turned back once more.

"I cannot leave you here," he said in a rather strangled voice. "It would be on my conscience. Something is wrong in this house, Megan. I sense it. I tried to get Fiona to leave, but she refused. She is a grown woman, however, and should know her own mind. You … you are a young girl."

"But I cannot go away!" Megan's eyes were wide with surprise at his words. "There's Lea to consider. And she's doing so well —"

"Megan," he groaned, "I'm afraid for you. I fear for Fiona. It is this house!"

"If you are so afraid, then why do you come here? You needn't, you know."

He looked a little stunned at her words, then managed a wry smile. "For the little girl's sake," he admitted, "and Fiona."

Megan looked at him, pitying him. This gaunt country doctor looked upon her employer's sister-in-law with a simple, sincere passion. Much as a beggar would look at a queen. His love would be a deep and aching wound, while Fiona seemed incapable of more than gentle affection. How lucky a woman would be to be the object of such love as the doctor's, Megan thought wistfully. Perhaps someday he would turn to someone else. Someone more suitable.

After he had gone, she returned to Lea, who lay sleeping, her face angelic in repose. Megan sat beside her, thinking over the events of these last few days. She thought of the attack that came in the night, of the strong small hands that had closed about her own throat, shutting off her breathing, of the scratches on Lea's arms, now nearly healed.

If she'd had good sense, she would have discussed the situation with the doctor, at least. But the evidence against Lea seemed so incriminating that Megan felt compelled to protect her. She wondered at her own conviction that the girl was innocent. Was it some sixth sense that led her to her conclusions? Or the stubborn, wrongheadedness that was her own heritage? Dim in her memory, she could see herself standing before her father, returning his angry gaze with one that matched it. And she remembered him snatching her up, tossing her high into the air.

"You're a true Alisdair, girl," he said, laughing uproariously. "An Alisdair!"

Right or wrong, she had committed herself to be this frail child's champion. And she would stick by her beliefs!

That night, for the first time in several, she was nervous about retiring to her own room. The house seemed, as Edward Potts described it, filled with evil. Yet it was impossible to keep up a day-and-night vigil always. She would have to trust in God and take her chances. She was careful to leave a tall candle burning by her bed.

It was burning when she woke, though it was past the halfway mark. Angus had whimpered. She smelled smoke. A wisp curled from the closed door that separated her room from Lea's.

The closed door. And Megan had left it open!

Leaping from her bed, she ran to it, turning the knob, throwing her weight against it. It refused to move. Dully, she recalled there was a bolt at the other side.

Seizing the candle, she rushed to the door that opened onto the balcony, throwing it wide. And as she did, she caught a glimpse of a wraith-like figure drifting along the darkened hallway.

"Who are you?" she called. "Wait!"

But the figure had entered the stair room, Angus yipping behind it. Megan felt an urge to give chase, to discover the identity of the night-time intruder. But now, her chief concern was Lea.

She hastened to the girl's open door. As before, the room was filled with smoke. Setting her candle down, Megan threw the window open wide, then turned to the sleeping child. The thing, whatever it was, had not awakened her, thank God! As Megan bent over Lea, she smelled a familiar scent: Morna's scent, stronger here than the odor of smoke.

"Mama," the child whispered in her dream, and the pale lips smiled.

Megan felt her knees grow weak. She thought back to Aherne's words. *"She's come again! ... You don't think she would hurt Lea, do you?"* His face had been white with fear.

Morna? The ghost of a dead woman come to plague a child who was responsible for her death? Megan swallowed. It could be!

With an effort, she forced herself back to sanity. Someone had closed the door between their rooms, had shot the bolt. And that had to be the act of a human hand.

As if to reinforce her line of thinking, Angus returned. He had a scrap of material in his mouth, and he fought a mock battle, worrying the thing as Megan tried to retrieve it.

A shred of filmy gray material, so fine it was almost invisible, but material nonetheless. Megan's ghost was not an apparition, but a reality, someone attempting to frighten Lea. But who, and why?

As she and Doctor Potts had done this afternoon, Megan ran through the list of people in the house, discarding them one by one. Unless...

Unless Morna Stewart was still alive! Driven mad, perhaps, by the loss of her little boy. Hidden somewhere in this dreadful house!

Wearily, Megan rubbed at her eyes, as if the act might restore her own good sense. Morna Stewart was dead. Yet Lea had recognized the intruder as her mother. And there was the gentle drift of sweet perfume, too. Megan was faced with three choices: Morna Stewart, dead, come to avenge her son; Morna Stewart living, and a madwoman; or someone masquerading as Lea's mother, attempting to frighten the girl so that she'd never tell whatever dreadful thing was dwelling in her memory.

Megan carried the shred of cloth to her room and hid it away, then returned to Lea's room. The smell of smoke had cleared, but surely it had to have a source. A small fire had been left burning on the hearth to keep the night chill from the sickroom. Megan knelt before it. No, the chimney was drawing well.

Frowning, she moved to close the window. The room had cleared now except for Morna's scent, which seemed stronger than before.

Blocking the door to the hall with a chair, Megan sat beside Lea, keeping another all-night vigil. And during the night, she thought of what she knew of the people in this house. Any or all of them could be suspect, except for Craigh Stewart. For he was gone to Boston, was he not?

And when he returned, much as she hated him, Megan would go to him for help, for the dark knowledge in her Celtic blood filled her with foreboding. There was death in this house, death in the night wind that had now risen and was sobbing at the windows.

And she was responsible for Lea.

CHAPTER 12

At a small sound, Megan awoke instantly. She had drowsed as morning neared, and she was stiff and cold. A glance at the window showed the pale light of dawn. Turning, she looked at the door, from whence the sound had come.

The knob was turning, though the chair she'd placed against it still held.

Rising, her mouth dry with fear, she approached the door. "Who — who is it?" she whispered.

"Aherne," was the answer. "Please, Megan, let me in."

Reluctantly, she opened the door to him. He stood before her, his face an odd mixture of defensiveness and joy. "You said I could see Lea," he told her.

"But at this hour?" Megan was bewildered.

"I was afraid *they* wouldn't let me. And today's her birthday. I have to see her! Please?"

His eyes pleaded, and she stood aside. After all, what harm could there be?

Aherne entered, dragging some contraption with him. Megan had no time to identify it; her eyes were fastened on the figure on the bed. For Lea's eyes were round with wonder and delight. The thin little body had risen to almost a sitting position, bony arms stretched in a gesture of love. Lea's pale lips moved, and Megan could have sworn they mouthed Aherne's name.

The boy ran toward her, clasping the frail young girl against him. After a long while, he turned to face Megan, his eyes brimming with tears.

"I haven't been allowed to see her for three years," he choked.

"But why?" Megan was bewildered.

"I don't know. She was getting better. She could say a few words. But *they* said I upset her."

"They? Who, Aherne? Constance? Fiona? Craigh?"

"Craigh Stewart gives the orders around here," he said dully. "I guess he knows what I could tell, if I wanted to. And with Lea to back me up —"

"What *is* it you could tell, Aherne? I have to know. It's important!"

The boy looked at Lea, and his lips closed tightly. "Not now," he said hoarsely. "Not here. It's her birthday, Megan. And I've brought her something."

He turned toward the object he'd brought with him and removed a cloth that covered it. Megan gasped. He'd made a wheeled chair from what appeared to be a cast-off bit of furniture. The seat had been carefully padded with faded velvet; and the back was soft and comfortable, suitable for a headrest.

And perched on the seat were two small chests: the one she'd seen him making for Lea, and one with Megan's own initial.

"How lovely," Megan said, overcome at the boy's thoughtfulness. "Oh, Aherne! I — I suppose no one has given me a gift since I was a child!"

"It's nothing," he said, his ears reddening. "I've made a lot of them. One for Morna, one for Fiona. It gets easier. And I thought … the chair…"

"The chair is going to help Lea get well," Megan said, swallowing tears. "I promise you. And I'm going to talk to

Craigh Stewart. Tell him you're to be allowed to see Lea! The very minute he returns."

Aherne paled. "He's back now," he said. "His horse is in the stable. I guess he came home sometime last night." He shot a frightened glance at the lightening sky. "I'd better go," he mumbled. And with a hasty peck at Lea's cheek, he scuttled out of the door.

Megan stood, her hands pressed to her cheeks. She had absolved Craigh Stewart from any part in last night's activities, but he had been here! In this house. Yet she had no other recourse than to go to him with her tale of an apparition, the story of the intruder who had attempted to strangle her, her sense of impending doom.

She turned to Lea. The little girl lay quiet, though her cheeks were glistening with tears. *Her birthday,* Megan thought. Her fifth birthday in this dreary room. Would the household take note of it? Would there be gifts? A cake with candles? Megan herself had nothing to give her.

Then she remembered. Going to her own room, she found the amber necklace that had been her mother's as a child. Returning, she fastened it about Lea's throat, beneath the high-necked nightdress. "It is called a lamer," she whispered. "It is for good luck, to protect you from all harm." Megan kissed the tear-wet cheek.

When Constance arrived to sit with Lea, the wheeled chair and Aherne's other gifts had been removed from sight, tucked away behind Megan's bed in her own room. They, especially the chair, would be her own secret for a while. She would lift Lea into the chair when they were alone, wheel her to the window. And one day, this house would be due for a surprise!

Constance, when she came, was laden with bundles, all of them for Megan except for one. Craigh Stewart had not forgotten his daughter's birthday. Making much of his gift, Megan unwrapped it before the girl, her heart sinking at what the package contained.

Three nightdresses, white and plain. Exactly like those Lea already owned. *You are an invalid,* Craigh's gift said, *and will never be anything else.*

Megan felt her face grow hot with fury at this man who did his duty and no more. Taking her own packages to her room, she tossed them on the bed. They would be the dress materials Fiona had suggested Craigh Stewart purchase. She would not stoop to even look at them!

Angrily, she went downstairs to breakfast.

Only Aherne and Fiona were at table. Craigh had gone out to ride. Aherne kept his eyes down, not looking at Megan. She knew he feared that she would give his morning visit away. And Fiona, to her surprise, had remembered Lea's birthday. She gave Megan a little book to give to her.

"I didn't bother to wrap it," she said, "since after all, she would not know the difference. But I do like to give her something every year."

The book was a slim little volume, with a pretty pink cover that announced it as *A Young Girl's Book of Days.* It contained readings for each day in the year, Bible verses and little poems, exhorting the reader to piety and virtue. A more inappropriate gift could not possibly exist, Megan thought. Still, Fiona had tried. The doll-like woman looked anxiously at Megan for approval.

"It — it's lovely," Megan lied. "And will there be a cake?"

"I ... I hadn't thought of it," Fiona admitted. "Surely, in the child's condition, it does not matter."

"I believe it will," Megan said, her voice steely.

Fiona made a gesture of helplessness. "Well, if you think so, dear. Why don't you speak to Cook?"

"I shall. I think we should have a real celebration." And Craigh Stewart would be there, Megan thought grimly, if she had to drag him!

After bolting her breakfast, Megan announced that she intended to ride. Gesturing to Aherne to remain where he was, she said she would saddle her pony herself. Half an hour later she was on the forest path, hoping to intercept Craig Stewart on his return. Hearing the sound of hoofbeats, she deliberately turned her little mount across the trail. Craigh would not pass, not until she'd had her say!

She caught her breath as man and horse appeared from among the trees. Here, sun-dappled, blending in with the surroundings, the pair seemed one, less than human. She thought of the old pagan gods, but she stood her ground. The master of Wyndspelle looked surprised.

"Riding alone?" he asked. "I thought I made it clear —"

"But I am not alone," Megan said, sweetly. "I am with you, am I not? At least, that was my intention. I rode to meet you; I must talk with you."

Craigh sighed. "I believe we've discussed all that needs be said. Can you not leave me in peace?"

She did not speak, but remained as she was, her jaw set with determination. At last, he groaned and dismounted.

"Very well," he said, seating himself at the base of a tree, leaning against its trunk, eyes closed. "We might as well get it over and done. Say what you have to say."

Megan slid from her horse and went to stand before him. "I have reason to think," she said, "that someone in your house is a murderer. Someone — or something — intends to destroy your daughter. And there has been an attempt on my life."

The man's eyes flew open, their strange blue blazing in such a way that it almost stopped her voice. But she went on doggedly, telling of the night she had been nearly strangled, of the ghostly visitor of the night before.

He listened to her tale, his face blank. And then at last, he burst into laughter, reaching out his hand to take hers.

"I'm sorry," he said finally. "I suppose it all seems very real to you. You are young, impressionable, imaginative. I suppose you've heard tales of the history of this house?" He raised his brows, questioningly, then went on. "And this is not the ideal situation for a young lady. I expect it seems secluded, gloomy. I can see why it would weigh heavily upon you."

Megan faced him squarely. "What you say may be true, but it has nothing to do with the things that have happened."

"Has it not? You say you were attacked. Can you show me your bruises?"

Megan flushed. "They have healed."

"And last night's intruder. Have you any proof?"

"A bit of material. Angus followed the figure and brought it to me."

"And it could have come from anywhere. A shred of drapery, perhaps, from one of the servants' rooms above. No, Megan, I fear the isolation here is preying on your mind. And, by heaven, I cannot stand another hysterical female on the premises! Constance tells me you have been filling the child full of mystical tales, making her promises that cannot be kept. I would say you have let your imagination run away with you."

"Lea is improving," Megan said, hotly. "Even Doctor Potts says so! And I feel her improvement is what is behind all this. The girl knows something. Something about the death of her mother and brother. Someone is trying to keep her from speaking of it."

The man's face closed against her. "I pray to God the girl knows *nothing*," he said in a flat tone. "It would be far better than to have to live with the knowledge of what she has done. I warn you, Megan. Do not try to delve into matters that do not concern you." He frowned. "I do not suppose that anything I say will still your imaginings; therefore, I will give you the option to stay or go, once more. If you stay, there will be no more of this feminine foolishness."

Megan turned and flung herself on the little pony. Seated, she looked straight into his eyes. "You will hear no more from me," she said, her voice shaking with anger. "And you will not be rid of me, either. I intend to stay!"

Turning her mount, she bent low over its mane, digging in her heels, so that the startled pony took off at a full gallop, along the trail, down the path that curved to the foot of the cliff. She could hear the hooves of Craigh's mount pounding along behind her.

Reaching the stables, she dismounted, but she was not quick enough. Craigh Stewart had caught up with her. He, too, leaped to the ground. Taking her forearms in his hands, he looked down at her soberly.

"I know you're doing the best you know how," he said. "'Tis just that I question its wisdom. And I'm equally sure that there's nothing in this house to frighten you. Please — please keep my daughter as comfortable as possible."

There was an aching sound in his voice, and the blazing eyes were wet with tears. *He does love her,* Megan thought, trembling before the depth of his emotion.

"I will try."

"Thank you." His tone was formal, but a smile of indescribable tenderness hovered at his lips. Only for a moment, then it was gone. For she had said, "I want permission for Aherne to visit Lea from time to time."

Craigh's face stiffened, his eyes growing watchful, guarded. "The boy's half demented, Megan. He was barred from her room for making insane accusations and upsetting her."

"I think it best they are allowed some time together."

The man bowed in mock acquiescence. "Very well, as long as you remember he is unbalanced, and act accordingly. Now, promise me, no more wild imaginings and fantasies —"

"I only spoke the truth!"

"Indeed? And as I recall, some few nights ago, you referred to me as a murderer."

Megan looked up at him helplessly, seeing his sardonic half-smile, trembling beneath the hands that held her fast. She wanted to lash out at him, to accuse him of her Uncle Ian's death, but now it seemed only important to get away from the spell he seemed to cast upon her.

Whirling to hide her streaming tears, she hurried into the house. She stopped suddenly as she saw Aherne kneeling before the fire in the large fireplace. He seemed hypnotized, bemused, as he stared into the flames. At last, he carefully withdrew a burning brand from beneath the cookpot, and held his free hand close to the heat. Surely he would sear his fingers! Megan caught her breath, then the rustling of skirts announced Fiona's presence on the steps that led down from the dining room.

"Aherne!" Her voice was frightened, sharp, for once filled with command. "Put that down! You've been told to leave the fires alone!"

Docilely, the boy replaced the piece of burning wood. He rose and came toward Megan, moving like a sleepwalker as he passed her in the doorway.

It was Fiona who seemed embarrassed and confused at Megan's appearance. "My — my brother has been a little odd since Morna and the baby died in the fire," she said, finally. "He seems fascinated by flames, as if he were trying to know how it *feels* to be burned. But there is nothing really wrong with him, Megan. It isn't as if he is…"

She stopped, looking pleadingly at Megan, who said, quietly, "I'm certain he's all right. I suppose it is a natural thing." But on her way upstairs, she was shaken. Was it possible that Aherne, not Lea, had set the fatal blaze? That perhaps Fiona *knew*, and was protecting him?

Craigh had referred to him as a half-demented boy. And she had seen his hands, his slender, clever woodcarver's hands. She could imagine how they'd feel about her throat —

CHAPTER 13

The days passed slowly as Wyndspelle lay quiet, drugged with summer. And with each day, Lea improved. Gone were the fits of temper, the frustrated lashing out of emaciated arms. Health began to fill the sunken cheeks, and more than once, Megan spotted a smile on the girl's face.

Each day, when Constance was gone, Megan blocked the door with a chair and lifted Lea into the wheeled chair that Aherne had made for her, pushing her to the window that overlooked the sea. There they would sit, companionably, while Megan stitched at the materials Craigh had brought from Boston. Her first instinct, to refuse them, had been overcome in her delight at his choice.

There were bolts of fine lawn, batiste, dimity, in tiny prints of yellow and of green that complimented her coloring. And in one packet, she had found fine hand-sewn underthings, threaded through with delicate ribbon, and a pair of soft kid slippers. How had he guessed at their fit?

Her feeling of annoyance that the man had not done as well by his daughter was diminished as she gauged the amount of material he had purchased. There was enough for only one dress in each bolt if she emulated Fiona's sweeping styles. But those, she knew, were outdated. She would make her dresses in the fashion that was current in England at the time she left there: Empire waist, a slight fullness to the skirt — and only long enough to reach her shoe tops. There would be enough on each piece to make a matching gown for Lea.

119

As she stitched, she had visions of the girl, her hair dressed as a young lady would wear it, clad in a becoming gown. When Doctor Potts came next, he would see her that way, sitting in the wheeled chair, rather than lying in bed. He would be confounded! And Craigh Stewart, if he allowed himself to see Lea, might be shocked back into his senses.

A small sound of delight from Lea drew Megan's attention. The girl was leaning far forward, her face alight, pointing down. Megan joined her, following her gaze. Below, on the stone strewn beach, a tiny sandpiper hopped and skittered at the edge of the waves. It disappeared, and Lea's joy faded. Her mouth worked for a moment, then she said, "Me."

Megan hid her excitement at the spoken word. "What is it, Lea? What do you want?"

The girl leaned forward again, pointing downward. Then she pointed to herself.

"Me," she said. "Me."

"You want to go down there?" Megan asked, carefully. The girl nodded with growing eagerness, and a plan began to form in Megan's head. Suppose she could manage to get Lea down there some way? And on that day, she could persuade Craigh Stewart that he should call Doctor Potts to look the girl over. When the doctor came, they would be on the sands below, she and her charge. It would be an effective setting in which to show how Lea had improved.

Possessed, Megan thought, laughing to herself at the sight of Lea's sunny face. Doctor Potts would have his proof that she was not. And Craig Stewart would know his daughter did not do the thing of which she was accused!

But would it be possible? Megan bent forward to study the beach below. The only access to it was a rickety set of wooden steps built long ago. She must check them for stability. The wheeled chair could be lowered by ropes, but Lea? Could she carry her down?

She would enlist Aherne's help.

"I promise you," Megan told the girl. "We will go down there — within the week."

From that moment on, Megan stitched furiously. And at last, two gowns from each bolt were finished. One for herself and one for Lea. Then one evening she managed to catch Craigh Stewart as he was on the point of descending to the chasm.

"I believe Doctor Potts should have a look at Lea," she told him, decisively.

"What's the matter? Is she ill?"

Megan felt the blush that colored her cheeks. "N-no," she stammered. "I just feel that it is wise."

He looked at her curiously. "Does Lea need to see our good doctor? Or do you? He is not an unattractive man."

"Master Stewart!" Megan's anger flared. "I have no interest in any man. I have only the child's best interests at heart."

He studied her levelly for a moment, then said, "I will ride in to fetch him in the morning. You can expect him sometime shortly after noon."

The next day Aherne, having already lowered the wheeled chair to the sands below the house, carried Lea down the steps from her room and through the front door. Megan followed, thankful that they had not been seen. Once outside, Aherne managed to get his burden down the wooden steps. Soon they were comfortably settled on the tiny, isolated strip of beach, Lea making small babbling sounds of delight at the feel of the sun, the small waves curling inward almost at her feet.

"Go now," Megan told Aherne. "And when the gentlemen arrive, send them here." He left reluctantly, his face somber and disapproving.

Megan had carried Angus along with her. When Aherne had gone, she put the little dog down. He dashed foolishly along the shore, barking at the waves, defying the entire ocean as Lea laughed her new-found laughter. Megan busied herself finding shells, placing them in the young girl's lap, observing Lea's enjoyment as she turned them in her fingers, now and again lifting her face, like a flower, to the sun.

Lea did look lovely, Megan thought, in the delicate gown, sprigged with yellow flowers. So far removed from the skeletal creature she'd been at Megan's coming, soon she would be able to walk — to talk — to say what was in her mind.

The thought of what might be bottled up inside the girl gave Megan a momentary feeling of depression. As if to add to her mood, Angus, nosing around a tumble of rock on the sand, began to growl and back away stiffly, his fur bristling.

"'Tis naught," Megan assured Lea, walking to where the little dog had been. "A crab, or some sea creature, no doubt."

But there was nothing there. Nothing but a pile of stones, stacked in a strange symmetrical fashion. Suddenly the hair rose at the back of her own neck, as Megan recognized the stones for what they were.

Here the witch of Wyndspelle had stood, surrounded by a cairn of stones, crying out her commands to wind and wave, creating the curse that damned this bit of land.

Suddenly, there seemed to be an odor of decay in the air; the sun simmering down upon the beach intensified the smell of rotting seaweed and of fish. The waters no longer seemed friendly and playful, but deep, dark, secretive, a damp shroud for the dead. Megan, drawing a deep breath, returned to Lea, who seemed to sense her moment of depression.

"Did I tell you about the games we used to play?" Megan cried out, with forced gaiety. "See, this is called *skiffin*." She skipped a flat stone along the water's surface. "And this. Watch me!"

Waiting carefully until the waves ebbed, she ran onto the wet sand. *"Willie, Willie Weet-feet,"* she cried, *"Dinna weet me, and a'll gee ye a Scots bawbee!"*

As a wave came washing in, crested with white lace, she leaped backward, triumphantly, her skirts still undampened, and behind her Lea laughed again.

The time dragged on as Megan strove to keep the girl amused. It was plain Lea was wearying, and Megan was concerned that she had so miscalculated the time. At last, having drawn on all the sea games of her memory, she sat down upon the sand beside the wheeled chair and began to tell tales of her childhood, pranks she'd indulged in, and how her Uncle Ian had been a co-conspirator.

"So we stole the cook's drawers from the drying-line," she finished one tale, "and hung them from the turret, where they waved in the wind like a flag. Oh, but she was angry!"

Lea's face had come to life once more, and she was trying to speak. Megan watched her lips carefully.

"Fiona?" she finally asked, and was rewarded by a nod. Lea pointed a finger upward, toward the bell tower. At last, Megan was able to understand. The girl, with a look of impishness that was new to her, was suggesting such a trick be played upon the ladylike Fiona.

"Oh, Lea," Megan laughed, scandalized. "We can't do that. It would never do!"

Lea's face clouded, tears brimming the eyes that were so like her father's. Her mouth set in an angry line, she flailed out at Megan. She hadn't indulged in one of her rebellious actions for so long.

Megan sat back, thinking. Surely, if the girl retreated into one of her frustrated sulks, the whole plan would be spoiled. She wanted Craigh and the doctor to see how much Lea had recovered, that she had the ability to be a healthy, happy girl. And it would only take a moment.

She stood. "I'll do it," she said. "Will you be afraid here with just Angus while I'm gone?"

Lea clapped her hands and made a little crowing sound.

Reluctantly, Megan left her charge. She could not bring herself to touch Fiona's things, but there was something among the purchases Craigh Stewart had brought from London — something with lace and blue ribbons. She would let it fly for only a second, long enough for Lea to see from below, then take it down and return.

She was smiling a little as she climbed to the third floor, the garment in her hands, for this bit of mischief convinced her Lea was quickly recovering.

However, when she climbed the ship's ladder that led upward, she had a momentary qualm. Her hand, touching the trap door that led to the bell tower, seemed to come in contact with a sudden cold. She jerked it away, then recognized the feeling for what it was. Here, too, something had happened in the past that had left its aura.

Something dreadful!

Forcing herself to open the door, she climbed upward and found herself in a small square room. The place must have once had glassed-in windows, but they had been removed. In the center of the room hung a rusty, cracked bell. A new rope had been affixed to it, but the clapper had fallen to the floor.

Quickly Megan tied the drawers to the bell rope, hanging the end of it over the side so that it could be seen from below.

Then, leaning over the low parapet, she looked down, eager to see the laughter in Lea's uplifted face.

Instead, she saw a knot of struggling figures. *Fiona!* Dear God, what was she doing? It looked like she was attempting to push the wheeled chair and its occupant into the sea! Angus was barking dreadfully, and above the sound came a scream. Constance was racing across the sand, her black skirts flying.

Megan tumbled through the opening in the bell tower and rushed downward, taking the steps two at a time. When she at last burst out on the promontory and descended the wooden steps, she found the wheeled chair back on safe ground, Lea unconscious, and Fiona in a dead faint. Constance, breathing heavily, could only stare at Megan with accusing eyes.

From above them sounded a shout. "What in the name of God are you doing there?"

Craigh Stewart and Doctor Potts, at last, had arrived.

CHAPTER 14

Inside the house, there was a flurry of confusion. Fiona was taken to her room in a half-dazed state to be rid of her soaked gown, Constance in attendance. Doctor Potts examined the drenched, semi-conscious child, his face grim.

"What was she doing down there?" he asked. "Whatever possessed you? Of all the foolish things to do! The girl's an invalid!"

"But she was so much better! I wanted you to see —" Megan's voice quavered. "I only left her for a moment, then when I looked out —"

"Never mind." The doctor replaced his instruments in his case and snapped it shut. "She seems well enough. Only time will tell. Get her out of those wet things and into —" he frowned at the sodden gown Lea was wearing — "into something more suitable for a sickbed. We will discuss this further when you come downstairs."

Megan did as he asked, smarting under his words. She deserved them, she knew. Instead of caring for her charge, she had been indulging in a silly, childish prank. Doctor Potts had been quite correct in doubting her maturity.

When she descended for the dreaded conference, she learned what had happened on the sand in her brief absence. Fiona, learning from Aherne that Megan and Lea were on the strip of beach, had gone, disbelieving, to see for herself. She arrived just in time to see Lea propel the chair into the water. Racing down the steps, she had caught at the chair, but it had been a struggle against the strength of the waves. Only the arrival of Constance saved the child.

Megan looked drearily from Craigh to Edward Potts. "Why?" she asked. "I don't know why Lea would do that. Unless … we were playing games..." The thought of her own voice singing, *"Willie, Willie, Weet feet"* sounded in her ears.

"It wasn't that," the doctor said. "I think the child is suicidal. Perhaps some memory came back to her. Something from the past."

Megan looked at Craigh. He was white-lipped. She saw in his face that he agreed.

"I can't believe it," she said, brokenly. "Only moments before she was laughing, sunny —"

"You'll have to believe it," the doctor said, "if we're to keep her safe."

It was a thoroughly chastened Megan who returned to Lea's side. Lea, once again, looked drawn, ill, her vulnerable mouth pale and bloodless. And it was all her fault, Megan knew. She had thought of the girl's brief move toward recovery as her own handiwork. She had been vain about it, showing off, saying, in effect, *See what I've done!* And it had turned on her.

She bent to kiss the girl's cold forehead. "Please, Lea," she whispered, "be all right. Get well!"

She wandered to the window, thinking moodily of the fate that had led her here.

Leaning out of the window, she looked down at the sands below, then covered her lips to shut off an exclamation of dismay. For far below her, Doctor Potts and Craigh Stewart were walking at the edge of the sea, looking at the tracks the wheeled chair had made in its journey. And as she watched, Edward Potts looked up, his face a fiery red, even at this distance. He turned to Craigh and spoke, and the master of Wyndspelle followed his pointing finger.

The drawers! The frilled, beribboned drawers flying from the bell rope. She had forgotten them!

For the remainder of the day, Megan remained in her room. Even though she was certain Doctor Potts had returned to Wychboro, she dared not face Craigh Stewart. It would be impossible to explain the prank, in the first place. In the second, it had had such drastic consequences. For the third, no decent woman would display her undergarments in public.

What would Doctor Potts think of her? Suddenly, it seemed to matter very much.

Megan sat by Lea through the night. Toward morning, the girl's eyes opened and Megan leaned forward, fearful of what she would see written on her face. With a vast relief, she saw that Lea's recovery had not been too much hampered, for she wore a look of impish mischief. She pointed upward and managed a very sensible, childish giggle, her lips saying a soundless *Fiona*.

"They're still there," Megan said, fighting back the tears that threatened. There could be no connection between this girl and a guilt-ridden child who tried to take her own life. "Lea," she said, unsteadily, "Lea … *why?*"

There was only a look of bewilderment on the girl's face in answer to Megan's questioning. It was clear she recalled nothing beyond the fulfillment of their prank.

"Sleep," she said, squeezing Lea's hand. And Lea slept.

In the wee small hours, Megan, still sitting on the hard chair beside Lea's bed, suddenly came awake. For she had heard a noise, a whining, a snuffling sound. *Angus,* she thought, agonized. She had left him on the sands below the house, forgetting him in the confusion the previous day. But the sounds came from her own room, where she had closed the connecting door.

Tiptoeing to the door, she opened it. A frantic Angus bounced like a rubber ball, leaping into her arms, covering her face with damp dog-kisses. Someone, possibly Aherne, had rescued him. For that, she would be forever grateful.

Then she saw the object on her bed. Folded neatly upon her pillows was a froth of white. On closer inspection, it was exactly what she'd feared it to be: her incriminating drawers.

Craigh Stewart was responsible for their return, she was certain of it. How, she wondered woefully, would she ever be able to face the man again?

CHAPTER 15

Morning came in a blaze of morning-glory blue, touching
Wyndspelle's haggard grounds with a compassionate finger.
Megan, from the window of her own room, caught her breath
as the sun gilded the tops of small ridges, purpling the hollows,
outlining each skeletal tree with gold.

Dressing in one of the new gowns, she moved on into Lea's
room. The girl was sleeping a natural, restful sleep. Megan
went to the window here, too, looking out on the seaward side.
The waves curled in lazily, laced with a froth of white, and
Lea's sandpiper skittered down there along the sand.

There was something else there, too, a memento of
yesterday. For the chair upon which Aherne had worked many
loving hours still lay there, tipped upon its side. *A broken dream,*
Megan thought, tears blurring her eyes. The wreckage of her
hopes for Lea. It had been a means of escape from the
sickroom, a coming back to living —

Megan's jaw set with purpose. Lea had not been suicidal, as
everyone seemed to suppose. She was merely trying to play
games with the waves, as Megan had done. From now on, she
must be more careful in leading the child into such activities.
But that need not stop her from her goal, which was to make
Lea into a normal, active girl. The chair had been useful, but it
was not necessary!

Megan turned, feeling Lea's eyes upon her. *"Tis a glorious
morning,"* she sang, whirling in a silly little dance, snapping her
fingers. *"Heist yer knee t' boggle a flea, t' shinny —"* She burst into
laughter as Angus joined her excitement, bounding madly

about her, tugging at her skirts. "Ye wee divil," she said, when she could catch her breath, "stop it, now."

To her delight, the girl's infectious giggle joined in. They were still laughing when Constance appeared at the door with Lea's breakfast tray. The woman looked stricken, but only for an instant, her face growing grim again.

"I am to feed Miss Lea this morning," she said sullenly. "You are to join Miss Fiona at breakfast."

Megan, a little flustered at being caught acting the fool, hastened downstairs, fearful that Craigh Stewart might have chosen this morning to add his presence to that of the rest of the family.

To her relief, he was not there. Fiona, pale and a little cross-looking, occupied her usual chair. Aherne, with an expression that was both guilty and chastened, promptly rose and left the room.

"I have been scolding him," Fiona said, in her thin, sweet voice. "He confessed he constructed that — *vehicle* in which Lea was nearly drowned. I told him he is completely at fault for her accident, and I shall inform Craigh of that fact."

"Oh, no!" Megan said, startled. "It was my own idea! I thought of taking her down to the beach. She wanted so to go!"

Fiona stared at her. "*Lea* wanted to go? However did she manage to convey that to you?"

"She speaks, occasionally. Just a word or two. And she can gesture."

"It is difficult to believe," Fiona said after a moment. "But if what you say is true, you are good for the child, Megan."

"Except for yesterday," Megan said in a wry tone.

"Except for yesterday," the woman echoed. "But, of course, you are not to be blamed. How could you know the girl's propensity for self-destruction?"

Megan opened her mouth to refute Fiona's words, but the woman forestalled her, reaching for the teapot with her slender, be-ringed hands. "There is something else I wish to discuss with you, Megan. The gown you are wearing — is it made from the materials Craigh purchased?"

Megan nodded.

"Highly unsuitable," Fiona said in a whisper. "I suggested something dark, more durable. And the manner in which it is sewn! There is not enough fullness to the skirt, and it is plain that you are wearing no lacings. The length, too — tell me, was there not enough material? One does not show one's ankles, dear."

Megan looked down, the fresh sprigged gown that had seemed so appropriate for a summer's day suddenly uncomfortable. She looked at Fiona, back erect, tiny waist cinched in, flowing skirts spread about her chair. "I had not thought," she said in a small voice. "They are dressing like this in London."

Fiona's eyes widened. "Are you sure, dear? I really must go down to Boston and check with some seamstresses. I cannot believe it! For I will admit, seeing you yesterday, I was shocked. I could not believe you would appear in something that — well — outlines your *form*. Not in front of Craigh or Edward." Her cheeks reddened. "It seems deliberately provocative."

Megan hid a smile, for now she realized the reason for Fiona's statements. Fiona was a woman, after all, a creature of flesh and blood, with a human vanity. Elizabeth, too, had spoken in such a manner whenever Megan wore anything that might be deemed attractive. It had dawned upon Fiona that her own things, though lovely, were quite out of fashion, and she was striking out in a very feminine way.

"I am certain no gentleman will look in my direction if you are in the same room," Megan said impulsively. Fiona blushed and bridled like a girl, and she knew she'd hit the right note. Though she disliked flattery, she meant what she said sincerely. She'd begun to feel sympathy for Fiona, tied here by duty, far from the social life she must crave. Tied to a child who was not her own, dancing to the tune of an embittered man who had been her sister's husband.

Fiona excused herself, and Megan finished her breakfast quickly. The summer day that waited outside was too beautiful to miss. This morning she would ride for the time allotted to her, returning to Lea's room refreshed and renewed. For she had some new ideas on how to help the ailing girl.

Stepping into the yard, she felt a flutter of misgiving. Craigh's horse was saddled and waiting. She looked toward the stables, ready to flee should he appear. He was nowhere in sight, and the copper-colored mare tossed her head impatiently. Apparently, the horse had been standing there for a long while.

Megan went closer to her, speaking soft words of affection, reaching out to stroke the velvet muzzle. The stocky little pony she'd chosen for her own mount was perfect for her needs, but, oh, to ride an animal such as this, just once! Megan closed her eyes, flying up the cliffside in her imagination, soaring like a bird —

And why not? she asked herself. Why not ride to the stone at the edge of the cliff and back? The horse's owner had left her to stand, waiting. He might be a long time in coming, and there was no one to see. He would never know!

Eyes sparkling, she swung herself up on the tall horse. The skirt of her new gown was constricting, so she pulled it above her knees. The animal started nervously beneath her, and she steadied it with her voice as it turned, prancing at the feel of an unfamiliar rider.

She held the mare to a walk until they were beyond the stables, then gave it free rein. Given its head, the horse lengthened its stride, and they were off and away, Megan's hair whipping loose, streaming behind her. They neared the stone and she didn't have the heart to halt the animal. She bent low over its mane as they fairly flew to the top of the horseshoe cliff.

"You beauty," she cried, delightedly, "oh, you beauty!" Leaning forward, she smoothed the silken neck. "If only I didn't have to take you back," she said. "If we could just run forever!"

Ruefully, she turned the mare's head toward the path, marveling at its surefootedness. Reaching the base of the cliff, she could not resist running the horse once more, arriving at the spot where she'd mounted, her hair in her eyes and her face rosy with laughter.

Before she could dismount, a hand clamped over her foot. She looked down, startled, into Craigh Stewart's blazing eyes. Reaching up, the man grasped her arm and tumbled her from the saddle into his arms.

"I am the only one who rides this horse," he gritted, setting her on her feet, turning her to face him.

The fury that flared in her at his touch faded. Again, Megan was in the wrong, and she knew it. "I'm sorry," she stammered. "It is only that the mare is so beautiful. I did it on impulse."

"And your impulsiveness could have killed you," he said harshly. "This is a spirited animal, worthy of only experienced riders. The way you were racing up the cliffside! Supposing she had gone down? You would have broken your neck!"

"It is *my* neck," she said in confusion. "I would have been responsible for my own actions."

"And supposing the mare had broken her own neck? Had you thought of that? Or a leg! How easy do you think it would be to replace her?"

Megan looked at the horse, her eyes widening with horror at the idea of doing her an injury. Turning to Craigh, she spread her hands in a futile gesture of apology, and his bleak face softened.

"I did not intend to speak so harshly," he said unexpectedly, "but since I've done so, supposing I make amends. I plan to take my morning ride now, and I would be pleased to have your company.' Seeing the negation in Megan's eyes, he amended his request. "I would like to discuss Lea's … accident with you. Though it may be difficult for you to believe, I am most concerned."

Megan weighed her decision carefully. She disliked this man for what he'd done to Uncle Ian and to his own daughter. Even more, she was appalled at her own reaction to his touch. There was something about him, a magnetism, that set her nerve ends shivering. And, too, his questioning might prove an embarrassment. With difficulty, she kept herself from looking upward toward the bell tower from which she had flown that unmentionable garment yesterday.

"And I will be pleased to accompany you," she said finally. For there might just be a possibility that she could bring Craigh Stewart and his daughter together in a more normal relationship. If that could be accomplished, her personal wishes did not matter. She turned away. "I will saddle my pony," she said.

"Aherne will do it for you. He is in the stable now."

Ignoring his words, Megan entered the long building. Aherne was leading the stocky little horse from its stall already.

"You were listening," she accused him, with a smile to take the edge off her statement.

"I was worried for you," the boy admitted, the triangular face beneath his pale hair reddening. "He," Aherne gestured toward the door, "doesn't go along with anybody meddling with something he thinks is his. Be careful, Megan. I ... I don't want anything to happen to *you*!"

Megan was flustered at the boy's worshipful gaze. "I appreciate your concern," she said, laughing a little, "but I did deserve a scolding. I expect I'd be quite possessive, too, if that mare were mine! And as far as something *happening* to me, what do you mean? Surely Master Stewart wouldn't do me harm!"

In answer Aherne flinched, burying his head against the stocky pony's body as he tightened the cinch. Megan whirled to see Craigh Stewart standing in the doorway, his lithe, broad-shouldered figure blocking out the light as he slapped his riding gloves against his knee. He stared at Aherne coolly for a moment, then turned and stepped outside again.

"What were you going to say?" Megan asked the boy in a harsh whisper.

He shook his head hopelessly and slapped the saddled pony on the rump, sending it out of the stable. "Nothing," he said sullenly. "I wasn't going to say anything."

Their moment of rapport was gone.

Megan left the building and mounted her pony, spurning any assistance from Craigh. They rode together in silence, through Wyndspelle's barren grounds, up the cliff path and into the trees. Reaching a spot where the crowding forest parted to show a sunny little glade, Craigh Stewart stopped his horse and dismounted, coming to give Megan his hand.

"We can talk here," he said.

Leading her into the small clearing, he took off his coat and spread it at the foot of a tree, motioning for her to be seated, then sat down beside her.

She trembled a little inside at his nearness, and at the beauty of their surroundings. The grass in the meadow was lush and starred with flowers that scented the air, making Megan almost dizzy. Birds trilled in the branches above. Sun slanting through leaves turned Craigh's hair to copper and made a golden mask of his face. It was a place of enchantment.

"Lea," Megan said, faintly, in an effort to break the spell. "You wished to talk about Lea."

The man started, as if he, too, had been held in thrall. "I wanted to talk about yesterday," he said quietly. "Why did you take her down to the beach? I cannot understand your actions."

"Two reasons, actually," Megan admitted. "She wanted to go there —"

The blazing eyes met hers with sudden interest. "And how did you know that?"

"By word and gesture. She is beginning to improve, you know. And that was the second reason. I wanted to show you … to show you…"

She stopped, too choked with emotion to continue, and he said, "To show me she is getting well, correct? That out of the sickroom atmosphere, she can become a normal, healthy child?"

Megan nodded, grateful at his perception.

"Then, tell me, why did she try to drown herself?"

"She didn't," Megan flared. "It was my fault. I had taught her a game. Or perhaps the chair rolled of itself!"

The man leaned forward, plucking a blade of grass, pulling it through his brown fingers, reflectively. "Then she showed no signs of malaise? Of depression?"

"On the contrary," Megan said, angrily, "she was happy! Laughing! Filled with mischief. She wanted me to play a prank!" She stopped, hand halfway to her lips as if to halt the words she'd already uttered. Craigh's eyes began to glint with an amused twinkle.

"I see," he said. "And that explains your absence at the time."

"It does," Megan said loftily.

"It makes sense," Craigh said, his face thoughtful. "Before her illness she was a happy child, a little minx. I suppose, though, that it is possible her memory returned in a single brief moment and she could not live with it."

"I do not think so," Megan told him, her voice filled with ice.

"Or that she saw Fiona coming and tried to run away."

"Fiona?" Megan was bewildered. "I do not understand."

"Did not Fiona tell you? Lea's malady has taken the form of animosity toward her entire family. My presence, Fiona's, Aherne's, all seem to send her into spasms of anger and frustration. Only Constance seemed able to calm her — prior to your coming, of course."

This put an entirely new light on the family relationships. Craigh Stewart was unable to bear the sight of his daughter, and perhaps the feeling was mutual. But Fiona! Megan thought back over the days she'd been in charge of the child. Just once had Fiona entered her room. And on that day, Lea had struck out at Constance, who was feeding her! It was the day she had spat upon Megan.

"Aherne has seen her," Megan said, remembering, "and there were no problems."

"Then perhaps she is improving. And it may be because the boy failed to launch into one of his wild, frenzied accusations."

"Accusations? Of Lea?"

"Of myself," Craigh said glumly. "Sometimes I feel the lad is in worse case than Lea. He has talent. He is good with his hands. I have suggested setting him up a shop in Boston or Gloucester, but Fiona will have none of it. And speaking of accusations, I feel you owe me an explanation. Upon two occasions you have accused me of murdering someone. I would suggest you produce a body as proof. Or failing that, I would like to know which of my many victims you are referring to. You did not mention the name."

"Then I will, now!" she said, angrily, her burr growing thicker. "The Reverend Ian Mackenzie, and if 'tis his body ye're wanting, ye'll find it i' the kirkyard at Wychboro!"

He stared at her, taken aback. "I don't know what you are talking about. I've only seen the man once! Shortly after I brought the remains of my family here."

"And ye turned him awa', ye did. He came to offer ye his prayers and condolences when ye were grievin'. An' ye sent him awa' the night I come here! Out into the rain an' the storm!"

"That's enough!" His voice was sharp and his hand went to his head. "Let me think. I did not see the man, I tell you. How——?"

"'Twas by yer orders. Nae man o' God is welcome in yer house, ye said. An' they turned him awa'. To die o' the wet an' cold!"

Megan was crying now, and he reached out for her distractedly. "Hold your tongue, girl! Give me a chance to speak." But when she was silent, looking at him with great, accusing eyes, he could only sigh.

"It is true," he admitted. "Or at least partly true. I confess to saying something of the kind, but good God! I would not consciously have allowed the thing you describe!" His face looked ravaged as he went on. "My life these last years has not tended toward thankfulness to any God. Yet there are those who would constantly intrude with their beliefs. Your uncle, Fiona, Constance. Even the physician I employ to serve my daughter's needs must put his long nose into the affairs of my soul. In truth," he said huskily, "I do not believe I have one. Or if I do, it is already damned to hell."

"Please," Megan said, torn by his agony despite herself, "oh, please!"

"You have helped me much," he said soberly.

Megan's eyes misted. "I have done so many wrong things, made so many mistakes!"

"But you have tried, which is more than we here have been doing. I have even caught myself smiling of late, a difficult accomplishment for one who has lived in a madhouse for a number of years."

He smiled now, the golden mask breaking up and becoming suddenly human. Megan looked at his lips, tender as they curved, oddly vulnerable, and caught herself to let her guard down so.

"We must go," she said sharply. "I promised to return within a certain amount of time. Lea will be waiting."

Turning, she stumbled toward the little pony. She was up and away before he had an opportunity to mount his own mare. As she went down the trail that led from the cliff, she could hear hoofbeats close behind her. When she reached the stables, Craigh was at her side to lift her down.

He held her for a moment, hands clasping her waist, blue eyes yearning into hers. And at last he said, "Thank you for what you've done for Lea — for all of us." Bending, he kissed her cheek, the lightest of kisses, tender as the brush of a night-moth's wing.

As she drew away from him, knees weak with the knowledge of the emotion she found within herself, Megan saw a face in the shadowed stable door: a white face, triangular, that seemed to hang there like a lantern, then disappear.

Aherne, his face contorted with fury and with hate.

CHAPTER 16

Megan returned to Lea's room, dazed and bemused. Craigh's kiss had stirred her more than she cared to admit to herself. The man was only showing his gratitude for her care of Lea, her mind kept telling her. But her traitorous body kept insisting the kiss had meant more ... more!

Finally, her sense of humor came to the fore. What a silly goose she would be to read anything into that brief embrace! Why would Craig Stewart look twice at a great gowk of a girl who had made such a ninny of herself, time after time? He had been quite right when he accused her of having a vivid imagination! It had been the glade, the lovely summer day. Perhaps the close proximity of any man would have put romantic thoughts into her mind.

"Aweel!" she said to Lea, when Constance had gone. "Still abed, are ye, little lazybones? We'll soon take care of that." Moving a chair to the window, she lifted the girl and carried her to it, lowering her so that she stood for a moment, feet on the floor, supported in Megan's arms. "We do not need a chair with wheels," she told her. "For one day you will walk. And today is the beginning!"

When Lea was seated, Megan placed Angus on the child's lap, then sat on the floor, massaging the pipestem legs, pleased when she ran a finger teasingly along Lea's bare foot and felt a reaction. There was feeling, then! Again, and Lea giggled, drawing the foot away.

At length, deciding the new exercise had gone on long enough, Megan carried Lea back to her bed, once again letting her stand for a moment. This time, it seemed she stood with more assurance, dragging less heavily on her arms.

"Give us a week," Megan said in a choked voice, "and you will be standing all alone. Another, and you'll be able to take a step or two. And soon, Lea, ye can run me a race — and win!"

The blue eyes, so like Craigh's, were sensible and smiling. Megan thought of the furious little face she had seen at her coming, the glazed eyes of the girl as she lay in a semi-coma. How far they'd come! God willing, and with Megan's aid and protection, this child could be well!

Constance appeared at the door with Lea's noon meal. "I am to feed it to her," the woman said, huffily. "Master Stewart is at table with the others and requests your presence below."

Megan looked at the woman in disbelief. Was it coincidence that the man would change his habits after their ride this morning? That he chose to dine with the family because he would be in her company once more? The blood coursed hotly through her body at the thought.

Her face set stubbornly. She was making a fool of herself — and over a man she had cause to despise! He probably sensed the emotions he'd aroused in her this morning, and it amused him to have her come running when he crooked his finger.

Well, he was wrong!

"You may tell Master Stewart," she said coldly, "that I am weary from our ride this morning, and that I have little appetite. I shall remain with Lea." She took the tray from Constance and set it down. "You need not return to sit with the child this afternoon, either. I shall be here."

Megan closed the door in the older woman's face. Now she had done it! Shut herself off from any escape from the sickroom this day. But it would be well worth it. She had no wish to see Craigh Stewart, in her present mood, and it would be as well to avoid Aherne. The memory of his angry, spying face still haunted her.

After feeding Lea her lunch, Megan sat beside her as she slept, enwrapped in a sort of daydream of her own, a dream of two people, a man and a girl, in an enchanted flower-starred meadow.

The sound of angry voices intruded upon her consciousness. Male voices. Craigh? Aherne?

Rising, Megan went to the door and opened it. The argument was emanating from the great hall below. Stepping out onto the balcony, she leaned over the railing. Below her she could see Craigh Stewart and Doctor Potts. Both of them appeared to be livid with rage.

"Dammit, man," Craigh was saying, "I did not send for you! When I think we need a doctor, I will call you out!"

"'Tis but a friendly call," Edward Potts answered stubbornly. "I wish to see how the girl weathered yesterday's problems."

"I have never pretended our relationship was a *friendly* one," Craigh scoffed. "You are a professional, and you are well paid."

"I wish to see Lea, if at all possible." The doctor scowled. "I have ridden all this way —"

"To see Lea," Craigh asked, suggestively, "or to see the young lady who is her companion? To try to win her over with your sneaking, sanctimonious ways?"

"Sir!" Doctor Potts doubled his fists, and the two men faced each other like a pair of fighting cocks. With a rustle of silk, Fiona appeared from the dining room and rushed between them, looking small and helpless.

"Craigh! Whatever's got into you? I myself let the doctor in. I appreciate his coming all this way for a second look at the child. To accuse him of having designs on our Megan! Why, that's the silliest thing I've ever heard! Our good doctor, who is a most eligible bachelor — and Megan?" Her laughter at the absurdity of the situation trilled upward.

Megan backed into her room, closing the door, her cheeks hot with humiliation. Fiona had quelled the disturbance most effectively, but she had also reduced Megan to her proper place. Returning to the chair beside Lea's bed, Megan looked down at her long-boned wrists, hating them, keeping her eyes averted from the mirror that would look back at her with a freckled, snub-nosed face. How could she have ever thought *any* man would look at her?

It was the new gown, she thought, smoothing it over her lap. Perhaps she had believed it might work a miracle.

She was still sitting there when there was a tap at the door. Edward Potts stepped in at her invitation, and she looked at him helplessly. The red of anger had not yet faded from his face as he approached the sick girl's bed and made a pretense of examining her. At last, he turned to Megan.

"I had to come," he blurted. "This is the last time. I dare not come here again."

"Master Stewart?" she guessed in a low whisper.

He shook his head. "That, too. Megan, Unity Deaton is dead."

Megan looked at him, uncomprehending.

"Ian Mackenzie is dead. Unity Deaton is dead. And they have both had dealings with those who live at Wyndspelle. The people of Wychboro are concerned about the evil eye —"

His words had washed over Megan like a wave. Unity Deaton dead! The kind and gentle old woman who had given her tea. So thin a line between life and death.

The evil eye — the sense of what he was saying finally penetrated her mind. "You don't believe that," she said in a choked whisper. "You cannot! 'Tis superstition!"

"I do not know. I only know that some of my patients fear to come to me. Anne Farmer died last night in childbirth. I was not called. Benjie Killam nearly bled to death from a scythe wound. As for myself —"

"For yourself?" Megan prompted him when he paused.

"For myself, I believe what I said the other day. This house is steeped in more than a century of evil. All who enter here are cursed. I believe that, Megan. The old tales of murder, witchcraft, and betrayal are true. My people have seen them happen from the beginning, even before this house was built. And I —" He paused, swallowed, and began again, the tight-drawn lines about his fine mouth even more pronounced. "I have a premonition that if I enter Wyndspelle grounds again, I, too, will die."

"What if Lea should become ill?" she asked, her voice trembling. "I know only simple remedies."

"Forget about Lea. It is too late for the child. This house, the deed she did, all have too firm a grip on her. It is *you* I am concerned about, Megan. Despite what they say about Unity Deaton's death, I cannot believe you are anything but fresh, unspoiled. We will go away from here, from Wychboro! I will give up my friends, my practice. And if what I feel for you is the result of some evil spell, we will pray together!"

Megan found it difficult to breathe. "You cannot mean … you cannot be saying…?"

"That I love you and wish to protect you, to make you my wife!"

Megan put out a staying hand and he mistook it for a beckoning gesture. His arms went around her, and he pulled her stiffly to him, planting a dry kiss upon her lips.

Behind them, the door flew open. Craigh Stewart stood there, his dark face murderous. Edward Potts dropped his arms, guiltily, and stepped back.

"Forgive me," the doctor said, his voice anguished. "I forgot myself in my ardor. I did not intend —"

"You have presumed too much upon the lady's good nature," Craigh Stewart interrupted. "Now, if you will be kind enough to take your leave!"

Doctor Potts looked at Craigh, his gaze steady. "Not until I have my answer," he said quietly. "Megan?"

"I cannot leave Lea," she said, her eyes blurred with tears.

"Then I will remain in Wychboro. Should you change your mind, I beg you to come to me. And if you are ever in danger, call, and I'll come to you."

He shouldered past Craigh, bowing a polite farewell to Fiona, who stood just behind her brother-in-law, and was gone.

Craigh Stewart was not finished, however. As Fiona disappeared to usher the doctor out, Craigh stepped into Lea's room and closed the door behind him. "As for you," he said in an ugly voice, "you are like all the rest, aren't you? Out to gather all the hearts you can, breaking them one by one. A cheating little slut!"

Megan came alive. "Oot," she demanded. "Oot o' this room! I canna say what I think of ye! There are nae words for it! Gang oot o' here!"

"Gladly," the man said, mockingly, "but only because I do not care for the company."

The door slammed, and Megan stamped her foot. "Oooo!" she breathed, too furious to make sense. Then a soft, wailing cry from behind her caught at her ears.

"Meeee-gan."

She whirled toward the bed. Lea was sitting upright, her eyes filled with horror, her whole body trembling.

Megan ran to her, putting her arms around the girl, drawing her head against her breast, stifling the awful moaning sound.

"Meeee-gan."

"'Tis all right, hinny! Dinna fret, now. Dinna fret!"

The child pushed her away, looking desperately into her face. "M-m-m-mama," she said. "M-mama, she … f-f-f…" Then she bent backward in a kind of spasm, her face twisted with frustration.

"'Tis all right," Megan said again. "Just rest now. Whatever it is, you can tell me later. I'll no' leave you, Lea. I promise! I'll never leave you!"

At last Lea stopped shivering and fell into a natural sleep. She was still sleeping when Constance brought her evening tray, and Megan decided to leave her as she was. She sipped at the child's tea and nibbled a piece of buttered bread. If Lea woke, she would prepare something for her herself. For now it seemed better that she was at peace.

Megan's own nerves were jangled as she paced back and forth. Why had Craigh's anger produced such a violent reaction in the girl? What were the relationships in this household? Was it possible that Wyndspelle, itself, aggravated ugly emotions?

She was nervous, overwrought from the day's happenings. She needed something to do with her hands. And there was an unusual chill in the room. Lea's face, and her hands outside the coverlet, felt a little cold.

The fire was laid in the sickroom fireplace. Megan took the lighted candle and set it burning. The flames, which should have been cheery, brought Lea's tragedy to mind and left Megan with a feeling of depression. She forced herself to think of practical things. It would be cool tomorrow. She would wear her gray woolen dress, putting off the thin sprigged print she had come to hate. But it needed mending —

With a rush of relief, she realized that here was something to do. She would sit here by the fire where she could watch over Lea. If she took very tiny stitches, she might be able to make the chore last until bedtime.

Going into her room, she took down the frock. She had not realized until now how very unbecoming it was — bunchy and drab! But surely suited to her station as the sprigged prints had never been. Seating herself beside the sickroom hearth, the gown over her lap, Megan threaded a needle, then turned the garment to find the torn place. Something solid struck her knee, something in the pocket. She drew it forth, to discover the diary she'd found in the stair room when she'd brought down Lea's rag doll.

Should she read it? For a moment she wavered. Lea would have been quite young when she wrote in it, but still, even a child deserves privacy. It was just possible, however, that there might be something written here that would resolve the questions that plagued Megan's mind. If so, she should read it, for Lea's sake.

Still, it was with a sense of guilt that she opened the cover of the little book. *For Lea,* was written on the flyleaf in an ornate hand, *from Aunt Fiona, on her seventh birthday.* Each page was topped with a Biblical verse. Only the first three or four held a line or two of a child's irregular writing.

Ant Fiona loves me, the first page read. *Even if I am not pritty, nor smel nice, like Mama. She wishes I was her little girl.* On the next page, *I do not like my brother. He makes Mama and Papa fite, and yell at each other.*

Poor thing, Megan thought, her eyes blurring. No wonder the girl couldn't stand the sound of voices raised in anger! She turned to the next page.

Papa is mad becas Mama likes men, an they like her. What is a bassterd?

"God in heaven," Megan breathed. "Dear God in heaven!"

Then: *Papa is gone to find a house where there is no fort an no young ofissers. He yelled a lot, an Mama cried. I think it is my brother's falt. I do not think I will writ anymore in this book. I hate it. I hate everbody! I wish they were ded!*

Oh, Lea, Megan thought helplessly, tears running down her cheeks. Poor little girl, caught up in a web of marital anguish, unable to understand! The violence of her emotion was there to be seen, the remaining pages slashed across with violent strokes that scored the paper.

For the first time, Megan admitted to herself that there might be truth in Edward Potts's surmise that Lea herself had set the fire that destroyed her mother and brother. But though she was repelled by the deed, she could not hold it against a little girl who was more sinned against than sinning.

Kneeling at the fire, Megan tore the pages from the little book and fed them to the flames, one by one.

Night fell, and the gray gown was mended. Megan took one last look at the sleeping girl and went to her own room. The wind outside had risen a little, and the house had begun its labored breathing. For some reason she could not determine, Megan was suddenly afraid. Shadows lurked in the corners of her chamber, creeping out furtively, only to retreat again, waiting.

For a long time, Megan sat, big-eyed, in the middle of her bed, Angus huddled close to her side. The little dog jerked in his slumber, making little whimpering sounds.

"You are supposed to be my protector," she scolded him. Then she whispered, "I know how you feel, wee Angus. Nothing here is what it seems to be. This house, the people. Haunted and doomed!"

At last she left her bed and did something she had not done since she was a child. Kneeling beside her bed, she folded her hands in prayer, for herself and for Lea. Satisfied that she had called upon the only aid available, Megan crawled beneath the comforters once more and slept, to dream.

To dream of a man in a golden mask, a mask that melted in the sun, the hard, straight line of mouth becoming vulnerable, tender. But the sun was merciless in its heat, a white-hot ball in the Wyndspelle sky. The corners of the mask-mouth softened and became molten gold, flowing downward until the thing became a mask of tragedy.

CHAPTER 17

One minute Megan had been asleep, dreaming, the next she was awake. There was no line of demarcation. Something had brought her upright in her bed, something that whimpered and scratched at her door.

Lifting the small remnant of candle that burned at her bedside, she saw that the noise came from within her room, rather than from without. The little dog had left her bed and was industriously trying to claw through the door that led to the balcony. "What is it, sir?" she scolded. "You know you may not go out until morning!"

Then she caught the strong scent of the perfume that always accompanied the evil visitations, and saw that the door between the rooms was closed against her. And it would be bolted again, she was sure of that!

Snatching up the candle, she ran toward Angus and the door that led outward. This time, she intended to trap the intruder. Whoever or whatever it was, she would not allow it to escape. It might still be in Lea's room!

But when she opened the door, Angus fled toward the stairs leading down into the great hall, barking madly. Megan hesitated, but only for an instant, between going to Lea's room and following after. She chose to follow the little dog, praying that Lea was safe and unharmed.

By the time she had descended the stairs, Angus had already disappeared into the dining room, thence to the kitchens. And at last, Megan found herself in the wine cellar, standing as she had once before at an open trap door, looking down the rock-hewn steps into the sea. The sea was angry this night, what with a rising wind, and even here her face was wet with flying spume.

She thought of Unity Deaton's tale: *"'Tis said the house itself ran red with blood, and that on stormy nights, the bodies of the dead attempt to climb the steps in the chasm below, seeking vengeance —"*

Supposing the intruder was not a thing of flesh and blood as she had believed! Supposing…

She could not allow herself to think like this! Angus had followed something down here, and it was up to her to discover the thing's identity.

Grimly she went down one step, two, shuddering a little at the slimy feel of the stone beneath her feet. Three. She stopped, wondering if Craigh Stewart was working at the stone in the cavern. If he were, he would have seen the thing, whatever it was, human or worse. Or it might be possible that he himself…

She did not finish the thought, for at that instant something pushed at her from behind. Two hands shoved at her hard between her shoulder blades, and she found herself falling toward the angry waters that boiled below.

With a small scream, she threw herself sideways, striking against the wet, jagged walls with her head and shoulders, tumbling into the cavern to lie crumpled on the floor. Above her, the torches blazed, their light splintered into far-off fragments, then all was dark.

Megan came to her senses at the touch of something warm and moist against her face, opening her eyes to see Angus wagging frantically and liberally bestowing dog-kisses. Dazed, she sat up, remembering the hands that had pushed her, the fall toward the hungry, foaming waters. It had been close this time. Too close.

And there was something in this cavern beside herself and Angus! She could sense it. Clutching the little dog to her, she backed against the rock wall, seeing the stone figures Craigh was molding as a monument to his wife and son. In the torchlight, they seemed to move, to take on life.

Then she saw it. In the far corner of the cavern where the light did not reach, a pair of green eyes were fixed upon her, glaring, demonic —

Her knees went weak, and her grip on Angus loosened. In a flash, he was gone, back into those shadows. There was a screeching, yowling sound, and Fiona's cat shot past Megan and up the stairs.

A cat! Only a cat! Megan pressed her hand to her lips to suppress a giggle that trembled at the edge of hysteria. Yet, as she turned to follow after the battling pair, dog and cat, dragging her bruised body up the stairs, she was conscious of a new and horrifying fear.

Someone had pushed her down these jagged steps with the intention of sending her to her death. And that someone might still be up there waiting!

It did not matter now. For even more compelling was the thought that Lea was alone, and therefore in danger.

Reaching the trap door, she discovered it was closed. One of Megan's arms was almost useless from her fall, but gritting her teeth, she heaved at it, feeling something soft and yielding that lay across it roll away.

Mounting the steps, she entered the wine cellar, tripping over the object as she did so. It was a living body, warm to the touch — small — Megan's fingers searched the face in the darkness, a terrible awareness growing within her.It was not—! It could not be —!

Then she felt the thing around the body's slender throat. A string of beads. The lamer that had once belonged to Megan's mother; the gift she herself had given to Lea.

Had it been Lea who pushed her down those awful stairs? Had Lea's small hands pressed against Megan's back, shoving her to her death?

With a strangled sob, Megan lifted the child from the floor, struggling up the steps that led to the kitchens. There, in the big room still illuminated by a banked fire, she leaned against the wall, trembling. It would be impossible to get Lea back to her room without aid. But who was she to call upon? She dared not leave her here, alone. Yet if she screamed for assistance, she would wake the entire household, and there would be explanations to make.

What could she say? That her imagination had led her to follow Angus to the chasm? And that Lea had tried to kill her?

Gritting her teeth, she tightened her hold upon the girl and dragged her up the stairs into the dining room, at last emerging into the great hall. Only one more set of steps to go, thank God! Only one more set! Again, she paused to rest, her whole body quivering with the effort she'd expended. Then her breath caught in her throat.

For along the floor of the great hall lay a monstrous, slanting shadow, and as if in answer to Megan's screaming nerves, the house gave a heaving sigh.

"The ban sith!" Megan whispered through dry lips. Then, slowly, carefully, she tore her eyes from the inky blot across the floor, raising them upward toward the balcony. There, on the railing, sat the black cat, looking down. A faint light from Lea's partially opened door behind it cast the elongated shadow that had frightened Megan so.

Even so, Megan approached the spot with trepidation. For tonight, more than any other, she sensed evil around her, the same cold chill as of the castle at Alisdair. Her head throbbed from her fall and, putting a hand to it, she felt the stickiness of blood. Grimly, she tugged Lea's body across the floor and, with the aid of the railing, managed to get her up the stairs.

Megan reached the girl's room to discover the door to her room was unbolted. It stood open. The window had been opened, too, and the draperies billowed with the cold wind.

Heaving Lea onto the bed, Megan hastened to close the window, then returned to the child. Lea's thin face was pallid. A bruise at the hairline showed the effects of her fall. Unless, Megan thought, Lea too had been struck down.

Getting the basin of cool water from Lea's nightstand, Megan carefully sponged the unconscious face. The gown, too, must be changed. It was covered with dirt from the wine-cellar floor. It was while Megan was in the process of making the girl comfortable that she discovered what Lea held in her hand.

A shred of some sheer, gray material, such as the piece Angus had returned with on that other night. So Lea, too, was a victim, as much as she!

If Master Stewart needed proof that something untoward was taking place in this house, then she now had it! Complete with cuts and bruises. Megan touched her battered face, feeling the blood that still flowed from a laceration, and grimaced. Surely he could not lay this at the door of her imagination!

Lea stirred and whimpered a little, a word forming on her lips. "Mama," she said, "the smoke…"

Megan's blood ran cold, for she seemed to have caught a drift of faint perfume. She shut her eyes tightly, unable to stop the throbbing in her aching head.

"It's Megan, hinny," she said, finally. "Don't be afraid." Taking the cold little hand in hers, she said, "I will not leave you this night. Now go to sleep."

CHAPTER 18

When dawn appeared, gray at the window, Megan disengaged her hand from Lea's and went to her own room. She was stiff and sore, one arm almost useless, and the face she saw in her mirror gave her a fright. One eye was blackened. There was a long laceration from high on her temple to her cheekbone; the surrounding area showed varying shades of yellow and green. Her hair was matted with blood.

Gingerly, she managed to cleanse her cuts with cold water, to sponge her matted hair until she was able to arrange it neatly. Dressed at last in the gray gown she'd mended, she looked at her image. With her face milk-white, the freckles on her nose standing out, and one side of her face badly battered, she herself might hire out to haunt a house! If Edward Potts could see the way she looked, he would retract his ardent proposal.

She thought of him now. He would be the person she would go to, if she dared. Yet, feeling the way he did about this house and its occupants, it would not be fair to him. She could see his face as he had looked yesterday: the deep lines about his fine mouth, his eyes that would be so kind if they did not hold just a wee trace of fanaticism. He would be a good husband. With him, one would be safe, protected. Such a marriage would be truly a blessed one.

Except, when he had kissed her, she had felt nothing. While with Craigh Stewart, though she despised him, she had felt — Megan closed her mind against the thought, feeling a tinge of guilt. It was not fair to compare the two men, especially when Doctor Potts was by far the better, without doubt!

She must see Craigh Stewart today and report on last night's happenings. And through it all, she must be calm, logical, impersonal. If he refused to believe her story, then she would take matters into her own hands. She had shilly-shallied long enough! The fireplace, for example, had been burning at the other time the intruder appeared. But when she set the fire, it was drawing properly. Could someone have reached the chimney from the roof, blocking the draft, and then removed the barrier later?

It was worth looking into. And the bolt on her door, she would remove that today. Why had she not thought of it that other time?

She returned to Lea. The girl was awake and did not seem too much affected by her night-time adventure. She looked up at Megan with slightly dazed eyes, and her hand went questioningly to the bump on her forehead.

"You had a very bad dream last night," Megan said, briskly, "and fell right out of bed. *Blue-eyed Blunderhead, fell out of a trundle bed!*"

Lea giggled, and Megan was careful to keep the battered side of her own face turned from her. She would concoct some story for *that* a little later in the day.

When Constance knocked at the door, Megan called to her to come in, then hastened to her own room so that there would be no comment made on her appearance. "Just put the tray down," she called through the door.

"I'm to feed her." Constance's voice seemed filled with a malicious glee. "Master Stewart says you're to come down this morning, and he won't accept no for an answer. Something's happened."

Something has *happened,* Megan thought, fiercely. *Something more important than he knows!* Still, she wondered what was afoot as she braced herself to face him.

She was halfway down the stairs when she heard the shot. It seemed to come from outside, from the rear of the house. "Dear God," she breathed. "Aherne?" Rushing down the steps, she ran across the great hall and burst into the dining room. Aherne and Fiona were both at table, and she breathed a sigh of relief. "I heard firing," she said, "I thought —"

The two faces turned toward her. Fiona and Aherne both looked white and sick. Megan recalled how she must appear to them with her face in such sorry condition. She put a hand to it, covering her injured cheek against their shocked scrutiny.

"I — I had a fall last night," she said, helplessly.

"That is quite obvious," came Craigh's cold voice from the door that led down into the kitchens. "And you need not explain the circumstances. I am well aware of them. Henceforth, I suggest you curb your impulsive nature and keep out of sight."

"The mare," Fiona broke in, "will she be all right?"

"She's out of her misery now. I shot her." He looked at Megan, agony mixed with the fury in his eyes. "You might have informed me earlier!" Slamming the door behind him, he was gone, apparently back to the stables from which he had come.

Megan stood transfixed. "What was he talking about?" she asked. "His horse? Was she ill?"

It was Aherne who answered, his eyes fixed on Megan's face. "Someone rode her last night, hard and fast. I found her in the stable this morning, covered with lather, her mouth bleeding — and with a broken leg."

Megan swayed. "Dear God!" she said, helplessly, "and he thinks I did it? Ah, no! No!"

"Your face," Fiona pointed out.

"But I told you, I fell! I was not near the animal!" The words came out in a gagging sound; tears streamed down her cheeks.

Fiona turned an accusing look on Aherne. "If Megan did not do it, that leaves only you."

Aherne leaped to his feet. "You know I wouldn't do that," he hurled at his sister. "I have never hurt an animal in my life! And what's more, I do not believe Megan did it, either! If you ask me —" he swallowed — "If you ask me, he did it himself!"

"Craigh?" Fiona's voice was small and shocked. "But Craigh would have no reason —"

"*She* rode it yesterday, didn't she? That's enough reason! My dear brother-in-law prefers to keep anything he owns all to himself."

"Aherne!" Fiona stood up, but the boy was quicker; wiping his tear-filled eyes with his sleeve, he dashed from the room. They could hear his boots clattering on the steps that led to the kitchens, then the slamming of the heavy outer door.

Fiona turned to Megan, her own eyes wet. "I'm so sorry," she said, softly. "What a strange house this must seem to you. Craigh with his surly moods, Aherne with his warped ideas! There must be some explanation for Craigh's mare. Perhaps she got loose and ran free for a while, doing herself an injury, and returned. Please, don't let Craigh's accusations worry you. He is not himself."

"It is quite all right," Megan lied. "I understand."

"Then I believe I shall return to my room for a while." Fiona touched a delicate hand to her forehead. "With all this confusion I'm exhausted, and I fear I have another headache coming on. You look as if you could do with some rest, also. Perhaps you should lie down after you've had your breakfast."

Though she'd had little to eat since the morning before, the thought of food made Megan feel ill. After the scene that had just taken place, she knew she would not be able to swallow a thing. Her head, where she had struck it, was aching unbearably, and her thoughts were confused. "I — I believe I'll walk a bit first," she said, "and then perhaps eat a bite or two. If you will excuse me."

She turned toward the kitchen stairs, almost running as she reached them. At the foot, Mollie Sharp barred her way. "Well," the cook grinned, "looks like you got the worst of it. A midnight ride, maybe? Master's fit to be tied, he is."

"I was not riding his mare," Megan said angrily.

"Then who was it? Me an' Della don't sneak out of nights to meet no young man!" The woman gestured toward the warren off the kitchens where she and Della slept. "Heard a racket, I did, and got up just in time to see your skirt-tail whip out the back door. That gray thing you got on, it was. Told the master, too."

Megan felt a sudden, uncontrollable urge to smash her fist into the cook's malicious face. Then she thought, tiredly, that perhaps the woman *had* seen something gray — but it was not her woolen gown, of that she was certain. It would be a floating material, as light and filmy as mist.

"Excuse me," she said, "I am going outside. Please let me pass."

In the open air, Megan felt weak, drained. Fiona had been right in thinking she needed rest. Her head hurt so, and the injured arm was throbbing. But she could not force herself to return to that house!

No, she must find Craigh Stewart and tell him of the activities of the night. Somehow she must impress on him the reality of the midnight visitor and of the danger both she and his daughter were in. And in doing so, perhaps she might convince him she had not ridden the mare.

Megan turned toward the stables, then stopped abruptly. Craigh would be making arrangements for the disposal of the horse's body. If it were still there, she did not want to see. A little later, the man might be more approachable. For a while, she would walk.

Head down, she went along the path that led to the horseshoe cliff. The sun today was high and white in a colorless sky, and the wind off the sea was cold against her shoulders. She hurried a little to reach the site of the ancient grave that seemed so comforting. It would be warmer there in the lee of the stone where the path curved upward.

Rounding the stone, she stopped abruptly, a feeling of nausea rising in her throat. Craigh would not have brought his beloved mare here, leaving her to lie beneath the open sky in view of all who passed this way. Yet —

It was not Craigh's horse! The head of the animal, which was all that was within her view, was brown, not copper, the nose roman, the head not so delicately shaped. Megan forced herself to move to where she could see the horse in its entirety, pressing her hand to her lips to stifle a small scream.

Beneath the animal, a booted foot protruded, the leg showing enough to reveal trousers of a sedate and somber color.

Megan knew what she would find before she rounded the body of the dead gelding and dropped to her knees beside that of a man. Edward Potts stared sightlessly at the colorless sky, his neck awry, his fine mouth opened on a silent scream.

He had come once more to Wyndspelle. And, as he predicted, he had come to die.

For a long time Megan knelt beside him, too shocked to move, too stunned to cry. At last she bent to place a kiss upon his dead cheek. Then she rose with a grim purpose, walking about the body of the fallen animal, studying it carefully. And she found what she was looking for.

Across the two front legs were odd marks, like horizontal burns. Megan climbed the path that led upward, knowing what she would discover. And it was there: two trees stood sentinel at the top of the cliff, one at either side of the path. At the base of each tree, hidden in the underbrush, was a circlet of hemp, cut close to the knot.

The doctor had been summoned here by someone, perhaps in Megan's name. He had ridden in the night, and in a hurry, too concerned to see the rope that stretched taut across his way. Unaccountably, Megan thought of the quarrel between the doctor and Craigh Stewart the previous day and shuddered.

She would not go to Craigh with the tale of what had happened last night. And she would keep the finding of the trap at the clifftop her secret, too. Even if the hemp were removed, the evidence was still there in the scored bark on the trees. She would keep her counsel until she found out who was to blame for all the horrors here. That had been the flaw in her thinking since she came. She had been seeking someone on whom she could rely for help, but God helped those who helped themselves.

Returning to Edward Potts's body, Megan stood over him for a moment, uttering a silent prayer. Then aloud, she said, "I'm sorry! I'm so sorry! But I promise you —"

She did not finish, but turned away, fists clenched at her sides, and marched back along the path toward the house to tell the tale of her dreadful discovery.

CHAPTER 19

Craigh and Aherne were just leaving the stable as Megan approached the house. She told them what she'd found at the foot of the cliff, watching their faces. Aherne seemed to shrivel, but Craigh only gave her a long look, his mouth grim, then turned and strode along the path. Megan and Aherne followed.

Reaching Edward Potts's body, Craigh knelt, inspecting the dead face. Looking up at Megan with eyes that accused her, he said, "His neck is broken."

Megan knew what was in his mind. He had assumed that she was the rider of his mare last night, that she'd left Lea for a tryst with the physician, and this was the end result. She bit back the urge to blurt out a denial. One cannot deny what has not been said.

Craigh stood, dusting off his hands, frowning down at the corpse. "When a man dies where he has no business being," he said, "I suppose there's nothing for it but to return him to his own. Saddle three horses, Aherne, You and I will take him to Wychboro. We can tie his body across the third. While you are doing so, I suppose I should inform Fiona."

He walked back to the house, taking long strides, ignoring Megan and Aherne who followed him.

Fiona still lingered in the dining room. Looking up at Megan, she said, "I decided to have one more cup of tea and wait for you. I've been thinking of going down to Boston to choose material for winter gowns, and I thought that you might — why, Craigh! Whatever is wrong?"

Upon hearing the news of the doctor's death, Fiona fainted dead away.

Craigh carried her to her room, Megan following. "She will want Constance," he said. "I suggest you go to Lea. We will discuss your fitness to care for the girl when I return. But first, change your gown — there's blood on it!"

Megan looked down, seeing the bright splash that marred the skirt. Edward Potts's blood. The blood of the man who, just yesterday, had asked her to come away with him and be his wife; who had held her in his arms, placed his living mouth on hers.

She swayed a little, then stiffened. She would not let Craigh Stewart think her weak. "I will change it," she said, haughtily, "and I wish to make a request. I should like to know when Doctor Potts's burial service is to be held, and I plan to attend it. I will make up for my absence on another day."

He eyed her steadily. "I suppose your request is one I cannot, in all conscience, deny. But you must remember the terms I set forth before. Should you ride to Wychboro, you do not ride alone."

"Aherne will accompany me."

His eyes narrowed. "I do not think so, in this case. You must settle for my company if you intend to go."

Speechless with anger at his high-handedness, she whirled and left the room. Going to her own chamber, she opened the adjoining door and told Constance to attend her mistress. Hastily, she changed into one of her sprigged gowns and, donning a smile that belied her true feelings, went in to Lea.

The girl seemed none the worse for the happenings of the night, and Megan managed to concoct a hilarious tale of how Lea had fallen out of bed in the night and Megan, hearing the thump, had hurried to her, tripping over wee Angus on the way. Thus she explained her own battered condition. Head aching, arm throbbing, she kept up a flow of bright conversation, while all the time her mind was upon the scene that must be taking place at the rear of the property.

Edward Potts would be leaving Wyndspelle for the last time.

It was an interminable day. Darkness had fallen when Craigh and Aherne returned from their sad journey. Megan, sitting beside Lea's bed, whirled at a sound from the partially open door that led to the balcony. Craigh Stewart stood there, clothes dusty, face lined with fatigue.

"We were longer than we thought," he said quietly. "We could find no one who would receive the body. It is with Reverend Saunders now, at the church. The burial will take place tomorrow."

No one who would receive the body! Megan thought of what the doctor had said the day before. Because he was associated with Wyndspelle, because Ian Mackenzie and Unity Deaton were dead, his patients had forsaken him. He had been right! The curse of Wyndspelle had touched him, too. In death, he was bereft of friends.

Her eyes brimmed with tears. "I shall go," she said.

Craigh Stewart studied her, his eyes somber. "Forgive me for what I said earlier," he said, heavily. "If there is any fault here, it is my own. You are young, willful. I suppose I should not have brought you to this lonely place. And though Doctor Potts and I had our differences, I suppose he was a good man. Attractive to a girl in your position —"

Megan opened her mouth, then closed it again. He still believed she'd met Edward Potts in a romantic rendezvous. Well, let him!

With a weary, apologetic smile, Craigh Stewart closed the door and left her. Megan put her hands over her wounded face and wept. Not because she had loved the man who had died at the foot of the cliff so much, but because she'd been unable to bring herself to love him at all.

The next morning, she donned the unbecoming dark dress that had been her second best, the weather being too chilly for her newer ones. Looking at herself in the mirror — her blackened eye, the bruises on the side of her face — she was a little daunted. People would be staring at her in the church, wondering at her appearance. Perhaps, she thought wryly, Aherne would be the one to accompany her, after all. Craigh Stewart might not wish to be her escort!

But when she descended the stairs, she found him waiting. Silently, he walked ahead of her to the stables where two horses were saddled, her own small pony and a tall black stallion that pranced and fought the rein as Craigh mounted. He moved out before her and she followed. Today had brought a cold gray mist, and Craigh appeared and disappeared before her in a ghostly manner.

Megan shivered a little as the mist penetrated the thin cloak she wore over her shabby gown. *The end of summer,* she thought. *It is nearing the end of summer.*

Ahead of her, the hooves of Craigh's horse were muffled by the first fallen leaves. Craigh did not speak. It was a silent journey.

When they reached the edge of the forest, the mist had become a light, dreary rain. Craigh pulled up his horse. "Go ahead," he said, quietly. "I will wait for you here."

She looked at him incredulously. "But I thought you were coming with me," she said. "You cannot —"

169

"I can, and will. My presence will not help the dead. And I do not think Edward Potts, if he could, would thank me for it."

She glared at him. Just sitting here, waiting, under the dripping trees, he would be soaked to the skin. Well, let him! She had not pleaded that he come with her. With a tug at the reins, she turned the pony toward buildings around the square that constituted the little town, noting as she rode that the houses all seemed closed and shuttered, and that no one was in sight.

Her heart rose a little. In spite of her concerns, she was certain the people of Wychboro would be at the church to honor their good physician and departed friend.

The church, when she arrived, was empty. She stood for a moment in the dim room, staring at the vacant pews, wondering. Perhaps she had arrived too late — or too early. Or Craigh was mistaken. Or he had lied. She turned blindly to leave, then heard the Reverend Saunders's voice from the rear of the structure.

"If you have come for the Potts service," he said, eagerly, "it is to be held at graveside —" Then, his voice cracking a little, "Oh, it is you!"

Megan managed a smile. "I thought perhaps I was late," she admitted. "I suppose the others —?"

The minister seemed flustered. "Follow me," he said. He kept glancing over his shoulder a little fearfully as he led her on the route he'd taken her to find Uncle Ian's grave.

Far ahead of them, across a sea of mud, Megan saw the grave site. A pile of wet earth, a yawning hole. And as they drew nearer, she saw the long box, crudely made of raw lumber. It was dark with moisture. Surely it hadn't been sitting here through the night!

Leaning on a shovel beside the grave stood a large man. "The sexton, Billy Wills," Reverend Saunders introduced him when they reached the site. Megan looked at the man's face, seeing the vacant eyes, the foolish grin, and her heart sank. Surely they would not hold a service, just the three of them.

"Well," the minister asked, nervously, "shall we begin?"

Megan's voice was flat. "Where are the others?"

"I'm sorry," the man said, sincerely. "I am truly sorry. Perhaps it will help if I tell you this may be my last act as pastor of this church. I'm certain I shall be asked to leave. The citizens of this town seem to be of a particularly superstitious character, and it does seem that by some strange coincidence—"

He was almost babbling now, and Megan looked at him squarely. "Let us get on with it," she said.

She stood silent in the rain that dripped like tears, her skirts draggled with mud, as the minister said a few hurried words over the box that contained Edward Potts's body. Finishing, he looked at Megan, who showed no signs of leaving, then he signaled to Billy Wills to aid him in lowering the coffin into the grave. A hammock of hemp had been fashioned for that purpose.

As the minister moved to one side, Megan glanced up, startled to see a child's face peeping over the fence. The sight was followed by a woman's frantic scream. "Hen-ree!" The face disappeared.

Licking his lips nervously, Reverend Saunders looked toward Billy Wills. "Ready?" he asked. The man grinned inanely and moved forward. The two men set the coffin into the hemp cradle, releasing the guide ropes from the stakes that held them, and began to let the box down into the pit.

Suddenly a flash of lightning cracked in the sky above them, a low roll of thunder accompanying it...

The Reverend Saunders jerked back, and the box tilted. Billy Wills made a low moaning sound that made the hair rise at the nape of Megan's neck.

The man's arm was crushed between the coffin and the wall of the grave.

Reverend Saunders stood holding to his ropes, goggle-eyed and helpless. Megan sprang forward, using the shovel handle as a lever to free the sexton's arm. He fell away. Her body flung across the shovel to compensate for the weight of the slanting box, Megan called out to him, "For God's sake! Give me the guide rope! Give it to me!"

"Eh?" the man asked, vacantly, holding his arm.

"The rope," Megan said furiously. "Take my place here, and I will take yours!"

The sexton's face was twisted with pain, but he obeyed automatically at the command in her tone. Now Megan turned her attention to Reverend Saunders, who seemed petrified with fear. "I will help you," she said, crisply. "Now, Billy, *you* let up a little. And you," to the minister, "let that end down a few inches. That is enough. Now it's level. Steady, now. A wee bit at a time."

At last the box settled into the sucking mud at the bottom of the grave. Megan's body trembled with fatigue, her clothes soaked from the inside with perspiration despite the chill of the rain. She looked at the minister, who was still blank-eyed with shock, and then at the whimpering sexton.

"You and I," she told Reverend Saunders, "will have to cover the grave."

He was instantly galvanized to life. "No," he stammered nervously, "there is no hurry. It's the living who require our first attention. Yes, the living. I must attend to Billy's arm. Someone else will see to this later, I am sure."

He backed away from Megan as he made his babbling pronouncement, and she knew that he was terrified, that he would never return.

"Reverend Saunders!" Her firm voice stopped him. "Surely you do not think Billy's accident had anything to do with the Wyndspelle curse? You are a man of God, and we are on church property. Do you not have faith?"

"This is not church land," he mumbled. "The boundaries are there." He pointed toward the area of ancient graves, mossy-green in the dripping rain. "This is unconsecrated ground."

"Unconsecrated!" Megan turned, looking about herself. Not too far from the spot where Edward Potts rested in his rain-soaked coffin was another plot, some months old, where Uncle Ian lay. A newer one, its raw earth running with the wet, was nearby. No blossoms marked its stark outline, but Megan suddenly guessed whose it was. Unity Deaton, whose home had been a flowering garden filled with hummingbirds and butterflies —

Dear God. Oh, dear God!

"Then you believe in the Wyndspelle curse!" she shouted at the minister. "Say it! You believe!"

"I suppose I do," he said, reluctantly.

There was a small sound of approval, like the wind in dry leaves, and Megan whirled, looking toward the fence. A bevy of faces peered across it. Not children this time, but adult faces, avid and condemning. Megan raised an accusing arm toward them and suddenly her eyes went blind, turning inward in a sort of vision she'd experienced several times before and had guessed was second sight. Her voice, when she spoke, penetrated the misty rain with an awfulness beyond belief.

"I see waste," she intoned in that dreadful, prophetic sound, *"and desolation. Your young will go away, and the old will die! Your roofs will tumble in, and the wild things will inhabit the ruins. Grass will grow in your streets and brambles in your village square. One day there will be no one to guess that here was a town. Here once you lived! Wychboro is doomed!"*

The faces were gone. Shaking her aching head to clear it, Megan turned toward the minister and the sexton once more. They both stood rooted to the earth in front of her, but only for a moment. With an inarticulate cry, Billy Wills ran for the shelter of the church, cradling his injured arm. The Reverend Saunders was not far behind him.

Megan picked up the shovel. Unconsecrated ground or not, she would not leave Edward Potts to lie in an open grave. At long last she put down the muddy tool and stood back, pushing at her hair with a mud-streaked hand. Her cloak and gown were sodden, stained, her shoes heavy with wet earth. But the grave was decently covered. She turned toward the bare plots where her uncle and Unity Deaton lay, then, reeling with fatigue but upheld by determination, she left the site and walked stiff-backed, feeling the eyes of the town upon her drenched, bedraggled figure, to the little house where Unity had lived.

Already the small structure, its unpainted boards gray with damp, seemed to sag with the burden of age. Its windows were dark now. The rocking chair that stood on the porch was still. Yet the garden still held the touch of the old woman's hand. Great masses of blooms hung everywhere, heavy with rain. Megan took off her muddy cloak, spreading it on the grass, filling it with flowers. Then she left Unity Deaton's empty home for the last time.

Returning to the new graves, she went to each, covering the raw earth with fresh-scented blossoms. "'Tis consecrated now," she said quietly at her uncle's grave, "by God's own creations." She stood for only a brief moment, head bowed, then straightened her shoulders again. There was one more thing to do before she left this place for ever.

Edward Potts had lived in a small gray house at the far edge of Wychboro, she knew. And he had a housekeeper. She would have a word with the woman, should she still be there.

Leaving the cemetery, Megan mounted her pony and rode slowly down the street. There was not a face in sight, but she knew she was being watched. Dismounting at the dead man's house, she tethered the pony and knocked at the door.

There was no answer, but listening, Megan thought she heard a rustling from within. Turning quickly, she saw a face behind a curtained window. The curtain twitched and it was gone. Grimly she set her hand to the latch and walked in.

The room she entered was small, dark, austerely furnished. And a sour-faced, elderly woman cringed against the far wall.

"Don't be afraid," Megan said softly. "Nothing is going to harm you. I only wish to ask you some questions."

A few minutes later she was in possession of the knowledge she sought. A rider had appeared at the doctor's house on that fatal night, hammering frantically at the door. The housekeeper answered, unable to see the face of the messenger in the darkness. A note had been shoved into her hand. A note that sent the doctor galloping off into the night.

"Is the note still about?" Megan asked.

The woman looked frightened. "I suppose it is. Had I thought, I would have burned it." She led Megan into a small cubicle where there was a desk. The corner of a paper showed from beneath a book. The housekeeper would not touch it, but indicated it to Megan, who picked it up. *There is danger,* it read. *I need you.* It was signed, *Megan.*

Megan had not written it, but there was no point in arguing the fact. The mischief had been done. "May I keep this?"

"I wish you would. Just get it out of here! And yourself, too!" The woman's eyes were still frightened and hating. Megan turned to go, setting her hand to the door, opening it wide. And from the darkening, rain-wet sky, a bird flew into the house, crashing against the farther wall in its panic.

The housekeeper uttered a thin wail, her hand going to her throat. "A bird in the house," she moaned, "it means death! Oh, if I'd only gone before you came! I'm going to die!"

Megan looked steadily at the woman who had worked for the doctor, yet had refused his body when Craigh and Aherne brought it here. And again, there was that flicker of knowledge, of prescience.

"Yes," she said, "I believe you are. And soon. And you will not lie in consecrated ground. In fact, this very house may be your tomb. They might refuse to bury you at all."

Leaving the housekeeper sagging visibly against the wall, Megan left the house, mounted her pony, and rode stiffly through the village of Wychboro. It was nearly dark now, and the rain was coming down in a heavy drizzle. Craigh was where she had left him, still waiting, his dark-clad figure silhouetted against the dripping trees. He came to meet her, afoot, the reins of the stallion in his hands.

"You are late?" It was more of a question than an accusation.

"I know." Her voice was weak and thin. It sounded far away. The trees behind Craigh's tall figure seemed to blur a little, then to wheel and spin. Megan reeled in the saddle, then felt herself slipping. Craigh caught her as she fell.

"What have they done to you?" he asked in horror as he held her drenched, mud-stained figure in his arms. "God in heaven! What have they done?"

A shudder ran through her, then she relaxed, suddenly feeling warm and at peace. "Nothing," she whispered. "They did nothing at all. I am sorry I was so long, but I had to — had to bury a man."

Then, blissfully, she remembered nothing more.

CHAPTER 20

Megan awoke in the morning in her own bed. There were only hazy memories of the previous night. Craigh had lifted her, struggling a little, to his own horse, holding her in his arms and leading the pony behind them. Her face flamed now as she recalled the small endearments he'd whispered. Surely they had been part of a dream! Or perhaps she had been a wee bit out of her head after the happenings of the day?

Now, she ached all over, her body stiff and sore from her exertions at the doctor's grave. The arm she had injured in her fall in the chasm was almost useless. With a deal of effort, she managed to struggle to a sitting position. From here, she could see into Lea's room. Constance, evidently, had spent the night in there, sitting beside her. In the morning light, the woman looked tired and old as she slept in her chair, chin sunken on her chest.

The woman had been kind last night. She helped Megan rid herself of her ruined clothing and tucked her into bed. And Fiona had risen from her own sickbed, white-faced, to hover over Megan and attend to her needs. Aherne had been shaken at her appearance and had assisted her in reaching her room. And Craigh —

Megan shivered. They had all been warm, solicitous for her welfare. Yet one among them had striven to drive Lea out of her mind, had tried to murder Megan, and had succeeded in killing Doctor Potts. She thought of the note she'd found in the doctor's house, the note that called for help, signed with her name. Her eyes scanned the room searching for the garments she'd worn. She had thrust the paper into a pocket of her cloak.

The things were gone. Probably taken to the kitchens below for cleaning and mending. She must find them.

Rising, she stifled a moan. She could not recall aching so much ever before. Going to the wardrobe, she took out one of the sprigged gowns. It was not warm enough for this day, with the skies outside still dreary, but it must do. The gray, with its bloodstains, was beyond reclaiming. Somehow she managed to dress, despite her helpless arm, but she could not do up her hair. She had to settle for letting it hang down her back, like a child's.

"Mee-gan." It was Lea's voice.

Megan hurried to her side, bending as the girl lifted her arms, to kiss her cheek and envelop her in an answering hug. She raised her eyes to meet those of Constance, now awake. The woman's face reflected shock.

"She said your name!"

"Yes," Megan said carefully. "She says many things these days. But only to me."

"Does everyone know?" Constance asked hoarsely. "Master Stewart? Miss Fiona? The boy?"

"I suppose not, but I see no reason why they shouldn't. I intend to tell them."

Constance opened her mouth as if to say something, then closed it. It was clear to Megan that she knew something that she would not say. Perhaps she had guessed at the identity of the intruder in the night, if she herself were not the culprit.

At any rate, Megan had planted a seed. Let all in the house learn that Lea was talking, if only to Megan, and whoever was guilty of these criminal acts might grow desperate enough to make a clumsy move. For Megan was certain that the thing that person feared most lay buried in Lea's mind, that the girl was the key to Wyndspelle's present mysteries.

As for herself, she must remain alert. She must forget the kindness of the night before, the warmth and peace she'd felt lying in Craigh's arms. Never again must she be lulled into a sense of false security. Lea's life, and her own, might depend upon her vigilance.

When Constance went downstairs to give orders for Lea's breakfast tray, Megan went to her room and found a thin, flat coin. Using it as a tool, she removed the bolt from the door that opened from her room into Lea's.

When the woman reappeared, Megan went downstairs. The letter in her cloak was still preying on her mind. She would retrieve it and try to match the writing with that of the other people in the house. It would surely provide the proof she needed regarding the death of the doctor, at least.

When she entered the dining room, she found the entire family at table. Craigh rose at her entrance. "We did not expect you this morning," he said formally.

"I am quite well."

"You look dreadful," Fiona said, rising. "I will go and tell Cook we need to set another place. Sit down, dear."

"I will go myself," Megan said. "I am only looking for my dress and cloak. They must be cleaned. This gown is not adequate for cold weather."

Fiona's face fell. "I'm so sorry, my dear. Your things were quite beyond redemption. I fear I told Cook to burn them! Was it your only cloak? And I do recall you had a gray wool—"

Megan felt sick. Her clothing had been burned, the message with them. She closed her eyes, trying to form a mental picture of the written words, and failed. She'd been so upset at the time she'd acquired the note that she failed to take notice of the hand in which it was inscribed. Though the content would haunt her forever.

"Oh, my," Fiona said, troubled, "I shouldn't have taken it upon myself! But truly, I don't think your things could have been cleaned or mended." She looked helplessly at Megan, then at Craigh.

"I see no problem," he said easily. "In fact, it leads me to suggest a step I've been considering for some time. You yourself need new gowns, Fiona. And your headaches seem to have worsened of late. I suggest a journey down to Boston. You can replenish your wardrobe and pick up some winter materials and a cloak for Megan at the same time."

Fiona's face glowed. "Oh, Craigh! It would be so exciting! And you will accompany me?"

He shook his head. "I have no reason to. Besides, I feel quite out of place on a women's shopping expedition. No, I suggest you take Constance. Aherne can be your escort. I think he would benefit, too, with such an outing."

Her eyes showed a child's disappointment. Then they lit again. "But that is impossible, Craigh. Are you suggesting we leave Megan here with you, *unchaperoned*? That would never do!"

"I fear it is *my* reputation that would be endangered," he mocked her gently, "for I would be vastly outnumbered by those of the opposite sex! Cook, Della, to say nothing of my own daughter. Rest assured, Fiona, our Megan will be safe."

He smiled at Megan over his cup, and she felt her face turn red. The man was impossible! "Then it is settled," he said, positively. "I suggest you leave tomorrow. The weather shows signs of clearing."

"I won't go," Aherne spoke up. "You can't make me!" He left the table, slamming his chair against the wall, and ran from the room.

Craigh raised his brows, his face harsh with anger. "I leave him to you, Fiona. You cannot travel without a male escort, and — if you wish new gowns —"

Fiona's face was a mixture of emotions. It was clear that she wanted to travel in Craigh's company. It was equally clear that the outing and the promise of new things was so alluring that it was difficult for her to say no to the excursion. Finally, she said, "Aherne will go. I'll speak to him."

"Then it is settled," Craigh said, leaning back in his chair. "I think it will benefit us all. We live too closely here."

Megan had her doubts. Mollie Sharp and Della were hardly ever above stairs, and Lea would be of little use as chaperone. Craigh Stewart had forced his attentions upon her once. She most certainly did not trust him.

And even worse, she thought, a little fearfully, she could not trust herself.

That night, sitting beside Lea, a blanket wrapped about her own shoulders to keep off the chill, Megan jumped at a tap on the door,' Opening it, she was startled to see Aherne. The boy's face was pale, and he wore a furtive expression as he sidled in.

"I've got to talk to you," he whispered. "They're going to make me go, so I've got to warn you!"

Megan shot a concerned look at the girl on the bed. "Lea's asleep," she whispered. "Come with me." She led him into her own room, closing the door behind her.

"Now, what is it?"

"This." He handed her a piece of paper. It had been folded many times and was creased, a little soiled, yellowing with age. Megan unfolded it, recognizing the childish, irregular writing. The same hand had written the words in Lea's diary.

Dere Sir, it read. *Your wife is having a affare with a ofisser. Your son is a bassterd. I am sorry for you.* It was signed, *a friend.*

Oh, Lea! Megan thought. *Poor child, to hate so! Poor little girl!*

"Where did you get this?" she asked Aherne.

"I found it in *his* desk," Aherne jerked a thumb in the direction of Craigh's room, "before the fire. Right after he left to come here."

Megan's eyes were wet with tears. "I had so hoped there was some other explanation. That Lea had not been involved. Now I suppose there's nothing else I can believe. All we can do is try to help her forget."

Aherne looked at her with surprise. "Lea didn't do it! That's what I've been trying to tell you. It was *him!*" Again his thumb indicated Craigh's room. "He had a big fight with Morna before he left. He threatened her. I heard it all!"

"But if he was gone —?"

"He got back before the ashes were cold. He could have hid out for a while and pretended he just got home. Don't you see?"

Megan saw, and it made her feel cold all over. "What this note says, Aherne — could any of it have been *true?*"

He shook his head, wiping tears from his own eyes. "No," he said, finally, "it couldn't. Morna was beautiful, and she liked to have people tell her she was. She — I guess she flirted a lot, but she loved Lea and the little boy more than anything else in the world. She just liked to have fun."

"And Craigh? Did she love him?"

He shrugged his shoulders. "I guess so. I don't know. Like I said, they fought sometimes. Men liked to look at her, and it made Craigh mad."

"I see," Megan said, numbly. "This paper, may I keep it for a while?"

"I guess so. But do you see why I had to talk to you? I'm scared, with him sending us away —"

She stared at him. "Why, Aherne? What are you afraid of?"

"I don't know," the boy admitted. "Scared for Lea, I guess. I think she saw something that night. She tried to tell me once, then she had one of her bad spells. Scared for you —"

"He wouldn't harm me," Megan said without much certainty.

The boy looked at her squarely. "Doctor Potts is dead. I heard Craigh tell him to stay away from you."

Megan had a vision of Craigh Stewart riding through the night, giving the doctor's housekeeper a message from out of the darkness, returning to set his trap, riding hard, careless of the mare in his haste —

"No," she moaned, putting her hands over her eyes to shut out the horrible imaginings. "Oh, Aherne, no!"

"I had to tell you," Aherne said simply. "Fiona says I have to go, or it'll make trouble. But if you want, I'll stay anyway."

"Go with them," Megan said. "Go with them. I'll watch over Lea, I promise you."

"And yourself. I — I don't want anything to happen to you, Megan." The boy's heart was in his eyes, and Megan leaned forward, kissing him gently on the cheek.

"I will," she promised. "And — thank you."

Aherne, blushing a furious red, left her standing, the bit of folded paper in her hand.

Carrying it to Lea's room, she sat down, studying it. When she had read it before, sensing the hatred that would have to exist to make a child write such a poisonous thing, she had believed it proof of Lea's guilt. Aherne, however, saw it as something else, something that would madden a man to the point of killing his own wife and son. Forlornly, she realized she wanted Craigh Stewart guilty no more than Lea. But someone was persecuting the child. And there was the matter of the doctor's death.

The note, she admitted to herself, was undeniably written in Lea's hand. How she wished she hadn't burned the girl's diary! Like the message Doctor Potts had received, it too had gone up in flames.

Megan frowned. If someone had gone so far as to forge a letter with her name, might they not have done a similar deed before? The word *officer* ... in Lea's diary, it had read *ofisser*, Megan was almost certain. And in the diary, Lea had asked, *What is a basserd?* The letter stated, *Your son is a basserd.*

Immediately afterward she had written, *Papa is gone to find a house* —

No, the sequence was wrong. Lea had heard the ugly word when her mother and father were quarreling, which meant this ugly missive had already been received and read.

Megan looked at the girl's sleeping face. She still believed in her, she thought stubbornly. Lea did not set the fire that night, but someone would like it believed that she had. And if that someone were Craigh Stewart —

Sick inside, she made her preparations for the night, dragging a heavy chest across Lea's door, barring her own with a chair. Last of all, she shook her finger at wee Angus, admonishing him sternly that he was to stand guard through the night and bark loudly at any noise, however small. She, too, she promised him, would remain alert. She did not take the depth of her weariness into account, for after a few minutes, in which the

185

lines on the two notes danced before her eyes, forming and reforming to say different things, she fell into a deep, dreamless sleep.

In the morning, she woke in time to remove the barriers she had set up. And before long, Constance appeared, bringing Lea's breakfast. It was a different Constance than Megan had seen before. The woman looked almost elegant in the traveling gown she'd chosen for the journey. Megan couldn't help saying so.

Constance smiled, the first true smile Megan had seen on her face. "It is outmoded, I suppose," she said. "Miss Morna gave it to me." Her hands caressed the material, and affection for the dead woman was visible in her face.

"You must miss her very much," Megan said softly. To her surprise, Constance's eyes filled with tears.

"Yes, I do," she admitted.

"Tell me about her. What was she like?"

"Miss Morna?" The woman smiled again, her eyes dim with remembrance. "She was beautiful, she and Miss Fiona. Their parents took me from an orphanage, you know, to care for them. Oh, they were a pair! They made me take their lessons with them. I learned to read and write and speak like a lady. And once," her face reddened, "once, when I was walking out with a young man, they dressed me up in a frilly gown — mauve, it was — and did my hair high. The gown had a parasol to match —"

Mauve? Megan thought, trying to imagine the dark, faintly mustached woman in such a dress, with her sallow complexion. But aloud, she asked, "The young man — did nothing come of it?"

Constance flushed again. "He asked, but I would have none of him. I could not leave my girls. No more could they leave me. When Miss Morna married, I came with them, as did Miss Fiona and her brother."

"And Morna's gone now," Megan said thoughtfully.

Constance lifted her head proudly. "I've still got Miss Fiona," she said. "So I figure it's worth it all."

At that moment, Fiona called from the doorway. The small entourage was ready to leave. Stepping out to say farewell, Megan thought how lovely Fiona looked, her eyes sparkling now that she'd set her mind on the journey. "I shall look into all the latest styles," the woman prattled, "and I shall certainly bring suitable things for you, Megan. Something serviceable and warm."

Then they were gone and Megan returned to Lea's side, a fresh idea beginning to form in her mind. Supposing Morna had considered leaving her husband and shedding Constance as well? The woman was capable of violent attachments. That she had proved. But would she deliberately harm one of the girls she loved, through jealousy? Fear that she would be displaced in Morna's life?

"They made me take their lessons with them," Constance had said. *"I learned to read and write…"*

Had she used those lessons to advantage?

A short time later, Megan went to her room, where she could see through the window on the landward side. Four horses were wending their way up the cliff path. Fiona, Constance, Aherne, and Craigh were the riders. Craigh had made arrangements for a carriage to pick up the party at the far side of Wychboro, where there were the beginnings of a road. There he would leave them, returning with the horses. They would ride to Gloucester, and from there take ship to Boston. Craigh would ride out to meet them again in a week's time.

For now, Megan, Della, and Mollie Sharp were alone in the house. Craigh would be back before darkness fell. Megan thought about the things Aherne had told her and was afraid.

At last she turned to Lea. After she had dressed the girl in a day gown, Megan managed to get her into a chair despite her injured arm. While Constance was gone and there was no one to spy upon her actions, she intended to redouble her efforts on the child's behalf. If Aherne were wrong and Craigh himself were not the culprit, she intended to force the guilty party's hand. And Lea's evident improvement would be part of her plan.

Thoughtfully, she studied the fireplace, still certain that it figured in the smoke that accompanied the intruder. Somehow, before the others returned, she must find a way to get a look at the chimneys. But with Constance gone, she was tied to Lea's side.

Somehow, during their absence, she must find a way...

CHAPTER 21

Della brought lunch for both of them, bobbing and smiling to see Lea seated by the window, clad in a gown that was the twin of the one Megan wore. How Megan wished the deaf woman could speak. From the expression in her eyes, she knew she would be a friend. It was lonely when she had gone.

Pulling a small table toward Lea's chair, Megan said, "We're going to eat here today. Two grown-up ladies, having a party!" Placing a plate before Lea, she handed her a spoon, pressing it into her hand. The girl's eyes were bewildered. "You can feed yourself," Megan told her firmly. "You can do it, I know."

Trembling a little, Lea guided the utensil toward her plate, pushing at her food until she managed to fill it a bit, then, spilling only a little, managed to raise it to her lips.

"Wonderful," Megan encouraged her, wiping up the spills. Smiling, Lea reached for a bit of bread, but dropped it. Angus, at her feet, pounced on it, then stood with his paws on her skirt begging for more. Lea giggled, and Megan joined in her laughter. The girl dropped the next piece of bread on purpose.

It was a happy, companionable meal. But when it was over, Lea was very tired. Megan helped her to bed, and the child fell asleep almost immediately.

Mollie Sharp and Della were below in the kitchens; the other members of the household were gone. She could leave the girl alone for a few minutes, Megan thought. Lea would be safe.

Hurriedly, she left the room and mounted to the upper floor, going to the ship's ladder that led to the tower. Once again she experienced an eerie feeling, a reluctance to open the trap door to the room that housed the bell. Did the memory of some old crime linger here, she wondered? Or was it her own guilty recollection of leaving Lea on the sands the day she had almost drowned?

Whatever it was, she did not allow it to deter her. It was most important that she check the chimneys.

The moment she looked down from the tower, she knew that her theory was wrong. The roof pitched steeply, so steeply no one could possibly retain a foothold. With the profusion of chimneys, she could not orient herself. It would be toward the front of the house, facing the sea —

But could it be reached?

Holding to a frame that had once contained a glass window, Megan placed a tentative foot upon the roof itself. In addition to the sharp pitch, its shingles were slippery. She satisfied herself that it could not be reached in this manner.

Then how?

She shut her eyes, recalling Cousin Elizabeth's house in England. The master sweep would come with a grimy little boy and go to an upper floor where there were openings into the chimneys.

Hastening down the ship's ladder, she explored the servant's rooms on the third floor. At last, in a closet, she discovered what she was looking for. A small fire door. The hinges had been lately oiled and it opened easily, revealing an aperture of about thirteen by eighteen inches. Marks gouged into the sooty interior indicated that something — a flat piece of wood, perhaps — had been jammed into the opening to close off the draft from below, and then removed.

Megan's jaw set in anger. The mysterious intruder had not been supernatural, but very real.

Now she needed a few more answers. Who was doing this, and why? What connection did it have with the murder of Doctor Potts? And from whence had come the sweet scent she had identified with Morna's things? If, as she had once supposed, the woman were locked up somewhere in this house, disfigured, mad, then there was no better time to search.

Methodically, Megan went over the entire third floor. There was nothing there. Going down to the floor on which she and Lea slept, she gave a quick cursory examination to Fiona's room, Aherne's, Craigh's, feeling much like an intruder herself. The two rooms which were to have been Morna's and the baby's were locked.

She would get the keys. Constance normally wore them at her waist, but now they were hanging in the kitchen.

While there, much to the irritation of Mollie Sharp, Megan searched the warren of rooms that led off the kitchen, the storerooms, drying rooms, even peering into the tiny, dank chambers the cook and Della occupied. There was a feeling here that Megan did not like. One storeroom in particular seemed to stiffen her spine with a sense of horror. But there was nothing tangible that might add to the answers she was seeking.

Taking the keys over the cook's indignant protest, Megan climbed the steps again. Then, as she passed Lea's door, she heard a sound. A sort of bumping and scuffling. Heart in mouth she ran for the door, flinging it open. The girl was in her bed, head back against the pillows, and she was awake. But in her arms was the rag doll Megan had rescued from the stair room. Angus was tugging mightily at one of its limber legs while the girl giggled.

Megan looked at the doll, then at the bare spot on the chest where she had placed it. "How—?" she began. Then she saw the coverings on one side of the bed had been dragged off to the floor. Lea, herself, had managed to reach the poppet!

Eyes shining, Megan rushed forward to envelop Lea in a hug. "You did it!" she cried, "Oh, Lea! I'm so proud of you. But show me!"

Lea, eyes reflecting Megan's happiness, rose, leaning on her elbows, then slid from the bed. Holding to it, she moved to a chair. Two steps and she had reached the chest. Gleefully, she retraced her steps, falling into the bed to retrieve the doll from Angus.

"You'll be walking soon, and talking," Megan said, joyfully. "Oh, Lea! Think how wonderful it will be. You can go anywhere you want to — say anything you want to say!"

"Mee-gan," the girl said, her face darkening. "Mama — Mama —!"

"But not all at once," Megan said, hastily. "Don't try to make yourself do or say things, Lea. Just let it come. It will." And to distract the child, she went off into a flight of fancy. "Do you know what I thought when I saw you with the doll? I thought maybe the brownies had been here!"

She told her a fairy tale about the little men of Scotland who go about doing good deeds, cleaning houses at night. And how if one rewards them, setting out a saucer of milk, for example, they go away and do not return. For they only do things for people from the goodness of their hearts.

"They would not get a saucer of milk here, I fear," she said with comic concern, "for if we set one out for them, Angus would surely drink it. To the last drop!"

They laughed together. Megan could not recall when she had spent a happier day.

As the day turned toward evening, however, Megan began to be a little nervous. Lea showed no sign of drowsiness, and she did so want to complete her search of the house. The keys should be returned to the kitchen before Craigh came back.

"Lea," she asked finally, "would you lie here and be very quiet until I come if I should leave for a moment or two?"

Lea nodded, but her face clouded. Suddenly, Megan had a better idea.

"You walked a little today," she said. "Do you suppose you could take a *long* walk, if I put my arm around you?"

Lea nodded again, eagerly, and made motions as if to rise. Megan was a little shaken at her own temerity, for it had come to her that Lea might show some reaction to her mother's portrait. Was the child's memory really gone? Or was it still with her, and she was unable to communicate? What if the sight of the portrait was a shock and had an adverse effect?

Dared she take such responsibility?

It was only when they had reached the door to the forbidden room and Megan was inserting the key in the lock that she recalled the room might be occupied. Leaving Lea to brace herself against the wall, Megan entered, scanning it and the room with its adjoining door. Both rooms were empty. She returned for Lea.

The girl's response to the painting was electric. Every muscle in her body stiffened, and she gave a little moan that was a cry of agony.

"Mama! Oh, Mama!"

For a moment she stood, face ashen, tears running down her cheeks, then she turned to bury her face against Megan's shoulder, to sob heartbrokenly.

"Mee-gan," she said. "Mama!"

Megan held the shuddering little form, her own cheeks wet as she whispered words of consolation. As Lea quieted in her arms, Megan lifted her head, drawn from her absorption in the girl's grief.

For the air was permeated with that scent again!

Lea lifted her own face, her pinched nostrils quivering. Her eyes met Megan's with a wild surmise.

"Your mother loved you," Megan said unsteadily, "very much. She still loves you." She looked across Lea's head at the portrait. It still wore its painted, dimpled smile, but the eyes seemed alive, pleading for understanding.

Lea's mother had been beautiful, a bit vain, a coquette, but she had loved her children. Perhaps spirits did not cling to places, but to those they loved. Perhaps Lea's mother was still close enough to care, to try to protect her.

True or not, Megan knew she would not question that drift of faint perfume again.

Calmed, Lea turned her gaze to the rest of the room. At last her eyes lit on the golden harp. With a muffled cry, she moved toward it, Megan hastening to support her. It would not be Morna's own, Megan knew, but a replacement. Yet it had a meaning to Lea, for all that.

Seating herself beside the instrument, Lea leaned her cheek against the gilded wood, her thin fingers going out to touch the strings with a kind of wonder. A sound like a soft wind rippled through the room, a sound of sighing. Megan ached with pity as she watched the girl so completely absorbed in memories.

A sound behind her made her whirl about. There, in the doorway, stood Craigh Stewart, returned from his journey. His face was white and shocked. It slowly reddened with a growing anger as he opened his mouth to speak.

But Megan had sped toward him like an avenging fury, her hands flat against his chest, propelling him backward. Closing the door behind her, she glowered up at him.

"You willna say one harsh word," she said angrily, in her thickest brogue. "You have already hurt the child too much wi' yer shoutin' an blatherin'! Now you will shut your mouth an' gang awa', I'm tellin' you!"

To her surprise, he turned docilely, then turned back. The anger was gone now, replaced by bewilderment.

"Tell me," he said thickly, "what is she doing in there? How can she bear to be in there, after what she —"

"Because, you girt bloody fool, she didna! She's been blamed for some other body's doing, since she canna speak! An' she didna have a father to have faith an' to love her!" She glared at him for a moment, seeing the doubt that clouded his eyes, watching his face break up with some unknown emotion, then regained her poise. "I am going to take her back to her room," she said, quietly. "It might be better if you were out of sight."

Entering, she shut the door behind her. She allowed the girl to reach a point where what she was playing seemed to end on a harmonious note, then said, "Come, Lea. We must go back now. You mustn't tire yourself too much this first time. But we will come again."

As they crossed the room, she paused long enough to give Lea one last look at her mother's portrait, then turned her gently toward the door.

The hall was empty. Craigh Stewart was nowhere to be seen.

Megan led Lea to her own chamber. The girl was weary now, and their progress was slow as she leaned heavily on Megan's shoulder. Once more, Megan undressed her charge and prepared her for bed before Della brought in the evening meal.

Lea indicated that she preferred sitting up, but Megan feared she was already overtired, so she made a game of it. A bite for Lea, then a deliberate spilling of something for Angus from her own tray. The girl still delighted in the game, so apparently her trip to the locked room that was to have been her mother's had done her no harm.

In fact, the girl seemed so sensible and so much improved that Megan decided try another daring scheme. Taking the paper Aherne had given her, she folded it in half lengthways. On one side, the broken sentence read, *Dere Sir, Your wife* ... and below that, *Your son is a*...

Showing the folded paper, the harmless words turned to the girl, Megan asked, "Have you ever seen this note before?"

Lea looked blank and extended a curious hand.

"I guess you haven't," Megan said. She carried it to her room and put it away. It was one more link in the chain of Lea's innocence. Unless, as Constance believed, the child had no memory at all.

Yet had she not remembered her mother?

When Lea slept at last, Megan barricaded the doors and retired early. Her head still ached from her fall, and the injured arm throbbed with the strain of supporting Lea's weight. The day had been successful in that she was pleased with Lea's progress. Still she could not forget the sight of Craigh as he stood outside the door to Morna's shrine. When Megan had proclaimed Lea's innocence in her mother's death, the man had been close to tears for a moment.

What a pity there was such a barrier between father and daughter. Craigh Stewart, when he allowed himself to do so, had such a capacity for tenderness. Megan thought of the day they had ridden in the forest, stopping to talk in the little glade, of the way he had kissed her upon their return, and of how he had held her on the long ride home from Wychboro.

She brought her thoughts up short. Aherne believed his brother-in-law guilty of killing his wife and son, of the murder of the man Megan had helped bury that day. And Aherne had known him far longer than she! Until she had positive proof against one of the people of this household, she must keep up her guard.

When she heard the sound of booted feet in the hall, the blood seemed to drain from Megan's body. They stopped first at Lea's door, hesitating only for a brief space, then moved on to her own. She had visions of Craigh standing there in his dark clothes, waiting, raising his hand to the latch...

But the footsteps moved onward, fading as he approached his own room. She heard that far-off door open and close. And then she dared to breathe again.

CHAPTER 22

In the morning, Megan dressed Lea in one of her pretty gowns and seated her by the window. The air had a balmy feel to it, as if summer had returned. A spot of sunlight flickered on the carpet as the curtains moved in the gentle breeze. Angus crouched, barked, and sprang, doing battle to the death with the curtains, much to Lea's amusement.

Della came bearing only one tray and a note from Craigh inviting Megan to join him for breakfast downstairs. Megan read it and shook her head. "No," she said, "tell him —"

The deaf woman stared at her blankly and Megan remembered. There was a quill pen in the little desk in her room. Finding it, she started to scratch a refusal on the bottom of the note from Craigh, then thought better of it. Finding a fresh sheet, she wrote, *Thank you, but I prefer to remain with Lea. Della will bring another tray.*

She gave the paper to Della and pantomimed her desire for a second breakfast to be brought upstairs. The woman nodded and smiled.

When the tray arrived, Megan again arranged a table before Lea. They would eat their breakfast together. "You have been a very spoiled young lady," she told her teasingly, "but no more! From this time you must feed yourself every bite! Those are strict orders from —" she glanced down at the dog, who sat on his haunches, begging — "from *Angus!*"

Angus cooperated by barking and running in a crazy little circle before he returned to tug at Lea's skirt.

After breakfast, Megan helped Lea walk a bit, then massaged the girl's tired limbs. Later, while Lea rested, Megan returned to her own room to study Craigh's note. His hand was masculine, angular. She did not think she had seen this script before.

She put her palms over her eyes in an attempt to recreate the message Doctor Potts had received, now ashes along with the dress and cloak she'd worn that day. It was not written in this hand, she was certain. If she had only looked at it more closely! But she had been so tired, emotionally exhausted from the happenings of the day.

She put the paper in her drawer and thought how little real evidence she had to explain the strange happenings in this house; two shreds of gray material and the missive Aherne had given her, supposedly written by Lea. A few gouges in the soot-blackened wall of the flue to Lea's fireplace; a note in Craigh's hand which seemed to have no significance at all.

Yet there had been two attempts upon her own life, Lea was being terrorized at night from time to time, and Doctor Potts, Unity Deaton, and Ian Mackenzie were dead.

The Wyndspelle curse? Perhaps. But the doctor's death had been brought about through human conniving. The trap that killed him had been set maliciously, by someone with murder in mind.

The house suddenly seemed oppressive. Megan had been glad to see Constance, Fiona, and Aherne go, but she did not realize at the time what it meant. Until their return, she was a virtual prisoner here. Without Constance to relieve her, there would be no more morning walks or rides.

Wistfully, she eyed the horseshoe cliff where the vegetation came to a halt beyond the barren grounds of Wyndspelle. Some of the leaves had fallen, but those that remained were glorious in their reds and golds. With winter coming, they would soon be gone, leaving the trees standing skeletal against the sky. And from Lea's room she would view only a cold and wintry sea.

She shivered, realizing that her nerves were tightened to the breaking point. She must seek some form of activity. At last she sought out a scrap of material that matched the gown Lea was wearing, and began to fashion a new dress for the girl's rag doll.

It was completed by the time Lea woke, and the child was delighted with it. She was holding it in her arms, the sun from the window bright on her hair, when a knock at the door announced the arrival of the lunch trays.

Megan opened the door and stepped back in surprise. For behind the cook and Della, both carrying trays laden with food stood the tall figure of Craigh Stewart.

"You would not come to me," he said, quietly, "so I have come to you. I wish to invite myself to dine with —" he turned to Lea, an odd expression on his face — "my daughter and her companion."

Lea seemed to shrink for a moment, her face paling. Her eyes went to Megan for support. Then she said, questioningly, "Papa?"

A shudder seemed to run through the man's body. "You are looking well," he said to Lea, in a formal tone. "I wished to check your progress for myself. So," turning to Megan, "if I may presume?"

"You are quite welcome," she told him. "Now, if you will aid me in placing the trays over here. And there is another chair in my room."

The meal was a disaster. Lea's hand trembled, and she spilled much of her food. It was apparent she found it difficult to swallow what did reach her lips. Megan was acutely conscious of the girl's discomfort. She also felt self-conscious about the fact that she, Lea, and the doll were all dressed alike, and worried that he might find it offensive somehow. For his part, Craigh maintained his stiff formality, speaking of the weather with its Indian-summer quality, mentioning the things the travelers would be seeing on their journey to Boston, the textile mills, the most interesting bridge over the Charles, the Feather store. Perhaps even a stage play. Boston was much like an English city.

At last the conversation dwindled into an awkward silence. Craigh rose. "Thank you for letting me join you." He inclined his head first to Lea, then to Megan. "It has been most enjoyable."

Megan felt a twinge of anger at his words. Lea was no stranger to be put off with mannerly words. She was his daughter! Apparently the two hadn't met for a long time, yet there had been no gesture, no word of affection. Megan did not intend to let him get away with it!

"Before you go," she said crisply, "I would like to ask your assistance. Lea should rest for a time, and I find it difficult to lift her into bed."

Craigh stood for a moment, his composure shattered, his eyes filled with anguish. He approached the girl, reaching for her uncertainly. At last, one arm beneath her knees, the other behind her shoulders, he lifted her. He seemed unable to move. His voice broke through in a choked cry.

"Lea," he said, hoarsely, "oh, Lea! Lea!"

He buried his face in the child's hair with a ragged sob. Lea's arms went around him, her thin fingers digging into his shoulders. "Papa!" she gasped. "Papa!" Then, her words blurring together, "Mama — Mama — fire! F-f-f —"

Her body began to twitch as she strove to find words for what she wanted to say.

Megan moved forward. "It is all right, Lea. You can tell him at another time. Now you're tired." To Craigh, she said, "Put her down. Leave her with me. I know what to do."

When he had gone, Megan comforted the shivering girl, insisting that she lie quiet. "One of these days," she told her, "you will be able to speak out. Remember, I promised you. And we have all the time in the world."

As she said it, she wondered if she lied. At any time on any night this room might fill with smoke — the apparition might reappear. As long as Lea was frightened into silence, the child was safe. The situation might change when she was able to tell what she knew.

Megan stacked the dishes for removal to the kitchen and frowned a little. Why had Craigh come here? The expression in his eyes as he clutched his daughter to him was indelible in her mind. Yet might it not have been assumed? *"I wished to check your progress for myself,"* he had told the girl. He could as easily have said, *"I want to see if you are able to tell what you know."*

And Lea was upset by his visit, obviously so. Perhaps she had made a mistake in allowing him to dine with them. What should she do if he returned at the evening meal?

She worried uselessly. Craigh Stewart did not come back. She knew where he would be. In the chasm below, chiseling away at the granite figures representing the dead, when he owed his affections to the living! Her anger rose again. It was easier than admitting to herself that she expected him to return — and when he did not, she was sick with disappointment.

He did not appear that night or the next morning at breakfast. When Della brought the trays up at noon, however, she brought another written message. While Lea napped in the afternoon, Della would sit with her. Craigh requested the pleasure of Megan's company for a walk about the grounds.

Megan's first impulse was to refuse, though her troubled emotions urged her to accept. After a moment's mental turmoil, she capitulated. She had been cooped up here in these rooms far too long, she excused herself. It would be good to get some fresh air — to walk. Still, she blushed as she discovered she was taking special pains with her hair.

Craigh greeted her, still wrapped in that strange formality he had shown when he visited Lea's room. Silently he extended his arm, and she took it, trembling a little at his nearness. As they walked along the path that led to the stone at the foot of the cliff, neither spoke. It was only when they reached the site of the ancient grave, its grass still green with summer, that Craigh said a word.

"I come here often," he told Megan. "Especially when I am troubled. The place seems to have a certain peace about it."

"It is a tomb, you know."

He nodded. "Someone who died long ago. I have tried to make out the name, but it has been nearly obliterated."

"As all our names will be one day," she said softly, "Yours, mine." Then, recalling his earlier statement, she asked, "Are you troubled now?"

"I suppose so. Seeing Lea, yesterday, so much as she used to be. For a while, I dared to hope. Then she went into a state of panic at my touch —"

"Through frustration," Megan told him. "There is something she has been wanting to say. In a way, I suppose her inability to communicate is like being imprisoned. She is improving, however. She will talk one day, I promise you." She studied his face carefully as she made her pronouncement.

"Then you believe she *remembers*?" Craigh sank to the grass, his face moody as he gestured to Megan to sit beside him.

"I know she does."

He was silent for a moment. "How terrible it must be for her! I could almost wish —"

"Wish *what*?" Megan cried, indignantly. "That your daughter would remain a vegetable? Has that not been the aim of this entire household? You are all so certain that she set that fire. Can none of you have a little faith? A little trust? I told you —"

"I know what you told me," he said wretchedly. "But you cannot know! You were not there!"

"And you were? From what I was told, you were on your way to purchase this secluded property! To get your wife away from —" She stopped, horrified at what she had said. Craigh rose, staring bleakly down at her.

"You have been listening to Aherne, I see. He was always Lea's champion. He would much prefer to put the blame for the fire upon my shoulders. He has hated me for years, and perhaps not without reason." Turning he walked a few paces, as if to regain his self-control, then returned, kneeling beside Megan, holding her eyes with his own. "Perhaps you will understand if I tell you the whole story," he said. "I am not free from guilt."

He told of his marriage to Morna, both of them very young and in love, and of how quickly he discovered he had not known the woman he married at all. She was flirtatious and vain, thirsting for male attention even after the birth of Lea, whom she adored.

"Though she gave me no real cause to doubt her," he said, "I brought her to this country. Constance, Fiona, and Aherne accompanied us at her insistence. I had not considered the proximity of Detroit and its fort, nearby. First Fiona, then

Morna was drawn into its social whirl, beautiful women being at a premium. Then my son was born. I am not proud of what happened afterward," he said harshly. "'Tis not a pleasant thing for a man — to have one's wife the subject for gossip. At first, I was foolish over the boy. So much so that I may have neglected my daughter. Then, when tales began to reach my ears, tales I should not have believed, but did in my jealousy, our home became a battleground. I ordered Morna to stay at home, to give up her friends. She was a creature made for music and dancing, and she refused. I suppose Lea was forgotten in our arguments, neglected, cast aside."

He paused for a moment, then continued. "I did not realize how much of our quarrels had reached her ears, nor that she, too, was acquainted with the gossip that was circulating, until I received a note from her, purporting to be anonymous. I didn't know how much she blamed her mother."

He had ignored the missive, for at that time he was prepared to leave. War was imminent, and it was his decision to remove his family to the coast, believing it to be more of a haven. When he returned, it was to find his wife and baby dead, and Lea reduced to a total invalid.

But before he had gone, he and Morna had had their biggest quarrel. "If I find you've disobeyed my orders," he'd shouted, "I will kill you!" Lea, Fiona, Constance, and Aherne had overheard.

During his absence, Morna defied him, attending a ball. Shortly before his return, Lea was punished for playing with fire. The next night the house had burned.

"She did not do it," Megan said stubbornly.

Craigh spread his hands, helplessly. "I have proof, Megan. The thing she wrote —"

"What if she didna write it?" Megan asked, her accent coming to the fore. "Supposing," she fought for calm, "supposing it were someone else? Trying to put the blame on the child?"

He stared at her for a moment, then laughed wryly. "Oh, Megan! Faithful, believing Megan! Would that all women were as true-hearted as you are! No, don't turn away. I admire you for it. I will not ask you to change! The thing is, now what are we to do?"

"Do?" she echoed.

"For years, the approach of any member of the family has thrown the girl into a state. It has been the general opinion that Lea does not want to, and *should* not, recall the details of the tragedy. It is evident that we were wrong. Now, what am I to do? Seeing Lea again, today," he paused with a painful smile, "I realized I have used her as a symbol of my own guilt, my outbursts against Morna, my — my fears that the boy was not my own son. I would like to make amends, to be a true father to her. Yet I would not wish my overtures to upset the child."

He looked so perplexed and helpless that Megan's heart melted. "I'm sure your affection would be most welcome to her," she said.

Craigh's face cleared in a wave of relief. His hands went to her shoulders, drawing her close. "Thank you, little Megan," he said huskily. "Had you not come, I do not know what might have become of us!"

Megan trembled beneath his touch. *He is going to kiss me again,* she thought. And she wanted him to. She wanted him to!

But, as he bent his head, she saw something beyond him, trapped in a thicket of a long-dead bush. Something small, black, and instantly familiar. She drew in a ragged breath, and Craigh released her.

"I beg your pardon," he said stiffly. "I did not intend —"

But she had gone, moving past him like a sleepwalker. Reaching the heap of brush, she picked up the object. A Bible. A small pocket Bible. And she knew to whom it had belonged. Shuddering, she looked toward the spot where Edward Potts's body had lain, trapped beneath his dead horse. Murdered by someone who had reason to hate him.

Perhaps a man who had just confessed to the fault of jealousy?

She weighed the small book carefully in her hand, thinking how near she'd come to giving her heart to the master of Wyndspelle. Perhaps divine providence had placed this reminder of the dead man here, in this place at this particular time.

Perhaps it was an omen.

"I think," she said slowly, not daring to look back at the man she dared not love, "that we should be getting back to the house. I must see to Lea."

Not waiting for him, she hurried down the path, her fingers closed about the Bible in the pocket of her gown.

CHAPTER 23

If Megan feared Craigh would be a constant visitor to the sickroom, she was spared any concern. Several times in the ensuing days, he paused gravely at the open door and offered his best wishes. Other than that, perhaps because he'd sensed her stiffness at their parting, Megan and Lea were undisturbed.

And Megan was delighted at Lea's progress during these days. She'd learned to use a few more common words. "Tea," she would say, pointing to her cup. "Bread," to her plate. Even, when Megan showed her how to fold her hands and said a night-time prayer for her, "Amen."

Each day she walked a little more. During the others' absence, they made several forays into Morna's room. Craigh did not interfere.

As the week drew to a close, the false summer intensified. No air stirred, and the atmosphere was heavy, the heat enervating. Lea grew fretful, irritable, her frustrations more difficult to handle.

I'm cross, too, Megan thought, looking out of the window at a glassy sea that seemed to breathe, humping in greasy swells in the distance. Somehow she sensed that this weather was but a respite. Dead summer holding on; when it was over, true winter would set in. She mopped her wet face with an equally damp hand. Perhaps winter would not be so dreadful after all!

"Mee-gan," Lea said fretfully behind her, "tea!"

"You've had tea," Megan said, mechanically. "With your supper tray, remember?"

"Tea!" the girl repeated obstinately. Megan sighed. The little girl's recovery was making her demanding. Yet she could not blame her. What a joy it must be to be able to express her own desires.

It was not yet dark. Della and Mollie Sharp would still be in the kitchens. It wouldn't hurt to leave Lea for such a little while. Descending to the lower regions, Megan requested the drink. While the cook prepared it, she confirmed Megan's prediction about the weather.

"This is a breeder, all right! Never saw it so hot this time of year. Them other folks better get home quick!"

"They plan to return tomorrow," Megan said.

"May not make it," the woman said, gleeful at the idea of impending disaster.

Megan was glad to escape the kitchen. The blaze on the hearth, already set to tomorrow's cooking, gave off an almost unbearable heat. Even so, the walls seemed wet, slimy to the touch.

Returning through the great hall was even worse. She had always tried to avoid crossing it after darkness fell. The hearth was cold and dead and smelled of a century of ashes — and something else, something she could not define. Evil, she supposed. She laughed at her macabre thoughts, but hastened her footsteps, nevertheless.

Upon reaching Lea's door, she pushed it open. And there, on the edge of the girl's bed, Lea's slim figure held in his arms, sat Craigh Stewart.

"What are you doing here?" she snapped.

He rose, his eyes inscrutable. "Seeing my daughter. Is there any wrong in that?"

Megan hesitated for a moment. "No," she admitted. "I am sorry. 'Twas a surprise to me." As the man placed Lea's head tenderly upon the pillow, Megan could see that the girl's features were bright with happiness.

Craigh went immediately to the door, Megan moving around him to place the pot of tea she carried upon Lea's table. "This is probably my last night to have my little girl all to myself," the man said to explain his presence. "I shall be taking the horses to meet Aherne, Fiona, and Constance in the morning."

"I see," Megan said politely. "I hope they have a pleasant end to their journey. Cook says the weather will break —"

"I think not. A change is coming, but I believe it will hold through the morrow."

The topic exhausted, they stared at each other awkwardly for a moment, then Craigh Stewart excused himself and went away. Megan was still a bit shaken. The man's reasons for coming here in her absence might have been legitimate — but he could have as easily been trying to pump Lea to see what she knew. Her hands trembling a little, she poured Lea's tea, then set about barricading the doors for the night.

That night Megan slept poorly. Her skin was beaded with a fine perspiration, and her sleeping shift seemed to cling to her body. The sheets felt damp, clammy. And she dreamed. She greeted the morning sun with relief, though the day gave promise of even more heat and humidity. When Della came with breakfast, Megan managed to learn through the little pantomime they had contrived between them that Craigh had already gone.

The day was spent in walking a little, which included a trip to Morna's room, and romping with Angus. Yet Megan could not shake the feeling of something about to happen, something dreadful. It was as if danger were speeding toward her like a runaway horse with a careening carriage.

The heat, she thought, mopping her damp forehead. And perhaps the fact that Lea seemed to be so fretful. Poor girl, she felt it, too. How nice it would be if they could both go down to the little beach.

But that other time had almost ended in disaster. Besides, there was no one here to help. In order to occupy Lea's mind, Megan bathed her, dressed her in a fresh gown, and sat her in a chair in her own room. From there, the girl could look out on the landward side. The steep cliff that surrounded the property could be seen; the trail the returning cavalcade would take was in full view.

"We will watch for your father," Megan told her. "And when you see him coming, you can wave to him."

Time seemed to drag interminably. Megan was about to give up and return the cranky child to her room when the first horse of the small parade appeared. Aherne led, Fiona close behind him, followed by Constance. Craigh brought up the rear, leading the extra animal he'd taken to transport the Boston purchases.

Lea clapped her hands with glee. Then, as the procession neared, she leaned from the window, hair falling like a copper flood about her face.

"Papa," she called out to her father. "Oh, Papa!"

The faces below looked upward, blank and stunned, except for Craigh, who returned the child's vigorous wave with one of his own.

To those below, Megan knew, Lea appeared completely recovered. And there was surely one of the four who did not want her so.

It was Constance who carried up the dinner trays later that evening. Megan took them from her at the door. "I am certain you are tired after your long journey," Megan told the woman sweetly. "I have managed quite well. You must not even think of relieving me for the next few days."

Constance looked past her, seeing the radiant child in her sprigged gown seated in a chair, the table drawn up before her. "Megan," Lea cried, "tea!"

The woman turned a sallow, pasty white, her mouth working. "You have done it," she hissed at Megan. "You have meddled in something that was none of your business. I told you you'd bring trouble upon us all!"

Turning, she marched straight-backed down the stairs. Megan felt a flutter of nerves, though the sight of Lea had accomplished what she wished. Let them think she was well, able to talk. It would bring matters to a head, and soon would force the guilty party to act.

And this time, Megan would be watching. The apparition only appeared when there was a fire on Lea's hearth and it was possible to clog the flue so that the smoke would permeate the room, torturing the girl with a re-enactment of the tragedy and sending her out of her mind.

There would be no fire tonight, not in this gasping humid stillness. She need have no concern. And she was tired from her sleeplessness the previous night. She must be alert, rested, if she were to trap the intruder.

Barricading the doors, Megan went to bed, thinking how even the burning candle seemed to heat the room. For a long time she tossed restlessly, making plans for what she intended to do. On the first chilly night, she would sit beside Lea's bed, waiting for a hint of smoke. She would station herself beside the door with something heavy. A candlestick? Then at least one mystery at Wyndspelle would be ended once and for all.

Who would appear? Constance, Aherne, Fiona — Craigh? For a moment she even gave thought to Mollie Sharp and Della, below stairs.

At last she slept, miserable with the damp heat that invaded the room so suffocatingly, and she dreamed. Once again she was standing at Edward Potts's graveside, helping to lower the box, effortlessly, in a slowed-down dream motion. But the grave was too small for the coffin. It grated against the earth with a sound that set her teeth on edge. Megan reached up to push back the damp hair that seemed glued to her forehead. Something was crying, a mournful, whimpering sound —

Angus!

Megan sat upright, for a moment disoriented and confused. Her candle still burned, but the door to Lea's room was closed against her. She was paralyzed at the scent of smoke.

Dear God!

Leaping from her bed, she ran to the door, throwing her weight against it. It was firmly blocked against her efforts. Turning, she raced out onto the balcony and into the child's chamber. The small chest with which she'd blocked Lea's door had been shoved aside and stood aslant, leaving enough space for entrance. Someone had touched off the dry wood in the fireplace, and smoke billowed into the room. Megan ran to the girl, crying out her name.

Lea lay pressed into her pillows, eyes wild in a sunken face. She caught hold of Megan's arms with a strength born of fear and desperation.

"Lea? Who was in here? Who was trying to frighten you so?" Megan's own voice was ragged.

"Mama," Lea said through blue lips. "It was *Mama*."

"It cannot be," Megan said with a firmness that belied her inner feelings. "And I shall prove it!" She thrust Angus into Lea's arms. "He will protect you."

She ran to open the window that some malicious hand had closed, then hurried out into the hall, candle in hand. Her eyes turned to the stair room. She recalled that first time, when she had sensed someone in the dark hall with her; the second, when Angus pursued a nebulous figure up the stairs.

The chimney flue, of course. It had been stopped with something to produce the smoke in Lea's room. And the intruder had gone to remove the evidence.

"Megan?"

She whirled at the sound of a voice behind her. Aherne had come from his room, barefoot, clad in trousers and a shirt which he was trying to button with shaking fingers. "What is it?" he asked, his face white with fear. "I heard something —"

"Someone was in Lea's room. I think they went to the third floor." She moved toward the stair room.

"No!" the boy said, explosively. "No, Megan! Don't go up there! It will be of no use!"

She turned, studying his frightened eyes. "What do you mean?"

He gulped. "You will find no one. I promise you, there is no one there! Please! *She* won't hurt Lea!"

Megan's eyes narrowed. The boy looked so dreadful; his triangular face, dewed with perspiration, seemed to change in the flickering candlelight. And he was shaking all over!

"Who won't hurt Lea! Aherne, do you know who this person is?"

"Morna!"

For a moment, Megan stood frozen. The boy had given voice to her own secret fears.

"Then your sister is alive?"

He shook his head.

It took a moment for Megan to regain her equilibrium. At last she said, "This is sheer idiocy! Whatever is going on in this house, there's a human hand behind it. I am going up those stairs. If you wish to come with me, I will prove it to you!"

Turning, she hurried into the stair room, giving it a quick cursory examination. Satisfied nothing was hiding there, she hastened up the stair, not even looking back to see if Aherne were following her. In fact, she jumped a little to discover him at her shoulder.

They found no one, only Constance in her third-floor chamber, grumpy at being wakened.

"We are looking for someone," Megan explained. "There was someone in Lea's room. We think that person came up here."

Constance froze, her face an inscrutable mask. "Lea is unharmed?"

"Only frightened. I left Angus with her."

"Then I suggest you return. For you will find nothing, I assure you," Constance closed her door against them.

So Constance, too, believed in Morna's spirit. Unless Constance herself had been playing the part... She would have had time to make her way up here, feign sleep, and throw on that shabby robe to open the door.

"She is right," Aherne whispered. "We have looked everywhere. Shall we go back down?"

Megan set her chin obstinately. "Someone has planned this! I told you I would give you proof." She led him toward the closet in which the flue to Lea's chimney was housed, pulling open the small fire door. Instead of the cloud of smoke she'd expected, there was nothing — nothing except —

"Look!" she whispered to the boy. "Oh, look! Whoever put this here didn't have time to remove it." She tried to pry the board that had been wedged into the flue loose, fumbling in her haste.

Aherne, looking over her shoulder, gave a sudden sharp exclamation. "Let me," he said.

Megan moved back, her blackened hands at her sides, waiting until the flue was freed of its obstruction. In the light of her candle, she could see the thing for what it was. Not a mere piece of wood, but something that had once been intricately carved, now almost obscured by soot. It had been a lid to a small chest such as Aherne had made for her and for Lea. She could see where the hinges were once attached.

Megan reached for it, but Aherne thrust it behind him. He looked frightened, dazed, as if someone had struck him. And Megan knew that he recognized his own work, that he knew to whom the chest had belonged.

"You know, don't you?" she whispered. "You know who has been doing these things to Lea!"

"No!" Aherne said harshly. "No!" Megan forced him to look at her, holding his evasive eyes with her own. At last he said, "Yes, I suppose I do. But I cannot understand —"

"Who?" Megan persisted.

Aherne backed from her. "I can't tell you. I — I don't want to say, not until I talk to somebody first. Don't tell anybody about this, please! If it is who I think it is — it won't happen again."

"Aherne, give that to me! I must know, for Lea's sake!"

He retreated before her. "Whoever did this — I will tell you tomorrow. I promise."

She would have to trust him, she thought wearily. He did not intend to give up the evidence she'd found, and she doubted she was strong enough to wrest it from him. Besides, she must hurry back to the frightened child below. Tomorrow, she would force him to tell her what he knew. Unless — a terrifying thought struck her — Aherne, himself, were the culprit. He might have divested himself of the gray costume and met her in the hallway, hoping to divert her and cause her to return to Lea's room.

"You will find no one," he had told her. *"I promise you, there is no one there!"*

"Tomorrow, then," she told him. She led the way downstairs.

Lea still crouched in her bed, clasping Angus in her arms. When Megan entered, the girl flinched, then recognized her. Megan went to her bedside.

"That was not your mother, Lea," she said in a firm voice, "but someone playing a prank. Like the day I hung the drawers in the bell tower, remember? But this is not a nice prank — and I intend to put an end to it! Tell me — just nod your head — was it a man? A woman?"

The child still sat in a small, dismal huddle. *"Mama,"* she said, *"fire! F-f-f —!"*

Megan put her arms around her to stop the awful, chilling little voice. The girl's body was tense, shuddering. "Don't worry about it," she said, consolingly. "As I told you, I intend that it shall not happen again. And I will stay with you all this night. I will not leave you."

217

CHAPTER 24

In the morning, Constance appeared punctually, ignoring Megan's advice of the previous evening. "I knew you would change your mind," the woman said, "you having had such a restless night and all."

Megan considered the situation, pushing her damp hair back from her forehead. She wanted to escape from the hot, confining room more than she would care to admit. Yet that must not enter into her decision. The most important thing right now was to find Aherne and see if he had anything to tell her. All night she had sat, hating herself for letting every important clue slip through her fingers. The diary, the message Doctor Potts had received — and now this, the lid to a wooden chest with an incriminating initial no doubt inscribed on it.

Megan tried to smile. "You are right, Constance. I appreciate your thoughtfulness." Leaving the woman with Lea, she went downstairs.

Fiona was alone at the breakfast table. She looked wan and tired after her journey, but her face lit up at Megan's approach.

"Megan! I wanted to rush up straight away last night, to tell you about our exciting time. But Craigh insisted I retire." She pouted a little. "I suppose he was right in doing so. It has been an exhausting trip. So much hustle and bustle! I tell you, Megan, Boston is no place for a lady. Horses, carriages! Everyone in a hurry! And the *sailors*, my dear! I actually feared for our safety! 'Tis so good to be home."

"And it is good to have you back," Megan said sincerely. "Tell me, was your journey successful? Did you accomplish what you set out to do?"

"Too much so, I'm afraid." Fiona smiled wanly. "I fear dear Craigh is quite angry with me. I made so many purchases I was forced to leave some of them behind at the ordinary in Gloucester. He left this morning to retrieve them for me."

"It could be a difficult trip, should the weather change."

Fiona shrugged. "In that event, I am sure he will remain there for a day or two. I do not think he would have gone, had I not told him some of the parcels were for you." Fiona smiled roguishly as Megan flushed. "Well, my dear, are you not interested in the purchases I made on your behalf? Don't you want to know what they were?"

"I'm sure I will appreciate —"

Fiona interrupted her, leaning forward. "I managed," she said impressively, "after much searching, to find exactly what I knew would suit your taste! I knew you were sorely disappointed in the frivolous selections Craigh made, so I looked and looked until I finally found," she paused again for effect, "some of the same gray woolen as the gown you were wearing when you came. And I believe I managed to match that of the other dark one, also. I purchased a great deal of both, enough for dresses and a cloak! You might make it of one shade and line it with the other."

Megan managed to keep a look of dismay from her face as Fiona frowned a little and continued. "But a bonnet! I did not think of that. I do have one, however, that I wore in mourning. Perhaps if we remove the veil —"

"Lea?" Megan asked in a stifled voice, "Did you bring materials for Lea?"

"I did, indeed. Some lovely warm flannel for new nightdresses. Megan, you must not just stand there! Run down and tell Cook to bring your breakfast and another pot of tea."

Megan obeyed, thinking a little ruefully that she had no right to be disappointed in Fiona's choice of clothing for her. Flighty and unimaginative, the woman thought she'd done her a service. If she only knew how Megan *hated* the garments that had been ruined! But Fiona must never know. Perhaps made differently, and if she could find something that would do for a bit of trim —

Lea, though! Those colors would never be suitable for the little girl. Would she be doomed to flannel nightgowns through the cold winter months?

Megan returned to the table, trying to keep her mind on Fiona's prattle about her trip. Her eyes kept straying to the window from which she could see the door to the stables, seeking a glimpse of Aherne. As soon as she could extricate herself politely, she would go in search of him.

"Aherne," she asked, trying to sound unconcerned, "I suppose he went with Master Stewart?"

"No, Craigh went alone. And I have no idea where the boy is. Megan, you would not believe how my brother behaved on that journey. He was positively insufferable! Angry, sulking. But then," her voice softened, "I believe I know why. I think," she said archly, "the poor lad left his heart behind. Surely, you've *noticed*, Megan?"

Megan stood and made a mumbling excuse to leave the table. Fiona's soft laughter followed as the girl fled, crimson-faced, from the house.

As she approached the stables, Megan could hear the horses stirring restlessly. A shrill whinny greeted her as she entered the door, and heads turned toward her, ears erect. The animals made little snuffling sounds of anticipation. Had they not been fed or watered? Surely Aherne had not let them go this long! It was his first chore, early in the day.

Her fears were confirmed by a quick inspection. Where was the boy? Megan went to the small room at the end of the long building, pushing open the door. The dim light from the high window shed its dusty illumination upon an empty room. A carving knife, a pile of shavings, one glove —

She returned to the horses. Three were missing. How many would Craigh have taken as pack animals? She could ask Fiona, but she was sure the woman would not know.

At last, Megan led the remaining horses, one by one, to the watering trough, returning them to their stalls, giving each a wisp of hay. When she returned to Lea's room she was hot, tired, her skin itchy with the feed she had handled. She was also thoroughly cross with the boy who had neglected the dumb creatures who depended upon him for their care.

Lea, after her experience of the night before, was cranky, too. A bundle of nerves. Megan was almost glad when Constance came to spell her in the afternoon and she could be free of her charge for a while. The heat had mounted. When she left the house to walk upon the grounds, it seemed that the world around her seethed and simmered. Turning to look back, Megan could see that the sky had darkened across the distant waters. The very air around her seemed thick, muddy, and of an odd greenish-sepia shade.

The weather change. That black line against the sea was a line of demarcation between winter and summer. Megan breathed an unconscious prayer that Craigh Stewart might return before the storm struck. Where was Aherne? Her anger at his neglect of the horses had changed to concern over where he might be.

Megan walked slowly toward the stone at the curve in the path. When she had almost reached it, she stopped still. For she had had a sudden vision of Aherne, his body lying crumpled as Edward Potts's had been, his pale hair framing a bruised, face, eyes wide in death —

She stood for a moment, shuddering, then forced herself to walk on. She rounded the stone, heart in mouth.

Nothing! Thank God, there was nothing.

But her outing had been ruined. She could not forget that death had struck here once, nor that some of her visions had a way of becoming reality. She scanned the cliff above with anxious eyes. The trees stood still, their remaining leaves seemingly pasted to them. Nothing moved.

Head down, she walked back to the house, hurrying her pace as a gust of wind struck her. The wind flattened her gown against her body and loosened her hair from its moorings. Only a single gust, but she knew that more would follow.

The weather was breaking.

The feeling of tension remained in the air even after the storm struck, blowing a chill breath across the area where the previous days had been too hot and humid to bear. The wind brought sheets of rain that turned to sleet, rattling against the windows of the big house. And on every hearth, fires blazed to offset the sudden cold.

Something — perhaps the flames leaping on the hearth, or the sonorous breathing of the house due to wind and wave — had Lea in an agitated state. Even after the child had been bathed and tucked in for the night, with Megan's assurances that she would remain with her, she twitched and jerked in her sleep. *Like me,* Megan thought, *she has this awful sense of something terrible about to happen.*

But Megan was prepared. As prepared as she could be. For the room was alight with candles, and close at hand was a heavy silver candle holder. She did not think the intruder would repeat his — or her — performance so soon, but should it occur, she would be ready!

She sat drowsing beside Lea for a long while, then snapped her head up at a sound. Tonight she had not barricaded her own room, but the door on this side. And she had forgotten Angus, leaving him in her chamber beyond the door.

Should she let him in? It would mean moving that heavy chest again, but if he kept up his noise, he would awaken Lea. Rising, she tugged at the chest to let the grateful animal enter. But something — perhaps a sense that something waited in the darkness of her own room — made her lift her candle high.

Nothing. But there was something white against the bolster on her bed. A bit of paper? She went forward, picked it up, and returned to Lea's room, feeling relief when the chest barred the door once more. Then she turned her attention to the note in her hand, her heart pounding as she saw the signature. Aherne!

The matter is settled. Lea will not be bothered again. But I think I'd better explain what happened, and I do not want anyone to know. I will wait for you in the chasm until you come.

A postscript read: *Don't worry about leaving Lea. I promise, she will be all right.*

Megan stood for a moment, torn by indecision, studying the boyish script. Where had Aherne been all day? And why had he chosen this method of communicating what he'd learned? It was a little silly and childish. She could not leave Lea alone!

Then the corners of her mouth tilted up as she recalled how her brothers had been as children. Aherne was a very lonely boy, and it was true that he was attracted to her. Perhaps this suited his idea of high adventure. Unless —

Unless Aherne were the culprit himself. Unless there was a darker side to the boy she did not know. Though he was a strange lad, she found she did not wish to believe evil of him. Yet to go down to the chasm, leaving Lea, walking through the darkened house alone...

She set her lips. She would do it. Anything was better than sitting and waiting for horror to descend. Whatever the thing was, it had not injured Lea, but merely frightened her. And the deed had been accomplished when Megan was nearby. Surely Lea would be safe for a very few minutes. Aherne had sworn she would be.

Megan would make a hurried trip to the chasm, force Aherne to state his message at once, and return. In the meantime, she would leave Angus on guard.

Taking up a candle, she hastened down the stairs and into the great hall. There was a spitting sound from the hearth, and she stopped dead for a moment. Only green wood burning, but the coals seemed to stare out at her with the red eyes of insanity. She shivered. The sound of breathing was louder here below, and she thought of the Wyndspelle witch, the stake from her burning pyre forming the lintel of the fireplace that was the heart of this house.

Craigh Stewart had deplored such imaginings. Perhaps she did have more than her share of it. But the important thing now was not her own fear, but the fact that Aherne was waiting. And maybe what he would have to tell her would clear up the nightmare in which she had been living.

Down through the kitchens she went. The fire had not been banked, for the night was cold. Mollie Sharp would rise to replenish it when the huge log burned away. She went down into the wine cellar, the candle she carried a tiny star, its light blotted up by the darkness. The trap door was closed, but from beyond it came a distant thrumming sound of waves lashing against the rocks below. The sound vibrated through the cellar and along Megan's nerves as she bent to raise the door that led to the chasm.

The sight that greeted her eyes was a terrifying one. In the cavern, midway, the torches still burned, their lights flaring and diminishing. The steps leading down to the sea were black and wet, flecked with flying spume. The waters at their foot lifted, curled and crashed against the steps in a seeming effort to mount them.

Megan stepped down, dizzily, clinging to the frame of the aperture above, Unity Deaton's words resounding in her mind. *"On stormy nights, the bodies of the dead attempt to climb the steps in the chasm below, seeking vengeance!"*

As if to give credence to the story, something seemed to move, down in that black, sound-filled void. A languid hand, lifted to quell the wave that thrust it against the jagged stone —

A hand? Or froth? A white-capped wave? Megan stood frozen in horrified speculation. Then it lifted again, as if to protect the face that bobbed up beside it — a pale, triangular face with staring eyes, a wet open mouth, and pale hair like a drift of seaweed.

Megan raced down the steps, leaving the sound of her own screaming behind her.

CHAPTER 25

By the time she had reached the foot of the stair, the thing she had glimpsed was gone, swept away by the receding waters to meet another wave coming in, joining it, adding to its towering fury. Megan was rooted to the spot for a moment as she watched the waters coming toward her, the underside of the comber like green glass, curving over her as if to swallow her.

She turned, slipping a little on the wet steps as she tried to scramble to safety. She was too slow, and as the seas crashed into the chasm, something struck her from behind, knocking her flat, throwing her a little forward. When the waters receded, she discovered she was not alone. Someone lay beside her.

Turning, she looked into Aherne's drowned face.

For a moment, she went weak with shock, too horrified to regain the use of her limbs. Then she remembered the force of the storm-driven waves below, gathering themselves to surge forward once more. Unless she could manage to drag herself and the dead boy upward, they would both be swept out to sea.

Rising, she slipped her hands beneath the body's arms, pulling, tugging until she reached the cavern with its flaring torches, the raging waters almost tearing him from her as she reached it. Safely inside, she sat for a moment, drawing in great sobbing breaths. Then she turned to look at the boy she'd pulled from the waters. Aherne, who had tried to help her, whom she had come to meet.

The body was as cold as ice, and flaccid. It showed signs of having been in the water for a long time. He had probably been dead since he'd left her the night before!

Then who had placed that note upon her pillow?

Megan sat for a long moment, half sick with grief and terror, smoothing back the pale hair from the boy's dead face. And as she waited, wondering what to do, the crashing of a wave thundered in her ears, a far-reaching one, that sent a rivulet of water curling into the chasm like a snake.

Another such wave, and there would be no safety here. She must find help in getting Aherne's body into the upper rooms. Fiona? No. Constance? It would take too long to reach her third-floor room.

Mollie Sharp! She was a strong woman, and she slept just off the kitchens.

Leaving the boy where he lay, Megan hurried up the stairs. The trap door was closed — and she had left it open! She pressed against it, confused by the tumult of the storm. It did not move.

Dear God! She was trapped. The thing was blocked, somehow, from above.

Dazed, she made her way back down to the cavern, keeping her eyes averted from the seas that raged and growled below, frothing, like some mad beast. She could see the waterline where the last wave had crashed, leaving behind it a trail of slime and debris. She would do the only thing she knew to do. Somehow, she must drag Aherne's body to the top step. There, huddled beneath the trap door, they might escape being overrun by the waters and drawn down into the sea.

In the cavern, she once again tried to lift him. The body was heavy, waterlogged, and her strength was beginning to fail her.

Only her courage and indomitable will enabled her to drag the boy's body to the mouth of the natural cave.

There, she stopped in horror. A wall of water was approaching the rift in the rock, blotting out the lightning-streaked night sky.

And she knew that here, trapped like a rat in the hold of a ship, she too would die.

The wave struck with the force of a great hammer, knocking her backward, tearing Aherne's body from her arms. She felt her head strike against stone and was swept upward, clutching at some projection as the waters closed over her face. How long she held her breath, she did not know. But suddenly there was air, and there was light. Her face was above water, she was high in the center of the cavern, and one torch, thrust in a crevice high in the wall, still burned.

At last she knew where she was. The wave had thrown her toward the stone figures of Craigh's workmanship. She was clinging to the larger one, the sculptured Morna.

Had this last surge been the peak of the storm's fury? She did not know. And Aherne's body was gone. She had lost it! Megan began to cry softly, her lips moving in an incoherent prayer.

Then something nudged her, insistently, an arm going about her body. She stiffened and turned to look into Aherne's dead eyes, bulging, reflecting the torchlight, his face pallid, beaded with sea water. He seemed to dance toward her, curving about her in an awful parody of affectionate embrace, the open wet mouth, spilling water from its corners, pressing against her cheek in a flaccid kiss.

Megan drew back in revulsion, and reacting instinctively she pushed the body away.

It drifted back again, its eyes glinting, draping limp hands across her shoulders. It was a nightmare, horror absolute. Megan felt her hands slipping on the granite figure to which she clung, her mind splintering with terror.

"Oh, God!" she whispered. "Oh, dear God!"

She struggled against the awful embrace, once more shoving the body from her. This time, it seemed to pause for a moment, as if considering a third advance. She gazed at it, terrified, as it seemed to hang there for a moment, its dead eyes fixed on Megan's, mouth open in mute appeal. Then it bobbed as if in farewell, making a slow half-turn, moving silently toward the cavern mouth, one pale hand trailing behind.

The water was ebbing from the cave. And it was taking Aherne's body with it.

Megan's mind righted immediately. Dear God, what had she done? Clinging precariously to her perch, she reached out, grasping the limp hand. It slid through her fingers. There was an awful sucking sound, and Megan lost him. She, too, was nearly pulled into the vortex as the waters swirled back down into the sea.

Megan climbed down to the cavern floor and made her way wearily up the stone stairs, huddling beneath the trap door in a tight little knot of shivering, sodden humanity. Below her, the waves still leaped and snarled, the thrumming sound still shattering her brain. But nothing seemed important now.

She had lost Aherne's body to the sea. The boy would never lie in ground, consecrated or otherwise; And all because she had succumbed to a stupid, feminine hysteria. She herself would possibly die here, either from the sea or from the cold. And Lea — Lea was in her room, sleeping, secure in her trust of Megan, who had promised to stay at her side.

Lea was at the mercy of whatever madness had been loosed in this house.

Megan was still huddled on the top step, numb with her predicament, blue with cold in her soaked gown, a tight little ball of misery, when she sensed, rather than heard, a grating sound.

The thing that blocked the trap door was being moved!

A friend, she wondered, or her faceless enemy? Perhaps whoever had left her down there to die was checking, making sure… She was helpless now, her strength gone, and she had no weapon.

She clenched her fists, feeling the nails bite into her chilled flesh, and watched the door above her open slowly.

A pair of mud-covered boots met her eyes. The hem of a wet, mud-spattered cloak. Her gaze moved upward, coming to rest on Craigh Stewart's bleak and angry face.

The man knelt, reaching through the aperture, his hard hands closing about her shoulders. Megan's head fell back, her eyes half closing as he drew her upward. He stood her on her feet.

"What the devil," he asked harshly, "were you doing down there? And how did this get over the door?" He pointed to a wine keg.

"Aherne," she gasped. "I lost him! Oh, Craigh, I pushed him away!" Her voice rose to a peak of hysteria, and the man shook her.

"Stop it," he commanded. "Pull yourself together! None of this makes sense. If it hadn't been for that dog, I might never have found you!"

For the first time, Megan noted that Angus was circling her, pawing her wet gown, barking with delight at having found his mistress. A cold horror seeped through her veins as Craigh Stewart went on, telling of how Angus had been whining and crying at the door leading from the kitchen to the wine cellar when he came in from his journey, how he had opened the door and followed the animal, through curiosity, only to find the trap door blocked with a wine keg.

His words only touched the edges of her mind, for she knew where she had left Angus. She had left him on guard in Lea's room.

And she had closed the door to the girl's chambers behind her. Someone had entered Lea's room.

"My God," she choked. "Lea!" Breaking free from Craigh's grip, she ran toward the stairs that led up to the kitchens, turning at the top to say, "Come — help me!"

Then she was flying across the great hall, up the stairs to where the door to Lea's room stood a little bit ajar, sending a red glow out into the darkness of the balcony.

Fire! The girl's room was afire!

CHAPTER 26

Megan flung herself into the room. Her eyes went first to Lea's bed, where she saw the small, rigid form, eyes blank with shock, mouth open in a silent scream. Then her gaze went beyond, seeing the nebulous gray figure in a misty gown and the burning brand in the intruder's hand. The curtains had already been set ablaze. The apparition, caught in the act of reaching to touch fire to the canopy above Lea's bed, turned—

Morna!

She staggered back at the sight of the red-gold curls, a face that was so lovely and appealing in the portrait, but which was now a twisted mask of hate.

Megan hesitated, but only for a moment. She dived forward, striking the figure with all her weight, knocking it away from the fear-paralyzed child. It struck out at her with the torch it carried. The brand sizzled against Megan's sodden gown, and the creature retreated, falling back against the burning draperies.

Megan gasped, seeing a tongue of flame lick at the gray gown's floating hem. The woman, in her madness, did not know her dress was afire. Megan moved toward her, then heard Craigh's shout of alarm as he reached the balcony, seeing the flames for himself.

Morna heard Craigh, too. With an incoherent cry of rage and fear, she ran past Megan and out of the door. Megan heard the shock in Craigh's voice as he shouted, "Morna!"

It was followed by a thumping sound and an anguished scream.

Dragging at the draperies, flinging them on the hearth where they could burn out safely, Megan turned to find Lea gone. She rushed to the balcony where a white-faced Craigh looked down. Lea stood beside him, barefoot, looking small in her white nightdress, her face buried against her father.

"Mama," she was sobbing. "Oh, Mama!"

Craigh looked helplessly at Megan. "She fell," he said in a voice filled with horror. "She ran past me — and fell!" Then, to Lea, "It isn't Mama. Don't cry, sweetheart! Please, don't cry."

Megan left them, hurrying down the stairs, to where a figure lay crumpled, a figure in a charred gray gown. Pale hair spread like a fan about its white face. A red-gold wig lay at a distance from its hand. The woman was not unconscious. Blue eyes that had once portrayed only a shallow sweetness glared up at Megan malevolently.

"No," Megan choked, dropping to her knees beside the body, taking a small, seared hand in her own. "Oh, dear God, no!"

The hand jerked away. "Don't touch me!" the woman hissed.

Appalled at the venom in her tone, Megan drew back, then turned at a sound behind her. Lea was slowly, carefully making her way down the steps, holding to the railing for support. Her face was hard and cold as she approached the woman beside whom Megan knelt. Her hand went out, a pointing finger of accusation.

"Mama," Lea said. *"F-fire! F-F-Fiona!"*

"Little sneak," Fiona spat, "always spying! I should have finished you off the night of the fire! But I didn't think you'd be able to talk. And I thought Craigh would see you needed a mother —"

Megan was sick with horror. Fiona had set the fire, had tried to place the blame on Lea. Trying to terrorize the child into insanity! And Aherne, too. She had murdered Aherne! But why?

Fiona turned her gaze to Megan. "You!" she said, her light voice guttural with pain. "You were like Morna! You wanted them all, didn't you? Craigh, Edward —"

Doctor Potts! Megan had not thought of that. Fiona had carried that message to him, had tied the rope between those trees.

"Why, Fiona?" she asked, her voice deep with horror and pity. "You did not love the doctor!"

Fiona's mouth twisted. "Men are fools! Any pretty face... But I am prettier than you — and as beautiful as Morna!" Her voice became plaintive, childlike, "Am I not, Craigh?"

Megan shot a desperate look at the man who stood behind her, her eyes imploring him as she gave a little shake of her head to indicate the gravity of Fiona's condition. Craigh's face was dark with revulsion, but his voice was steady as he said, "Yes, Fiona. You are very beautiful."

Fiona gave a quivering breath and the malevolence faded from her eyes.

"Fiona!"

The woman stared sightlessly into the vaulted beams of the great hall.

Megan was conscious that Craigh had come to stand beside her, one arm supporting Lea. "How could I have been so wrong?" he asked in a dead, far-off tone. "So wrong!"

From the balcony above, they heard Constance's querulous voice. "What is it? What is all the commotion about?" And then they heard her scream.

Rushing down the steps in her flannel nightdress, the cloak she'd thrown about herself flying out behind like the wings of a bird, Constance fell to her knees beside the dead woman, tears raining down her dark face.

"Fiona," she sobbed. "Ah, Fiona! I didn't want to believe it! I never wanted to believe it!"

She laid her dark cheek against Fiona's pale one and uttered harsh, ugly sounds of agony. At last Craigh lifted her to her feet.

"You knew this, Constance? You knew Fiona was doing these — terrible things? That she killed Morna and the baby? Was frightening Lea? And you did not *tell* me?"

Constance wiped at her swollen eyes. "I didn't know anything for sure," she said, her voice catching with a gagging sound. "Maybe I guessed from something Lea said, but I didn't want to think it. And when she came in the night, I wanted to believe it was Morna, come back to us! I watched over Lea, trying to protect her. Then when I saw Fiona push Lea's chair—"

"My God," Craigh said, putting his hands over his eyes as if to shut out the sight of her. "My God!"

Megan put a hand to his arm. "Please, Craigh. I think Lea should be put to bed. And Fiona —"

Constance stiffened her shoulders. "I will take care of her," she said. Bending, she lifted the limp body in her arms and walked straight-backed toward the stairs, taking Fiona to lie in rest in her own room for the last time. And though the woman walked with a firm step, Megan knew that, once more, she was crying.

Waiting until Constance had reached Fiona's room with her burden, Craigh aided the white-faced Lea up the stairs. Megan went ahead, opening the door to her own sleeping chamber.

"She will sleep in here tonight," she said. "Away from the smell of smoke."

"And you?" Craigh studied her.

She was conscious of the soaked gown clinging to her body, of her damp hair fallen about her face, of the fact that she was still shivering with cold and shock. "I will sit beside her."

"You will not." His tone was commanding. "There is enough room in your bed for two. Get out of those wet things, and I will bring you something hot to drink!"

She looked at him, still wet and muddy from his journey, gray with fatigue. "You too," she said. "You must guard against a chill."

"We are quite a pair," he said wryly, "are we not?"

After Lea was made comfortable, Megan took off her wet clothing and put on a flannel nightdress. She had no robe or cloak, so when Craigh knocked at her door once more, she pulled a comforter about her and opened the door only a crack.

He handed her a pot of hot tea that smelled as if it were laced with something alcoholic. "Put it down," he said, "and step outside for a moment."

"I am not properly dressed —"

"It does not matter."

It could not matter. She must tell him what had happened to Aherne. Clutching the comforter around her, she stepped out onto the balcony. He, too, had changed to dry clothing, after rousing Mollie Sharp to make the tea. Now he wished to know what she'd been doing in the chasm in the first place.

Haltingly, she told her story. Of the discovery of the carved board blocking the flue; how Aherne had promised to reveal the ownership of the box from which it had been taken; of the message she'd found on her pillow.

She did not minimize her own fault in believing the forged note, nor did she fail to mention how she'd pushed the boy's body from her, losing it in the sea.

"It will return, won't it?" she asked, her voice tinged with remembered horror. "It will wash up — on the beach, perhaps, after the storm?"

He shook his head. "The sea here does not give up its dead, Megan. Only some freak condition of wind and wave carried it back in the first place. But you must not blame yourself."

His admonition was too late. Her eyes had already brimmed with tears. He pulled her close against him, and she wept in the comfort of his arms. At last he let her go.

"You must rest now," he said huskily, "and do not think on it too much. The conditions that brought all these things about were present when you came. Think what I must atone for. Five years out of my daughter's life! The death of my wife and son, of Doctor Potts, Aherne. All because I was conscience-stricken, sunk in self-pity. Blind, through neglect!"

When Megan attempted to deny his words, he shook his head, eyes dark with sadness. "I have much to consider this night," he told her. "I will see you in the morning."

When he had gone, Megan went into her room, still feeling the warmth of his brief embrace, hating herself for taking pleasure in it amid so much tragedy.

She drank a cup of the brew he'd brought and felt a glow of relaxation moving through her body. Climbing into bed beside Lea, Angus snuggled down between them, she was surprised to feel the girl's touch on her arm.

"I — love — you, Megan," the child said haltingly. "Don't — ever — leave — me."

The evil spell had been broken! From now on, Megan knew that Lea would be all right, becoming a normal, healthy little girl.

"I won't," Megan promised. "Not ever."

But what if she had made a promise she couldn't keep? Supposing Craigh decided, as soon as all was well, that they did not need her any more? She could not bear to lose this child. Her heart wrenched as she identified with Constance, now in Fiona's room just beyond. Constance, who had loved two children and had lost them both, who had lived in constant fear for Lea, torn between her loyalties.

Megan had thought she would be unable to sleep, but she sank into a dark, dreamless pit of exhaustion. The faint rays of a lemon sun were shining in her window when she awoke.

Rising, she went to her window. The wind had died, but the grounds, with their sparse vegetation, were a sea of liquid mud. At the foot of the horseshoe cliff, near the stone, she could see a figure diminished by distance. Craigh, and he was wielding a spade.

Today Fiona would be laid to rest.

That afternoon, the deed was accomplished. For a coffin, one of the chests from the stair-room storage had been used. Perhaps a hundred years old or more, it had been delicately carved and still smelled of some exotic, foreign wood. The parcels Craigh had ridden to retrieve from Gloucester provided a lining; the delicate silks and satins for which Fiona had shopped so eagerly would now be with her forever.

Only Constance, grim-faced now that she had recovered herself, Craigh, and Megan stood beside the grave. Della was with Lea. Mollie Sharp had gruntingly stated her refusal to attend.

Craigh said a prayer that came haltingly to his tongue; a seagull, late on its way to southern climes, circled, uttering a raucous cry; then, between them, Constance and Craigh lowered the chest into the grave Craigh had prepared that morning. It slid smoothly down and was covered. Yet Megan felt a sudden chill.

One more ghost to haunt this house, this land, she thought. *One more ghost.* Fiona, with her sweeping gowns, her seeming fragility; the flower drifting on a surface of a dark pond, poisoning its depths.

As they returned to the house, weighed down by the dismal errand they had just performed, Craigh put his hand on Megan's shoulder. "Must you go in?" he asked in a pleading tone. "I wish to speak with you. I took it upon myself to saddle a couple of horses before the — the burial, in the hope that you might ride with me." Seeing her answer in her eyes, he transferred his gaze to Constance. "You will relieve Della? Look in on Lea?"

The woman nodded.

Craig led the great black stallion and Megan's stocky pony from the stables. She followed him as he rode silently past the stone with its new grave and up the winding trail. Reaching the glade where they had talked before, he dismounted, helping Megan down. Leading her to the tree where they sat, he spread his cloak for her to sit upon. The leaves were gone from the trees above them, now, no birds sang, and the damp twigs made a rasping sound in the wind. But where they sat together, it was sheltered, the sun pointing a golden finger to rest on Megan's face.

"I should never have brought you to this house," he said, quietly. "Last night I tried to wrestle with my own guilt. And all I could think about was how near I came to losing you."

Megan's heart lifted at his choice of words, but she dared not read more into them than was there. "I am not sorry I came," she said in a level voice, "except that I seem to have been the catalyst that precipitated such tragic events."

"And I am not sorry you came." He paused for a space. "I had forgotten how it was to have someone merry in the house. I had to learn to laugh all over again. There is something I must tell you, Megan."

His voice dropped to such a somber note that she held her breath waiting for his next words. At last he began heavily, "I thought about a lot of things last night. I ... thought about Morna, and our life together. And I came to the conclusion that I am as guilty of her death as Fiona was —"

Megan gasped and he held up his hand for silence. "'Tis true," he said morosely. "Morna was fun-loving, flirtatious; we were ill-matched, but I believe she was true to her marriage vows. The gossip that reached my ears must have been planned, engineered, and I was stupid enough to believe it."

"Even the note from Lea," Megan said. "That was a forgery, too, I am certain."

"If I had not been angry, I would have taken them with me, despite Lea's cold. I suppose that note was the final straw. I thought, *Even my daughter knows!* And because of my stiff-necked pride, I left them to die."

"You couldn't know! And you mustn't blame yourself. It is over and done with. Now you must think of your daughter, her happiness!"

"I intend to. Lea, also, was uppermost in my mind all night. Detroit is no longer in British hands. I have been considering returning there, rebuilding my home and the small shipbuilding yard that was once my dream. I think it would be a more salubrious climate for Lea. And Fiona spoke one true sentence as she died: Lea needs a mother. I need a wife, and I have had someone in mind for a long time, someone quite unlike Fiona. A true lady."

So this was why Craigh had brought her here! He wanted to tell her that he was going back to where he'd come from, to get himself a bride. Apparently he already had the lucky woman picked out. Someone he had known before his tragedy.

He was letting her down easily before he told her he could dispense with her services.

Megan rose, her cheeks pink, and hurried toward the brown pony. "I canna stay any longer," she said in a flustered tone. "The wee lass will hae need of me —"

"Megan!"

His voice stopped her and she turned, her fists clenched defiantly at her sides.

"Miss Megan Alisdair o' Alisdair," he said, his mouth twitching a little, "can ye not stay still long enough for me to ask ye to be my wife?"

She stood for a long moment staring at him, then when he opened his arms wide, she began to run toward him, tripping on a tree root in her haste, and falling to her knees at his feet.

He shook his head, copper in the sun's rays, and the electric blue eyes glowed in his golden mask of a face. "Miss Megan Alisdair," he laughed down at her, "I believe I remarked once before on the strange way you have of entering a room. You have an equally strange way of entering my heart!"

Reaching both hands to clasp her own, he raised her up, and she went into his arms.

It was only moments later that she noted the faint drift of perfume that she'd come to know as a friendly, protective scent. Her senses reeling a little, she drew away from Craigh.

"What is it, love?" he asked.

"The flowers," she stammered. "They smell so sweet."

"Flowers? You ninny! The flowers are dead and gone." He laughed as his arms enfolded her once more. She leaned against him, secure in a message that had been meant only for her. Their union would be truly blessed.

CHAPTER 27

One week later, a small cavalcade set out from Wyndspelle. Craigh led, Lea and Megan followed, Lea sitting on the small brown pony. A subdued and oddly gentle Constance brought up the rear. Della and Mollie Sharp had already been sent on ahead with the few possessions considered important enough to transport: a portrait, a golden harp, a rag doll, two small hand-carved jewel chests.

All else would remain with the house, for the furnishings bespoke the touch of Fiona's hand. They would buy more, Craigh had said, when they reached Boston. There, also, Megan and Lea could indulge in shopping for a new wardrobe. The drab materials Fiona had selected had been left behind.

They would remain in Boston for the winter; then, at its end, they would begin their trek to the great lake on which Detroit was situated, in a smiling land of green grass and flowers.

They rode along the barren lands for the last time, passing the stone where the new grave lay, mounting the curving path to the cliff.

"Craigh," Megan called, "would you mind waiting for a moment? There is something I want to do."

She turned her horse down the path again, dismounting beside the plot of fresh, raw earth where Fiona lay. Kneeling at Fiona's graveside, she whispered a little prayer for the repose of this troubled soul.

"Rest in peace," she finished at last.

Standing, she looked toward the house. *I wonder,* she asked herself, *if it is truly haunted? Or if it only attracts haunted people? Souls in torment.* It looked truly evil, silhouetted as it was against the crimson morning sky.

Then she turned to the task she'd come to do.

From the carpetbag she carried she extracted a piece of carved wood. She had discovered it this morning when she'd taken a last tour through the house. It was wedged on the top step of the stairs that led through the rift in the rock, down the throat of the chasm to the sea. How it came there, she had no idea. But she liked to think that somehow Aherne had placed it there; that even in death, he'd tried to keep his promise, to protect Megan and the niece he loved.

She knelt beside the grave again, placing the lid of the chest Aherne had made with loving hands at the head of it, tracing the initial that was soot-blackened and water-soaked. The letter F. F for Fiona.

Then she rose and mounted her horse again, riding away without looking back at the only marker Fiona would ever have.

Up the path she went, following it among the trees to the spot where Craigh waited, Lea and Constance waited, and wee Angus barked his joy at her return.

EPILOGUE

The home of Doctor Potts, deceased, had been generally shunned. Now it had once more become an object of interest. Several of the braver souls of Wychboro leaned on the fence that surrounded it, their eyes avid with morbid curiosity.

"Last of the Potts line, wa'nt he?" one man asked another.

"Ay-yuh," his friend drawled.

"Pity. But he knowed better than to get mixed in with them Wyndspelle devils!"

There was a silence, then, "You think she's dead? The housekeeper?"

"Reckon so. Nobody seen her in some time, now."

"What you think we ought to do?"

"Leave her be, unless *you* want to go in there. Can't ask the preacher. He's gone. Left town." The speaker laughed as the other backed off with a negative motion. Then his expression grew sober.

"Ben, you think it'll happen, what that witch-woman said? That our young 'uns'll go off, and we'll all die out? The town'll fall down around us, with nothing left?"

"I dunno. My own boy left yestiddy."

"My two are thinkin' on it." The man stood silent for a moment, then turned, shaking his fist toward the eastern sky. "That place!" he shouted. "We've lived in its shadow all our lives! Wish it'd fall off into the sea!"

Wyndspelle stood on its promontory, oblivious of the man's fury. It had been here since before he was born. It would stand on. In the great hall, a shadow lay across the floor, a shadow

245

with no light to give it form. At Wyndspelle's foot, dead souls clamored at the mouth of the rift in the rock.

And from a rear window on the third floor, somehow forgotten and left open to the elements, fluttered a tag of misty gray material.

The wind rose, and with it the house began to breathe. Except it seemed more like a purr, had there been anyone to listen.

A deep and abiding purr of satisfaction.

BIOGRAPHICAL NOTE

My mother, Aola Vandergriff, was an American author in the 1970s and 1980s, writing twenty New York Times bestselling gothic and historical romance novels under her own name and a pen name, Kitt Brown. Reviewers compared her deliciously eerie gothic romance *Wyndspelle* to *Wuthering Heights*. The second novel in her 'Daughters' series, *Daughters of the Wild Country*, was recommended along with a handful of books for accurately portraying Alaskan history. She was humbled to find her name "right up there with Jack London".

Mom was born Lola Aola Seery on a college campus in Le Mars, Iowa, in 1920. Her mother once described her as, "a merry little pixie of a child with magic in her fingers and her eyes". Perhaps this daughter of a blue-collar craftsman and a teenage mother absorbed her love of books in this very environment. By the age of five, her talents, interests and abilities began to separate her from her humble beginnings when she stood before classmates and parents and read from Edgar Allen Poe's *The Masque of the Red Death*. By the time we, her children, were old enough to appreciate her special gift, she was our walking dictionary/thesaurus and our very own Scrabble queen.

As the Seery family followed my grandfather's work across the Bible Belt, they struggled through the Great Depression and eventually settled in Oklahoma. During these years, Mom earned small prizes in the Denver Post poetry contests. She was a voracious reader and prolific poet by the time she was twelve. She launched her writing career at seventeen with the publication of a book of poems, *Golden Harvest*, which she also illustrated. The book earned her the title of 'Oklahoma's Baby Poet'. Fresh out of high school, she received her own radio program where she read her poetry to a large audience.

In the early 1940s, Mom became protégé to Jennie Harris Oliver, Oklahoma's Poet Laureate. Impressed with Mom's artwork, Ms. Harris chose her to illustrate her book, *Pen Alchemy*. About this time America entered WWII and Mom married a young soldier, Bill Vandergriff, and saw him off to England when my older sister was only two months old. He returned to civilian life when my sister was two years old, eventually becoming a New Mexico State senator. Dad's post-war jobs took them through several states while Mom focused on raising six children. I was number three.

I have great memories of a woman other people never knew. She would chase us, screaming and giggling through the house, with cold cream on her face. She loved rock hounding and was fascinated with "Pecos Diamonds". We always kept an eye on her as she drifted from one desert ant hill to another where the little residents had discarded these worthless pieces of quartz from their homes. She loved to watch the dust devils spinning in the distance, and when she said she wished to be cremated, my youngest brother said, "And when we see a dust devil, we'll say there goes Mama." I still say that.

In the evenings, Mom would sit in a chair or on her bed, kids circled around, and read a novel, or perhaps it was back to Poe, but she just never stopped reading, and she never stopped writing poetry. It is the hundreds of poems she left us that warm my heart and bring her close to me. When I picture her, I see her with a book in one hand and a cucumber sandwich in the other on her way to a hot bath. It may have been the end of our day, but it was not the end of hers. We could hear her typing late into the night, using the only time she had to herself to craft her stories straight into the typewriter in near final form, seldom changing anything beyond the first page.

Mom did not make a leap from poetry to fiction, she just sailed into it. She used to say that when her children were nearly grown, she was leaning on a broom one day and thinking life is supposed to begin at 40. That thought spurred her to take a $3 creative writing course. Her novelist teacher, Ms. Ethel Bangert, immediately recognized her potential and pushed her forward. She began by writing "true" confessions and other short stories and articles. I hope I haven't spoiled the illusion that confessions are true. Eventually Mom published over 2500 of these stories. Now her long suppressed desire to write really caught fire. She sold the first novel she ever wrote, *Sisters of Sorrow*. It was so rich with exciting cliffhangers, Ms. Bangert suggested, "My dear, you must let the reader rest sometimes."

Mom paid the support and encouragement forward that she received from family, Ms. Oliver, and Ms. Bangert. She spoke at schools and various organizations and taught writing at American River College in Sacramento, California. She was also an associate editor for *Writer's Digest*. Mom was interviewed many times, including on a renowned nationwide television talk show where she was introduced, along with a racy novelist, as "Hot Blooded Writers of Lusty Novels". That was a misnomer for Mom to say the least and an affront to her genteel nature and passionate, but classy novels.

The unexpected reward of her career was when the woman who inspected every ant hill she saw in the desert and every dust devil whirling across the horizon now got to see the world with her husband and dive deep into history books so her novels would be as authentic as possible. Sometimes she had to come home and write, of course, and that is when she and Dad built an adobe hacienda in a haunted New Mexico canyon where they finished out their days, perpetually in love.

Rebecca Williams
Daughter of Aola Vandergriff

A NOTE TO THE READER

If you have enjoyed this novel enough to leave a review on **Amazon** and **Goodreads**, then we would be truly grateful.
Sapere Books

Sapere Books is an exciting new publisher of brilliant fiction and popular history.

To find out more about our latest releases and our monthly bargain books visit our website:
saperebooks.com